THE
DEMON SWORD
ASPERIDES

Also by Sarah Jean Horwitz

The Dark Lord Clementine

Carmer and Grit, Book One:
The Wingsnatchers

Carmer and Grit, Book Two:
The Crooked Castle

THE
DEMON SWORD
ASPERIDES

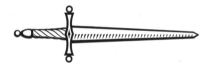

Sarah Jean Horwitz

ALGONQUIN YOUNG READERS   2023

Published by
Algonquin Young Readers
an imprint of Workman Publishing Co., Inc., a subsidiary of
Hachette Book Group, Inc.
1290 Avenue of the Americas
New York, New York 10104

Printed in the United States of America
Design by Carla Weise

The publisher is not responsible for websites (or their content) that are
not owned by the publisher.

LIBRARY OF CONGRESS CATALOGING-IN-PUBLICATION DATA
Names: Horwitz, Sarah Jean, author.
Title: The demon sword Asperides / Sarah Jean Horwitz.
Description: First edition. | New York : Algonquin Young Readers, 2023. |
Audience: Ages 9–12. | Audience: Grades 4–6. | Summary: Asperides,
an ancient demonic talking sword, tricks Nack Furnival, a bumbling
would-be knight, into battling a wicked sorcerer bent on summoning all
the evils of the underworld.
Identifiers: LCCN 2022050077 | ISBN 9781643752785 (hardcover) |
ISBN 9781523523832 (ebook)
Subjects: CYAC: Swords—Fiction. | Knights and knighthood—Fiction. |
Demonology—Fiction. | Quests (Expeditions)—Fiction. | Magic—Fiction. |
Fantasy. | LCGFT: Fantasy fiction. | Novels. Classification:
LCC PZ7.1.H665 De 2023 | DDC [Fic]—dc23
LC record available at https://lccn.loc.gov/2022050077

10 9 8 7 6 5 4 3 2 1
First Edition

FOR DAVID,

who always laughs when
I do the funny voices

THE
DEMON SWORD
ASPERIDES

The Resurrection

The demon sword Asperides was having a drink in the Wet Fang, well known as the coziest pub in the upper levels of the underworld, when he felt the long-forgotten tingling along his blade that meant that someone, somewhere, was about to create a zombie.

Asperides stared at the purple steam rising from his drink as it mingled with the smoke that rose from his own metallic body and tried to tell himself that he was mistaken. He was just having a funny turn, that was all. He'd been out of the game too long, coasting through the top levels of the underworld, letting his magical powers grow rusty with disuse. It was nothing one of the Wet Fang's infamous concoctions couldn't fix. Not that Asperides could actually drink them—he was a *sword*, after all—but he liked the ritual, and he liked to think that with so many human souls inside of him, he could still feel some of the same sensations as the living. He thought that sometimes, if he concentrated hard enough, he could even smell whatever hair-curling aroma was arising from Thom the barkeep's libations.

Another tingle ran up and down his blade, and Asperides shuddered. Fortunately, there was no one around to see him. Asperides was a regular at the Wet Fang, and Thom was always good enough to reserve his favorite darkened corner for him. Granted, the underworld—being the underworld and all—was chock-full of darkened corners, but Asperides appreciated the gesture all the same. Few would bother him as he hovered here . . . though few beings, whether they be renegade spirit, demon, human, or anything else, would bother a demon sword, period. Even a half-retired one.

Asperides hadn't returned his consciousness to his form in the daylight world for over three hundred years and had no plans to break that record anytime soon. He'd had enough of the humans and their squabbling and their grasping for power and their wars. He'd had enough of masters using him to cut down their enemies and power their dark spells, even if they all paid for their crimes in the end—and they invariably did, as the scores of souls writhing in agony in the depths of Asperides's underworld prison could attest. Asperides had been more than satisfied—happy, even—to lay down his burden and settle into this next phase of . . . well, he supposed he could call it existence, if not life.

He did not know if he had ever been precisely *alive*.

But when the third shudder passed through him, making him vibrate from point to hilt, he knew he could ignore the warning no longer. He turned his gaze inward, leaving the Wet Fang and his dark corner and his gently smoking beverage behind, leaving this part of the demon world for the small world within himself.

Only when he looked upon the smudgy, indistinct forms of the soul fragments there did he fully realize what was happening, though he was loath to accept it.

A piece of him was missing. Or rather, precisely, a piece of a *soul* was missing. And that could mean only one thing: some powerful sorcery had dragged it back to its rightful owner.

At that thought, another shiver passed through Asperides, though this time, it wasn't magical in nature: it was fear. Whoever had attempted to resurrect *this* soul's body—a body who just happened to be Asperides's last master—surely didn't know the consequences of their actions. No one in their right mind would think the world would be a better place with Amyral Venir back in the land of the living.

Asperides could only hope that the wards would hold. That the rumors would keep people away from the tomb. That the protections he and others had cast—others, who had bravely sacrificed their lives for this secret—would be enough. That whatever small piece of soul had returned to Amyral Venir would not grant the dark knight full strength, or even full consciousness. Amyral might be alive, but only just—and with Asperides's physical form thrust through Amyral's chest, pinning him to his tomb, "just" was as far as he would ever get. With any luck, he'd wither away inside that stone sarcophagus, as much a prisoner there as the rest of his soul was inside of Asperides.

The other souls were in an uproar over Amyral's absence, dashing about in blurry blobs of light and babbling their incomprehensible distress, but they quieted at one strong look from Asperides. (In the absence of eyes, it was more of a *vibe*, but the effect was the same.) He pushed the souls further back into the recesses of his consciousness and imagined placing an extra lock on the door. Heavy iron, it fell against the barrier in his mind with a satisfying clang.

And yet it didn't change the fact that a soul fragment had escaped, and that his day—or possibly his next several centuries—was downright ruined. Asperides returned his attention to the Wet Fang to find his drink stone-cold and a trio of pixies eyeing it jealously over the edge of the table. He sent a few tendrils of black smoke streaming in their direction, and they darted away, shrieking all the while.

If only pixies were the worst of his problems. But Asperides was a demon sword, and if his two thousand years had taught him anything, it was that the worst was always yet to come.

He didn't have a mouth, but since that had never stopped him before, Asperides flagged down Thom the barkeep. All he could do now was wait, and that definitely called for another drink.

A Nack
for Trouble

*T*he sounds of the battle rang in Nack Furnival's ears. Swords clanging and scraping. People yelling and grunting—sometimes in anger, sometimes in fear, and sometimes in pain. It was hard to tell which in the heat of the moment. Even the sounds of the nearby sea permeated the battle. Somehow, the crashing of waves echoed in Nack's head just as loudly as the violent din around him.

Or perhaps that was just the blood pounding in his ears.

He'd run inside Castle Clyffidil with the rest of the knights, encased in a protective crush of bodies. But now they had separated, the knight in front of him gone to fight one of Lord Solonos's men, the knight to the side of him to ward off the blow of another, until it seemed that only Nack was left, clutching his sword and running down a darkened stone hall without the slightest idea of where he was going.

Time sped up—or maybe slowed down?—and suddenly the boy was in front of Nack in the small courtyard. His lip quivered and his eyes were wide but defiant. He was barely Nack's age, if that. He had no sword of his own.

"Stop him!" cried a voice from somewhere above Nack's head. He turned and saw Declan, armor glistening and face scowling, on a balcony a few floors above them. Declan turned, perhaps to fight an enemy of his own, and Nack faced the boy again.

The boy stood, frozen with fear, perhaps not even realizing he could have taken advantage of Nack's distraction.

"S-surrender," Nack stuttered. His sword shook in his hand as he pointed it. He never imagined he'd be pointing this sword—this sword that was destined to become an angel blade—at another person. "Surrender and come with me, and you'll be taken prisoner with the others."

"Just kill him, Nack!" Declan's voice came again over the balcony, this time hoarse with exertion. "Do it now!"

"What?" Nack nearly choked in surprise, spinning toward the sound of Declan's voice. This time, the boy seized his opportunity. He rushed Nack, ducking under

Nack's sword and sending them both crashing to the ground. For a moment, they were nothing but a confusing tangle of limbs—a pile of boy, thrown elbows and jabbing knees and scratching fingers. A few grunts and curses. Nack's face pressed into stone and bits of dirt and straw; he spat some out and almost laughed when the boy made a noise that sounded suspiciously like, "Yuck!" And in the heat of the tussle, he quietly let the sword slip from his fingers, praying that neither of them would be so unfortunate as to fall on it.

He gave it a swift kick for good measure.

The boy paused above Nack, his fist raised, looking like he didn't quite know what to do with himself.

"NACK!" Declan shouted.

"Go," Nack whispered.

The boy's eyes widened, but after one last shove that rattled Nack's teeth, he clambered over Nack's bruised body—none too gently, considering his life had just been saved, Nack thought—and ran pell-mell into the corridor beyond.

Nack closed his eyes and took a shuddering breath that turned into a cough. He groaned, opened his eyes, and looked straight up at Declan glowering down at him.

He had never seen his older brother look more furious.

"BOY!"

The shout jolted Nack awake. His heart pounded in his chest as if his body still thought he was back in the heat of the battle, still running along the battlements of Castle Clyffidil. He wasn't sure where he was . . . until the smell of horse dung gave him a swift reminder.

"What part of 'we ain't got no rooms to let' told you, 'go ahead and make your own room, then'?" The burly innkeeper stood in the stable doorway, his stocky figure silhouetted by sunlight. He held a rake in one hand, and it didn't look like he was preparing to use it on the hay.

Nack rubbed the sleep from his eyes, wincing as he poked himself in the face with the hay that had stuck to his palms . . . and every inch of him, apparently. He spat some out and tried to brush the rest off his front, but it was a lost cause.

"I'm sorry, sir, but I didn't have—"

"Does this look like a room for rent?" demanded the innkeeper. "Or perhaps a charity hostel, considering you *haven't paid*?"

Nack stood quickly but kept his head down, unable to meet the man's eyes. He knew the only reason the innkeeper wasn't being even harsher was because Nack was still in the clothes of a young nobleman—a young nobleman down on his luck, perhaps, but a nobleman all the same. It wasn't so long ago that if Sir Declan Furnival,

Nack, and their retinue—and he'd *definitely* have had a retinue—had entered this inn, they'd have been given the finest rooms, perhaps even free of charge, if the owner noticed the knights' angel blades.

But those days were behind Nack now. He was quickly running out of the small amount of money he'd been given, and he had no horse. Last night, he'd faced the choice of either sneaking into the stable for the night or being stuck out on the roads after dark. Even under the light of the two moons, he'd have been mad to travel along the wooded roads alone. If stray spirits or other creatures weren't about—and that was unlikely—chances were, knights and soldiers involved with the interclan fighting were. And a warm bed of hay had seemed like the most comfortable mattress in the world after the past few days.

"I-I'm sorry, sir," said Nack to the innkeeper. "I won't trouble you anymore. I'm leaving right now. I just need to . . ." Nack glanced around his sleeping spot. His scabbard must be right there . . .

But the only thing in his dirty corner of the stable was a Nack-shaped indent in the hay.

"What you *need* is to leave my property before I set the dogs on you, boy!" threatened the innkeeper. He took a step forward and shook the rake in his hand.

"Sorry, I just . . . it must be here . . ." A cold, heavy feeling settled in Nack's gut. He fell to his knees, feeling desperately in the hay for his sword. The sword his father had given him on his twelfth birthday. The sword he had sworn to protect House Furnival with. The sword that had been the only thing he was allowed to keep other than the clothes on his back. The sword that was his only hope of salvation if he wanted to regain his honor and return to his family.

His fingers met only dirt and more hay. It wasn't until he felt the poke of the rake in his backside that he realized the innkeeper was still shouting at him.

"OUT. NOW."

"Wait—ouch—no, I'm going, I just—"

Another shove. Nack was about to protest when he heard the unmistakable clang of steel on steel outside. He ducked out from under the reach of the innkeeper's rake and made a beeline for the door.

"And may that be the last of you!" said the innkeeper behind him, but Nack was hardly listening. He had stopped short just outside the doorway of the stables. There in the yard was a group of older boys—locals, it looked like, and none wearing clan colors. They shoved each other, horsing around and laughing. In one of their hands was a sword that was unmistakably Nack's.

Nack groaned, gripping the sides of his head with his hands.

"No," he breathed. They must have taken it while he was sleeping. Some future knight he was, that his weapon could be snatched out from under him while he drooled on his pillow! "No, no, no."

Though they were far across the busy yard of the inn, one or two of the boys must have noticed Nack watching them, judging by the snickering and pointing.

The boy with the sword, tall and blond and pimply and at least fifteen, brandished it in the air. Nack, who was no great swordsman himself, cringed at the boy's form. At this rate, the sword's new owner was more likely to take his own eye out than anything else.

"Missing something, young sir?" asked the boy, putting on a horrendous imitation of a posh accent that Nack fervently hoped sounded nothing like his own. The other boys laughed, and another one with a blade made a feint for Pimply Blond, who was forced to pause in his taunting of Nack to block the halfhearted strike. The rest of the servants and townspeople bustled along their business in the yard and in the street beyond, thoroughly ignoring the group, which Nack admitted was probably wise. There wasn't much worth antagonizing a gang of miscreants waving around naked steel.

Except regaining one's honor, family, and place in the world.

Nack took a step forward, ready to . . . well, do *something*, and was surprised to feel a hand clamp down firmly on his shoulder.

The innkeeper stood next to him, scowling at someone other than Nack for a change. He shook his head at the boys.

"I'd leave it be, if I were you, son," said the innkeeper. "There's more where that lot came from, and you . . . well . . ." He looked Nack up and down, taking in Nack's skinny frame and half-ruined clothes.

"If you want it, come and get it!" taunted one of the boys.

"I *need* my sword," Nack said. He shrugged off the innkeeper's grip but stayed where he was. There were at least six boys—young men, really—and two of them had swords. Nack didn't stand a chance.

There was no retinue traveling with him now.

"I'm not a charity," repeated the innkeeper. He looked at the boys again and then back at Nack. Poking Nack in the chest with the handle of the rake, he warned, "And I'm not a mortuary, either." He patted Nack's shoulder and tottered back into his stables, leaving Nack alone in the doorway.

"There's a copper piece and a bowl of soup for you if you help me with the one that kicks," called the innkeeper from the back of the barn. Nack stood still, gritting his teeth against the tears rising in his eyes. There *were* too many of them. If he were injured—or worse—in a fight with some stupid bullies, he might never be able to fulfill his bigger mission. He might never be able to complete a quest grand enough to gain reentry into the Furnival clan.

The mocking didn't even last very long. The boys never came any closer—perhaps the innkeeper's prowess with the rake was a well-known deterrent of mischief on his own doorstep—and soon, another party passing by in the road caught their attention. They ambled away, lightly terrorizing everyone they passed. Nack didn't miss the last, smug look from Pimply Blond, though, and he didn't think he'd ever forget it.

"Once a coward, always a coward," it seemed to say.

Nack turned back to the stables with his ears burning, thankful for the innkeeper's kindness and resenting the fact he'd needed it in the first place. As he mucked out the stables in exchange for his breakfast, he took his frustration out on the hay, stabbing at it until he worked himself up into a sweat.

He didn't need his sword. It wasn't even an angel blade

yet—just plain steel. He would get another someday, and *that* sword would be the sword he was known for. He still wore his bandolier full of candles that the thieves had left surprisingly untouched—probably because they hadn't realized its value.

He could still find a quest.

He *would* still find a quest. He *would* prove himself worthy of being a Furnival. He'd put the events at Castle Clyffidil behind him and rejoin the fight against the evil House Solonos. Even Declan would welcome him back with open arms, after all the *very heroic things* he would certainly do. Slaying monsters. Exorcizing demons. Gallantly saving maidens from . . . whatever unspecified supernatural dangers happened to be lurking about at the time. Whatever it was, he'd do it.

It must be said that even a Nack in high dudgeon was not a very fearsome sight, and so even the nervous horse did not deem him enough of a threat to kick out as she usually would. She even treated him to an affectionate snort in the face.

"I think she likes you," said the innkeeper, patting the horse as Nack finished cleaning her stall.

At least someone does, thought Nack.

The Prophecy

Asperides was not sure how much time had passed since he'd first sensed Amyral's attempted resurrection. The tingling sensations were gone—departed with that small piece of soul, most likely—and now he only felt a sense of impending doom. Though only slightly different from his usual grim outlook on life, it was a distracting feeling. He decided to seek out company to distract himself from his distraction.

And so Asperides found himself floating toward a not-quite-so-dark corner of the Wet Fang, as opposed to his usual lonely haunt. He let the chatter of the pub—demon and human languages mixing with the strange squelching, screeching, or hissing sounds only the residents of the underworld could make—ebb and flow around him like a tide. He didn't even protest when a couple of ghosts glided right through him by accident; judging by their shudders at making contact with his blade, it was the ghosts who got the rawer deal. He simply sat, aware of his drink—something green apple–flavored, Thom said; Asperides would have to take his word for it—shooting off small sparks on the table in front of him. He tried to lose himself in the problems of two goblins attempting to resolve a gambling debt; a vengeful spirit who couldn't seem to scare her murderer no matter how much she shrieked at him; a mid-level demon who was excited for a delivery of new torture instruments.

This was how Asperides first learned of the prophecy.

"The Missing Moon, that's right" came a voice to his left. Two hags were shuffling to the other end of the long table where Asperides had parked himself. He couldn't exactly sit, but he always made sure to float at chair height, so as not to make people nervous. Nobody, even the technically immortal or already deceased, liked a sword floating above their heads (or below anywhere else). The hags lowered themselves to the benches with much sighing and creaking of their ancient bones. Once they were settled, the one with scraggly blue-black hair and a hood that might have once been velvet, cleared her throat. The sound was like frogs dying.

"There's a prophecy and *everything*," said the hag in

a stage-whisper. She took a great gulp of her drink and smacked her lips. "I heard it came from the priestesses themselves!"

"Could be a bit of wishful thinking though, couldn't it just?" asked the other hag, steepling her long yellow fingernails together. "'The Mission of the Missing Moon' . . . isn't that their whole schtick? Waiting around for the Missing Moon to return? Not a very solid foundation for a faith tradition, if you ask me—"

"Well, they'd be the ones to *know* then, wouldn't they? If the prophecy were real?" asked the blue-haired hag testily.

"Maybe they got tired of all the missing. Wanted something else to entertain themselves with."

"Oh, don't be such a spoilsport," said the first hag with a huff. "If it were true . . . think what it would *mean*. For the daylighters. For us. For *magic*."

Asperides kept himself very still while the hags continued their gossip. He knew very well the seriousness of anything to do with the daylight world's mysterious third moon. Their planet had been orbited by only two moons for so long that most of its inhabitants thought the third moon a myth. The Mission of the Missing Moon, however, believed otherwise. The order dedicated themselves to the magic of the third moon and the hope that one day, it might return to their skies. For most of his existence, Asperides had assumed their hope foolish at best and suicidal at worst. If the Missing Moon ever did return, it would upend the world as they knew it.

But he was getting ahead of himself. The hags hadn't said anything specific about the *return* of the Missing Moon—merely that there had been a prophecy concerning it. For all he knew, that prophecy could very well be, "No need to worry, the Missing Moon is going to keep floating around outer space all by itself for another twenty thousand years. Just checking in! Have a nice day."

Yet Asperides had his doubts.

The hags' conversation quickly strayed to other topics while they drained their drinks. Asperides quietly slipped away from the table.

He would have liked to ignore the hags' words, just as he'd tried to ignore the tingling feelings that preceded Amyral's attempted resurrection. He could have gone back to his dark corner of the Wet Fang and let another fifty years pass him by before he deigned to move again. Time passed differently for him, especially the last three hundred years or so, what with his physical form trapped in the land of the living. He had grown accustomed to being almost as much a ghost as the spirits that had passed through him earlier.

But news of the Missing Moon required investigation. That, combined with Amyral's stolen soul fragment, was too much of a coincidence for a demon sword worth his edge to ignore.

He started in the upper levels of the underworld first. He glided through the most crowded pubs—Bloody Mary's, Jack O'Lantern's, the Last Chance—and then the less crowded ones. He floated in the darkest corners of the darkest corners and up and down the main thorough-fares, listening. As he made his way downward, as the pubs and converted fairy-ring ruins and goblin markets gave way to the more industrial parts of the underworld, where down-on-their-luck demons and captured spirits worked in indentured servitude or punishment or simple captivity, he heard less and less chatter, but he still heard whispers.

"I heard the prophecy said the Missing Moon will return . . ."

There went that faint glimmer of hope, then.

"I heard the Missing Moon will raise all the dead . . ."

"I heard the Missing Moon will flip the worlds! Hope you're not allergic to sunlight!"

Each theory was more fanciful than the last, but the whispers persisted. They grew louder. And judging by the number of demons and spirits Asperides saw passing through the worlds, some of the rumors were true. He heard boasting from lesser demons who'd possessed new victims, and vengeful spirits who'd finally manifested after years of being nothing but a menacing aura or a cold spot in the daylight world. The barriers that kept them in the underworld were getting thinner, or moving, or both.

He eventually returned to the Wet Fang, turning over the various rumors in his mind. He hovered at the bar, hoping to hear more gossip, but the seats on either side of him stayed empty. It wasn't long before Thom the barkeep plopped a drink in front of him. The half-demon barman waved a thick and leathery hand through the wisps of black smoke emanating from Asperides and grimaced.

"You're scarin' away my customers with your . . . miasma of darkness, or whatever that is," Thom groused, shaking the black smoke from his sausage-like fingers. Some tendrils lingered, clinging to his fingers like sticky taffy, before he managed to wave them off. "*Paying* customers, I might add."

Most of the pubs in the underworld did not charge Asperides for his drinks. Firstly, because he was a demon sword. Secondly, because he didn't actually drink them, and they could then be served to less picky customers.

Thirdly, because most proprietors seemed disturbed when Asperides offered payment in the form of free labor from some of the souls trapped inside of him. He could not imagine why.

THIS IS THE FIRST LEVEL OF HELL, Asperides said.

Thom shook his head a little at the effect of Asperides's voice reverberating inside his skull and frowned, presumably at Asperides's use of the word "hell." It was the word many daylighters used to describe the underworld, and not one the underworld's original demonic inhabitants were very fond of. Despite what the humans thought, the underworld was not primarily in the business of being a human afterlife. With a few notable exceptions, only human souls with unfinished business when they died, or who died particularly violent deaths, became spirits in the underworld. The fate of the majority of daylighters' souls was as much of a mystery to the denizens of the underworld as anyone else.

The demons the humans feared were real enough, though, and so Asperides had never thought the label "hell" entirely inaccurate.

IF A BIT OF SMOKE IS ENOUGH TO FRIGHTEN THEM, THEN PERHAPS THEY SHOULD KEEP TO THE DAYLIGHT WORLD.

The barkeep huffed.

THOUGH I BELIEVE SMOKE EXISTS THERE AS WELL.

"Point taken, point taken," said Thom. "Stinkin' salt, I think that's the most I've ever heard you speak, old friend."

I AM NOT YOUR FRIEND.

Thom held up his hands in a small gesture of surrender and turned to "cleaning" his bar with a rag. Asperides was fairly sure he'd been using that same rag for about two hundred years.

"Did you find what you were lookin' for?" asked Thom as he wiped, his tone light.

Asperides let another tendril of smoke drift over in Thom's direction and settle down upon the spot he'd just cleaned. Apparently, despite his attempts at being as inconspicuous as possible, Asperides's wanderings had not gone unnoticed.

"All right, all right," said Thom, re-wiping the spot Asperides had just blackened with soot. "How much can I pay *you* not to sit here anymore?"

Asperides did not dignify him with an answer.

"Just heard you were hankerin' after the Missing Moon rumors, is all," continued Thom with a shrug.

"Believe you me, you're not the only one who wants to know exactly what that prophecy says."

SO THERE IS A PROPHECY. Asperides cursed himself for falling for the barkeep's bait so quickly, but he didn't have the luxury of feigning disinterest anymore. If the beams of the Missing Moon were to once again light the night sky . . .

TELL ME WHAT YOU KNOW OF IT, Asperides demanded.

Thom snorted and scratched at one of his horns.

"Gee, you're a friendly sort, aren't you?" the barkeep asked, chuckling. "What a wonder no one felt like spillin' their secrets with you lurkin' about!"

I DO NOT LURK.

Thom raised a furry red eyebrow.

I HOVER MENACINGLY.

Thom stashed his rag and flashed a brief look around the pub before lowering his voice.

"I'm only tellin' you this because I *am* a friendly sort," said Thom. "And I don't know much, mind, but I have heard this: the Seer who made the prophecy is a novitiate with the Mission of the Missing Moon. Just a scrap of a girl, by the sound of it. But she's caused quite a stir, even in the daylight world."

Asperides didn't doubt it.

"Word is, the Mission's tryin' to keep it quiet," continued Thom. "Well, some of 'em. And that's the problem. Half of 'em want to lock her up for heresy, and the other half want to ready the sacrifices for the moon's 'glorious return,' and a goodly portion of both want to sacrifice *her* to the highest bidder. You know how much a genuine prophecy can sell for. I almost feel sorry for the poor girl."

Asperides was itching to ask about the contents of the prophecy, but despite Thom's teasing about his eavesdropping skills, Asperides had many years of gossip-gathering under his hilt, and so he kept silent. In his experience, once you got them going, people—including demons—loved to talk. Hold a silence for just long enough, and they'd say something to fill it. Thom was no exception.

"This is all hearsay from outside the Mission, of course. Those folk may worship the Missing Moon, but they've got plenty of moon magic from the other two to keep their convent well-warded against our kind— hence the lack of specifics on the prophecy." He winked. "But if the rumors are true, and the third moon really is returnin' . . . well, that'll be somethin', won't it?"

Now it was Thom the barkeep's turn to look

expectant. Everyone knew the myths about demon swords being forged in the light of the Missing Moon—that only a handful had been made with its magic, and after its disappearance, none could ever be made again. That the power of the demon swords, as fearsome as it was, was only a fraction of what it could be should the moon return and shine its light again. That just as these swords had been made in the light of the third moon, so too could they be *unmade.*

It was this last myth that concerned Asperides the most.

Thom, unfortunately, would have to learn to live with his curiosity. Asperides gave him no answer, but the demon sword did rein in his various smoking bits for the few remaining minutes he stayed at the bar and attempted to make his gleaming black blade look a little less threatening. It was not nearly as successful as some of the glamours he could cast on himself in the daylight world, but Thom seemed to take it as the kindness as it was meant.

As a fresh wave of patrons entered the pub, Asperides thought of the girl priestess. The gift of prophecy was a significant burden to bear. If his physical form in the daylight world had not been bound by his duty to seal Amyral's tomb, he would have investigated the matter further. As it was, he could only hope the Mission would keep their secret—and keep it safe.

———— ◆ ————

A world away from the Wet Fang, Sister Dawn Therin tripped over her too-long novitiate's robes and stumbled into a rough stone wall. She gripped the stones for balance, skinning her fingers, and turned around as quickly as she could. The older woman who had shoved her into the cell was already retreating.

"Please, Sister!" called Therin. A small beam of light from the hall outside traced a glowing line on the floor, straight from her to Sister Luna Nan. Therin watched it grow skinnier and skinnier as the door closed, until with a *thunk* and the scrape of the deadbolt being lowered into place, the room was plunged into darkness. She imagined that glowing thread between them, her last link to the rest of her Sisters, snuffed out as if it had never been there at all.

"It's for the best, my dear." The nun's voice was muffled through the thick wooden door. "We need to keep you safe, until . . ."

Until they decided what to do with her. Until they decided if she should be burned as a heretic, dismissed as a willful and imaginative child, celebrated as a hero of their order, or sold to the highest bidder.

There were many who would pay a very high price for any knowledge of the prophecy of the Missing Moon. And they would want their information straight from the source: the unlikely twelve-year-old Seer who had channeled the prophecy. A Seer could not lie while prophesizing, and hearing the words from Therin's mouth would be the only way to completely verify their authenticity. Therin didn't know much about the state of the Mission's finances, but she did know that the last few years of patchy harvests, freak storms, and violence between the clans surely couldn't have helped their already fringe sect. It wasn't surprising that whether her sisters believed her or not, at least some of them would want to profit from the sale of a genuine prophecy.

Sister Luna Nan gave a great big sniff outside the door, which made Therin even angrier than being tossed in a dank cell. Why was Sister Luna Nan crying, when she'd been the one to do the tossing?

"Just go," spat Therin. Her own face crumpled, and for now, she was glad there was no light for anyone to see her by. She choked out the Sisters' customary goodbye. "And may the Third Daughter shine upon you."

She heard Sister Luna Nan turn away from the door with a sob and flee down the hall.

Her pleasure at making the other nun feel guilty was short-lived. Soon, the night's chill and the darkness began to press in upon her, and despite her best efforts, she shed some tears of her own. She huddled against the damp wall and sobbed into her hands until her tears made the scrapes on her palms sting. Her veil hung askew on her head. Messy tendrils of flaming red hair escaped from it and stuck to her wet cheeks; she brushed them away with annoyance. There was no point in tidying herself now.

Therin looked up at the high-set window of the cell. In the morning, it might let in a small trickle of light. But at this hour, not even the thinnest beams of the two moons could enter her prison.

Therin waited for sunrise, afraid even to close her eyes for a moment. She'd been afraid to sleep—afraid to dream—ever since she'd delivered the prophecy.

Unlike most people's, *her* dreams tended to have consequences.

Itinerant
Knights

After his meager breakfast with the innkeeper, Nack returned to one of his most common activities since being banished from his clan: loitering. He wandered around the village square, avoiding the pointed stares of tetchy market stall owners who would eventually tell him to *buy something or scram, boy*, shuffling his feet in the dust and generally trying to look like someone who was definitely using his time productively, thank you very much. He sidled up to groups of fellow travelers and visitors, listening with all his might for any hint of gossip that might point him in the direction of the thing he needed most in the world: a quest.

In the first few days of his exile, he'd just sort of walk up to people and ask if they needed any spirits or demons exorcized, or anything slain, or if there had been any extra grisly murders recently that were sure to leave some ghosts behind, but it turned out that most strangers were not particularly fond of this line of questioning. He had never really given much thought to how the knights of House Furnival learned of their missions. Sometimes, people came to petition his father, Lord Furnival, directly, or a messenger would simply ride up one day and hand a letter to Declan, who would solemnly open it and say something like, "There's reports of trolls under Rollingrock Bridge. I'll send a small party tomorrow," and then they would just . . . go. The Furnival knights were known throughout the land. They never had to hawk their services in the middle of village squares like bit players looking for a gig.

Nack quickly learned he was more likely to hear useful information if he simply let other people do the talking—hence the lurking—but most of his previous leads had been duds. A "possession" that turned out to be a little boy pulling a prank on his siblings. A restless spirit that crashed about someone's kitchen at night that had actually been a restless (and resourceful) raccoon, sneaking in the family's window. (He'd helped said family install some new shutters, for which they were grateful.) Nack felt a bit badly about being so eager to hear news of death and destruction, but death and destruction meant that someone, somewhere, might be in need of a knight.

Or a knight-in-training, in Nack's case. Close enough.

Of course, it wasn't lost on Nack that lately, a lot of the local death and destruction was happening *because* of the knights. Even before the disastrous attempt to recapture Castle Clyffidil, the power-hungry Lord Solonos's machinations to absorb or wipe out smaller clans had turned friends into foes and pitted knight against knight. The clans' energy was not spent fighting demons or spirits, but one another.

Nack had always been taught that the knights' angel blades were for fighting demons. A fatal blow with one was the only thing that could send a demon or evil spirit back to the underworld for good. They were sacred. Angels *chose* their blades and their wielders. To bond with one was to forever live by the knight's code, to use one's sword in service of the living, not the dead.

But at Castle Clyffidil, for the first time, Nack had seen angel blade clash with angel blade—not in practice or jest, but to kill. He had seen these sacred swords stained not with the black ichor of demons, but with red blood. Human blood . . .

"Arty, why don't you go and help those nice ladies? There's a good lad."

The voice jarred Nack back to the present. He had wandered next to a dumpling stall, where a stout woman was busy stuffing and folding dough at lightning speed. She gestured to a boy sitting across from her in the back corner of the stall. He was towheaded and thin, with a curious gray pallor to his skin, and seemed to have trouble meeting her eyes.

Nack looked from the boy to the "nice ladies" the proprietress had indicated and nearly gasped aloud. Standing before him were two of the most impressive-looking knights he had ever seen. The first was tall—nearly six feet, he was sure—with sparkling brown eyes and a voluminous coronet of black braids that made her look more like a queen than a demon hunter. Her companion was shorter and stockier, though no less lovely, with short brown curls that bobbed in perfect ringlets around her temples and a dimple in her left cheek. They both wore gleaming leather bandoliers fully stocked with a rainbow of colorful candles, and their coats of fine mail looked both impenetrable and light as air at the same time. They both had swords. Nack detected the slight blue aura peeking out of the taller knight's scabbard that told him hers, at least, was an angel blade.

Nack immediately noticed they wore no livery or colors he recognized—nothing to identify the house or clan they served. They were itinerant knights, then—rare, but not unheard of. These knights simply roamed the land, helping wherever help was needed, or stayed with one clan or court for a short time before moving on to another.

Though they lacked the protection of the clans, itinerant knights were free to do as they pleased. *They* would not be dragged into interclan hostilities, to use their angel blades against their fellow men, instead of demons . . .

The two women smiled pleasantly as they waited to be served at the stall. They carried themselves with the confidence and grace of the most well-heeled knights Nack had ever met. He stood a little straighter just by being in their presence.

The tall knight noticed Nack staring and gave him a small wink. His cheeks flamed with embarrassment as he ducked his head and stumbled away, taking his place behind them as if he, too, were waiting in line for dumplings. He angled himself to the side, the better to admire their swords and kit.

Nack didn't know how anyone could refuse service to such wonderful-looking knights, but the boy behind the market stall didn't seem inclined to help. In fact, he flinched and turned away from them with a shiver, as if their very presence made whatever malady he seemed to be suffering from even worse.

At the tall knight's waist, the blue light of the angel blade pulsed a little brighter.

"Arty, come now," said the proprietress with a worried frown, but the boy merely shook his head and retreated farther back into the stall. "You've got to start helping with the customers, son . . ." The woman sighed and finished crimping the last dumpling, dusted her hands on her apron, and bustled over to the front of the stall.

"Apologies, my la— my good sirs," the woman corrected herself, noticing the two knights' mail and swords. She gave a little bow and a tight chuckle. "You know how contrary children can be!"

The two knights ordered their meal quickly, and as the proprietress bustled about wrapping up their food, the taller knight spoke up.

"Is your son quite all right, madam?" Her voice was low and kind.

"Oh, yes," said the woman quickly. "You know, they get *moody* when they get to a certain age . . ." She laughed again, but the smile didn't reach her eyes.

"Or when they've been very frightened," said the tall knight softly.

The woman's face fell. She looked hurriedly around them, as if worried someone might overhear. The boy's eyes flicked, just for a moment, toward the knights.

"Did something happen to your son, my good woman?" asked the shorter knight. Her voice was higher than her partner's, though there was a roughness to it that suited her.

The dumpling-maker took a shuddering breath as she handed the knights their food.

"He ain't been the same since he went to that cave," she said, shaking her head. At the mention of the cave, the boy paled and backed farther into the tent. The woman continued, "I told him not to, but . . . you know how boys are."

"We do," said the knights in unison. Nack could have sworn the taller one glanced at him for a moment, just a hint of amusement in her eye.

"This is a peaceful place, you understand? But lately . . . frightening tales have been coming out of those hills." She looked beyond the knights and Nack to a ridge of tall, rocky hills in the distance, bordering the far limits of the town. In the calm light of day, it was hard to see them as anything other than unremarkable not-quite-mountains. But a life of training to be a knight had taught Nack that many things weren't what they seemed in the sunlight. Different powers reigned when the sun left the sky and the two moons came out to dance.

The woman continued. "Strange noises and cries in the night. Figures in the mist, stalking the trails one minute, gone without a trace the next. Piles of rocks getting up and marching about of their own accord—"

Probably trolls. Nack didn't think this area was particularly known for them . . .

"And worst of all, gasper-cats prowling this . . . this cave," she finished. "We didn't even know there was a cave *there.* At least, not big enough for a man to stand in. But there is one now, and those foul beasts almost got my Arty . . ." She looked back tearfully at her son, who shivered as he eyed the taller knight's glowing sword.

The knight pushed it more snugly in its scabbard and the glow receded.

"Well, that sounds like something worth investigating, don't you think, my dear Willa?" asked the shorter knight. Her partner—Willa—nodded, her face solemn.

"I do, my love," she said, placing her battle-scarred hand on the proprietress's stubby fingers and giving them a gentle squeeze. "I'm very sorry about your son, ma'am. I promise you, my wife, Barb, and I will look into the source of all this trouble. If we start out now, we can make camp at the foot of the hills in time for nightfall."

"Oh, I couldn't ask you to—"

"Nonsense," said Willa. She drew herself up to her full height, standing proudly, and Nack felt his face flush again for no apparent reason. "It is our duty as knights to protect all in this land from those that would pierce the veil between our world and the next. At the very least, if we manage to slay the gasper-cats, your son's breath may be returned to him." Willa smiled kindly at the mother and son.

The woman had tears in her eyes as she thanked the knights and sent them off with twice the number of dumplings they'd ordered. The shorter one, Barb, surprised Nack by turning squarely around to face him, a twinkle in her surprisingly blue eyes. She shoved the second packet of dumplings into his hands. He nearly dropped them.

"What . . ."

"You look like you could use them," she said simply. "Eat up, kid . . . and stay inside after dark tonight!"

And with that final warning, the two knights strode off, soon lost from Nack's sight in the crowd of the market.

Nack was thankful for the dumplings—two hot meals in one day was a rare treat, these days—but he had no plans to heed the knight's warning. This was *exactly* the sort of news he'd been waiting for. A mysterious cave appearing out of an otherwise normal hillside? Supernatural beings stalking the roads? Gasper-cats, who normally preyed on sleeping humans in only the oldest of haunted buildings, openly prowling the land for breaths to steal?

It had all the signs of a quest in the making. If he could find whatever hellish source the cats sprang from and defeat it, that would surely count as a brave enough deed to prove his worth to his family. He thought of his sword, swinging blithely from the hands of Pimply Blond, and nearly considered tracking down the meatheads who had taken it. Walking into a haunted cave without his blade seemed just as foolish as confronting those boys would have been, but he couldn't pass up a chance like this, could he? He still had his candles, which was better than nothing. And besides, his sword was no angel blade yet, and therefore almost useless against any spirit or even modestly powerful demon that might be lurking in the hills.

This was not exactly a comforting thought, but it would have to do.

Nack would have liked to try and get more information from the villagers, but if the knights were starting out for the hills now, then he had no time to waste. As lovely and capable as Willa and Barb seemed to be, Nack had no choice but to try and beat them to the mystery cave if he wanted this quest to be his.

The innkeeper did not look pleased to see Nack walking into his stables again.

"Excuse me, sir, but . . . can I borrow the one that kicks?"

4

A Call to Arms

It was with great reluctance that the demon sword Asperides returned his full awareness to his form in the daylight world. After he was plunged into his former master's sarcophagus so many years ago, he had not spent one more second than necessary in this physical form. To be fair, it wasn't like there had been anything to see for ninety-nine point nine percent of that time. After being used to pin down Amyral Venir inside the coffin, Asperides had immediately set himself to giving off such potent and perpetual get-thee-gone vibes that no living thing—never mind curious humans—had dared come near the cave in three centuries.

Amyral's sarcophagus lay in the cave's inner chamber, a guardian only slightly less fierce than Asperides stationed just outside. But before any interlopers could even get close, they'd have to avoid several carefully concealed booby traps in the outer chamber. And, before *that*, they'd need to get past the cave's first line of defense—a rocky and uneven cavern filled with fatal whirlpools disguised as placid ponds—as well as, of course, the pack of hungry gasper-cats.

They were sure to be starving for a meal of life's breath after so many centuries locked up.

Perhaps Amyral's enemies had gone a bit *overboard* with his tomb's defenses, especially considering the cave had been spelled shut with the most powerful moon magic they could muster and was essentially invisible to passersby. But they hadn't wanted to take any chances. There could be no risk at all that the darkest knight, the most villainous sorcerer of their time, would rise again. Those who had survived the battle had set the rest of their lives to scrubbing nearly all record of Amyral's misdeeds from history—lest any copycats be inspired by his legacy in the future.

And yet all their preparations might be for naught. Back in his true form inside the tomb, Asperides could feel Amyral's consciousness. He could feel the knight's body *moving* around the blade, gasping and twitching as Amyral tried and failed to free himself, which only served to make the gaping wound even wider. Asperides didn't know if Amyral felt any pain in his new, resurrected form—most revenants and zombies did not—but he found himself repulsed all the same. He almost felt sorry for the man. Or whatever Amyral was now.

Whoever had resurrected Amyral Venir had clearly not come riding in on their white horse to rescue him. No—for some inexplicable reason, they had chosen to leave him there in his tomb, by now fully conscious but hopelessly trapped under several inches of stone and enchantment, tortured by life in darkness and without the escape of death. It was, Asperides thought, a crueler punishment than the one he had helped inflict in the first place. But perhaps the necromancer did not know where Amyral's body lay, or somehow lacked the resources to retrieve it. Perhaps—and this was an overly optimistic possibility, but a possibility nonetheless— they had tried to get past the cave's other defenses and failed.

Or perhaps Amyral Venir had even older and more

powerful enemies than his former demon sword, and this was their revenge.

If so, it was a poorly thought out plan, because the only safe Amyral Venir was a thoroughly dead one. The mere presence of his life force, even without his entire soul, was enough to erode the protections the brave knights, sorcerers, and even necromancers who had imprisoned him had constructed. Just as the sarcophagus lid quivered with Amyral's attempts to escape, so, too, did the magical wards keeping him hidden.

Whatever shenanigans the Missing Moon was engaged in probably weren't helping matters of magical stability, either.

Asperides's awareness did not extend far enough from the inner chamber to detect exactly how much of the tomb's defenses had deteriorated. He did not know about the exposed cave entrance, or the prowling gasper-cats wandering outside their usual bounds, or the curious village children. All he knew was that Amyral Venir was very much alive again—and very, very angry.

"When I get out of here," Amyral whispered into the darkness, his voice a phlegmy rasp, "you are the first thing I will destroy."

Asperides believed him.

The demon sword retreated to the underworld, back to the comforting atmosphere of the Wet Fang—back to the world where *he* was the scariest thing in the room. But it was harder than usual to bring his consciousness back this time, and it was several moments before the cozy booths and smoky air of the pub materialized before him.

Something was pulling on his attention back in the daylight world—and despite his first thought, it wasn't Amyral.

Unbidden, the image of a boy came to his mind. The boy was young—barely thirteen, by the looks of it—and looked absolutely terrified. He was surrounded by darkness, his thin face covered in muck and scratches.

The vision quickly faded, but Asperides suspected he had not seen the last of this boy.

And before he could stop himself, Asperides thought, *YOU LOOK LIKE YOU COULD USE A SWORD.*

———— ◆ ————

Nack made it to the foot of the Thorny Hills, as the townspeople called them, by the latter half of the afternoon, due in large part to the death-defying gallop of the innkeeper's most ill-tempered horse, who was extremely inaccurately named "Sweet Bean." Sweet Bean took Nack, who was armed with a shovel from the stables (*"Not a mortuary!"* the innkeeper had reminded him), on a riotous and bumpy ride to within about three hundred yards of the hills before stopping short so suddenly that Nack was nearly thrown from the saddle, at which point the beast absolutely refused to go a step farther.

"Smart horse," Nack admitted as he caught his breath and dismounted Sweet Bean, his limbs quivering like jelly from the ride. He half-tumbled to the ground and was quite tempted to simply lie there in the mud until his heart stopped pounding, but Sweet Bean let out a snort that sounded so close to a derisive laugh that Nack was embarrassed enough to haul himself up.

Nack halfheartedly tied the horse's reins to one of the scrubby trees that littered the foot of the hills. He knew he should do a better job; Sweet Bean, however terrifying, might be his only escape from the even *more* terrifying things lurking in these parts. Yet Nack still felt guilty, leading an innocent animal into danger.

"If you know the way back, you should probably go home," Nack advised the horse.

"Nnnarrghghgh," snorted Sweet Bean, ending with a

little whinny, which Nack took to mean both *I laugh in the face of danger!* and *Of course I know the way home, foolish human.*

Nack hefted his shovel over his shoulder and began his ascent into the hills.

———————◆———————

Several hours and three and a half caves later, Nack was forced to admit that "mysterious haunted cave located in this general area" was not exactly a wealth of information to be getting on with. He wandered the hills for what felt like miles, waiting for the telltale chill that came with the presence of unsettled spirits and poking his head into every hole in the hillside. He was rewarded for his efforts by making the acquaintance of several hundred surprised bats, who were none too pleased to have their daytime rest disturbed by a noisy, curious human. (The shovel, unfortunately, came in quite handy in whacking his way to daylight and freedom.)

His second most hopeful lead came when he discovered the trolls—or, if he was being honest, when he nearly walked into them, having mistaken their hard, moss- and grime-covered limbs for an outcropping of stone. They were just stirring from their daytime slumber under a rocky overhang when one of them let out a snort that let fly such a giant booger, Nack considered himself lucky he hadn't lost an eye. He crept away as quickly and quietly as he could and fervently hoped the cave he sought wasn't in the trolls' path.

Though the way this day was going, he wouldn't be surprised.

Nack had hoped to fully investigate the cave before nightfall, when any spirits or demons lurking in its depths would be at full strength, but now the sun was setting, and all he had to show for his time spent demon-hunting was a guano-spattered shovel and some new blisters on his feet.

Declan and the Furnival knights would never have been caught meandering around a hillside waiting for demons to find *them*, Nack thought with a sigh. No, *real* knights seemed to have a sixth sense about where dangers lay in wait. Real knights had angel blades instead of shovels—angel blades that would light the way, glowing brighter and brighter as they drew closer to any evil presence.

Glowing brighter and brighter. Maybe that was it! Nack knew it was a slim chance, but he also knew that he was about to be stuck on a haunted hillside after dark with nothing but a shovel, a few candles, and his wits for protection. He increased his pace, eyes fixed on the top of the nearest—and by luck, one of the tallest—hills.

The two itinerant knights, Willa and Barb, had mentioned they would probably reach the hills by nightfall. If they, too, were searching for the cave entrance, Willa would surely have her angel blade out for protection—and the glow of an angel blade was something Nack could spot from miles away.

Sure enough, only about twenty minutes after he reached the summit of the hill, he spotted a familiar blue glow bobbing in and out of sight, wending its way along the paths only a few hundred meters below him. Nack watched until it disappeared from sight—presumably because the knights had entered the cave.

As full dark descended, Nack had no choice but to light one of his candles. He'd been trying to ration his limited supply, but if he even wanted to *get* to the possible demon-slaying portion of the evening, he was going to have to be able to see his hand in front of his face.

He held the candle up to the feeble light of the first moon and whispered, "Bless me brighter." The flame flared several inches taller for a moment before receding again, but now, the candle radiated a stronger overall glow, as if Nack were holding a small lantern instead of a single stick of wax.

He said a small prayer for clear skies and bright moons as he descended the hill.

———————— ◆ ————————

NO, Asperides said to himself, as if after all this time, he could resist his entire reason for existence by sheer force of will.

HA-HA, the cruel laugh of fate echoed in response. Or perhaps it was the damned souls inside of him, eager for another to join their number.

Because world-saving missions to lock up the evil-est sorcerer of all time notwithstanding, there was no getting around the fact that at his core, Asperides was a *demon sword.* He had one calling and one purpose to his existence, one impulse driving him beyond all others: to find someone to wield him. To prey upon the insecurities, the greed, the ambition of humans, and convince them that with Asperides in their hands, they could conquer all. They could get their revenge against those who had wronged them. They could amass enough power to bend the wills of spirits, demons, and men to their own desires.

And they could. While they were Asperides's master, they could do all that and more. There was just the *teensy* issue of the price for his special services: their soul.

In exchange for access to Asperides and all the magic he contained, for his obedience to any and all of their direct commands—no matter how foul—Asperides's wielders sold their very souls. Upon their death (and they usually died sooner rather than later, not least because owning an outrageously powerful magical sword tended to put a giant target on one's back), their souls were immediately cast into the deepest depths of the underworld, where they would stay for the rest of eternity, tormented and tortured by the sheer oppressiveness of that dark place, or else used as reserves of magical power for the sword's next master.

For *that* was the greatest source of Asperides's power: with each soul he imprisoned, the great pool of energy inside of him grew stronger. It was these souls he called upon to do his next wielder's bidding.

And so the cycle continued.

This had never *bothered* Asperides before, exactly. It was what he was made to do—or all he could remember doing, at any rate. A sword—any sword—needed someone to wield it. And demon swords needed souls to feed upon, just as much as humans needed food and water. The urge to make the contract, to bind another soul to himself, was as powerful and instinctive as the human urge to breathe.

Asperides did not know why he so often wasted time explaining his need for souls—even to himself—in human terms. He was not human, after all. As far as he knew, he was as much a demon as the foulest, slavering greater demons in the deepest levels of hell. He had no soul of his own. His . . . food chain, so to speak, was entirely divorced from the humans'. (In his grander moods, he told himself he was the *top* of the human food chain, but he did not feel particularly self-empowered today.)

No. Today, he felt . . . helpless. A prisoner of his own impulses, trapped just as truly as the souls inside of him. Asperides had had every intention, after sealing Amyral Venir's fate so many years ago, of settling into an early retirement. He was content to stand guard over Amyral's corpse for eternity, rusting inside that dusty tomb, and spend the rest of his days with his consciousness bobbing about in the upper reaches of the underworld, taking naps and staring at drinks and gently smoldering. Perhaps he'd have even opened his own pub, eventually, though mixing drinks without hands might have been a challenge . . .

But it seemed his retirement would have to wait. Because now he was beset with the kinds of visions he hadn't seen in over three hundred years, when the already haggard face of a young Amyral Venir had blasted into his consciousness, exuding confidence and ambition and *ownership*.

This new boy had not entered Asperides's mind with such a vengeance. But there was no doubt what the vision meant. There was no doubt their paths would cross—and soon.

Asperides knew that when a willing human crossed his path, he would not be able to resist the compulsion to make a new contract. To add one more soul to his never-ending, ever-ravenous collection.

Like it or not, the demon sword Asperides was about to get a new master.

5

Werecat-Witch-Mummy . . . Thing

"**B**ARB, WATCH OUT!"

Nack Furnival had expected to find Willa and Barb in the early stages of investigating the mysterious cave. He thought they might have surrounded themselves with alternating circles of summoning and protective candles, the better to coax out any spirits. Perhaps they might have trapped a gasper-cat or two in a ring of salt to figure out who—or what—might be controlling it. Or perhaps they wouldn't even be *in* the cave, judging it safer to come back in the light of day.

He did *not* expect to find the knights in the middle of a furious battle, swords flashing in the dim glow radiating from the cave's shimmering stalactites, surrounded by an entire pack of angry gasper-cats.

Barb rolled, dodging the ice-colored gasper-cat's attack in the nick of time. A candle fell from the curly-headed knight's hand and rolled into one of the many pools of water on the rocky cave floor—but rather than bobbing to the surface, as Nack expected it to, the candle was quickly sucked into a swirling vortex of water. The formerly placid-looking puddle had transformed into a frothing whirlpool the moment the candle had touched its surface.

FWORP. The candle disappeared from view with a noise that sounded suspiciously like a burp.

Nack gulped. Careful to avoid *those*, then.

Barb regained her footing and slashed at the advancing gasper-cat. Her sword, though beautiful and engraved with a variety of protective sigils, was a mundane one. With every strike, the cat simply dissolved into thin air, only to reappear again a second later, angrier than ever. She could only hope to hold the cat off until Willa, who was occupied with a breath-stealing monster of her own, could banish it for good with her angel blade.

"Here, kitty, kitty . . ." taunted Barb, leading the cat back toward Willa. "What's that . . . cat got your tongue?" The gasper-cat hissed at her and pounced again, but Barb dodged it easily. Nack stood rooted to the spot, watching both knights, transfixed by the fluidity and ferocity of their attacks.

Which meant he was totally unprepared when one of the cats launched itself at *him.*

WHUMP. What felt like a lump of burning cold ice collided with Nack's shoulder, toppling him to the ground. The innkeeper's shovel fell with him, skittering away with a clang. He missed one of the whirlpools by inches but managed to keep hold of his lantern candle. Pinned on his back by the cat, he threw his hands up in a desperate bid to protect his face and brandished the candle this way and that, hoping to at least keep the cat from getting too close to his mouth . . .

The cat hissed, a powerful blast of icy air that covered Nack's skin and hair in a thin layer of frost, and the candle went out.

Nack froze—whether from the panic or from the gasper-cat's influence, he couldn't say—and winced as the tiny, sharp icicles of the cat's claws dug into his chest. Its glowing white eyes hovered above his face, fangs fully extended. The cat inhaled, its face mere inches from his. Nack gasped as his breath was leached from his lungs . . .

"CLOSE YOUR EYES, BOY!"

Without thinking, Nack did as he was told. A great

crackling crash, like the sound of a dozen breaking windows, filled his ears, and even with his eyes closed, he saw a brilliant white flash burn bright around him.

Nack kept his eyes screwed shut as several hundred tiny pieces of gasper-cat exploded outward, raining down on him like bits of hail. They melted within seconds, leaving a cold and slimy residue all over him. Nack rolled onto his side, coughing, and gingerly wiped at the goo on his face before daring to open his eyes.

Willa stood over him, her face fierce and her angel blade gleaming like a beacon, bathing them both in its unearthly glow.

"What are you *doing* here, boy?" she demanded.

"Um . . ."

Another crash and a strange whumping sound echoed from across the chamber. Willa's head snapped in its direction before she trained her worried gaze back on Nack.

"Never mind that now," she said, reaching out a hand to help him to his feet. "Just get out of here!"

Nack would have liked to explain that he'd like nothing better, thank you very much, but there was the small matter of regaining his entire future and sense of self, when Barb's quavering voice cut him off before he could begin.

"Oh, Willa, dear . . ." said Barb, her voice growing louder as she backed into view. "I believe your and Lenira's services are required!"

Lenira, Nack thought. That must be the name of Willa's angel blade.

Barb turned to face them, careful of the slippery edges of the pools. She didn't look as surprised to see Nack there as Willa had—or perhaps she hadn't had time to notice him at all.

She grimaced. "It's quite possible I should have kept the cat jokes to a minimum."

"MROOOOOOOOOW." An unearthly cry rent the air, vaguely feline and somehow *metallic*-sounding at the same time.

Nack scrambled for his shovel—it *was* the only real weapon he had—as he and Willa skirted around the nearest pool, the better to see what approached them.

Nack wished he hadn't looked. On the far side of the cave, up a few stone steps where two more stalking gasper-cats crouched in wait, was a coffin-shaped door. This place wasn't just a cave, Nack realized; that doorway looked like the entrance to a tomb. And the secret behind these roving gasper-cats was probably behind it.

A stone figure was carved into the door's surface, and it was one of the strangest creatures Nack had ever seen. The figure was about eight feet tall, with the body of a woman wearing a moldering gown, her limbs wrapped with strips of linen. The statue's head, however, was decidedly *not* human. It was bulbous and unnervingly large, and appeared to be the mummified head of what had once been a cat. It was posed upright, its arms crossed over its chest.

"A werecat," Nack whispered. He had heard tales of such half-human, half-animal creatures, some of whom could supposedly shift completely from cat to human and back again, but he didn't think anyone had seen one in living memory.

Nack realized the door wasn't just coffin-*shaped*. It *was* a coffin. And it had been flung open to reveal this werecat, who was almost certainly *not* a statue.

A fact that became abundantly clear when, with another ear-piercing *meow* and the sound of ripping fabric, she flung out a hand, long black claws extended, swiping at anything within reach.

"A werecat *mummy*," Barb added, her forehead scrunched in confusion, which was not an encouraging sign. If Barb and Willa were just as confused as Nack, he didn't much like their chances of making it out of this cave.

Quicker than any of them would have liked, the

werecat mummy freed her other hand. Her back peeled off the coffin door with much yowling and shedding of what Nack hoped was just flaky bits of fabric, soon followed by each of her legs. Nack, Willa, and Barb stood rooted to the spot—as, fortunately, did most of the gasper-cats, who seemed surprised (and a little intimidated) to see their werecat guardian up and about. One of them took a few cautious steps toward her and was rewarded with a heavy backhanded swipe and a hissed cry of "Myaw!" for its bravery. The rest froze and looked between Willa with her angel blade and the angry mummy, as if hedging their bets on the more formidable opponent.

"WHO DARES DISTURB MY SLUMBER?" demanded the mummy, except her listeners did not speak werecat, and her teeth were not in the *best* shape, so all Nack and the knights heard was "*Myu mwrawr yeool grrrr mwooooor?*"

The werecat mummy began to lurch down the stone stairs, each step stirring up little clouds of desiccated flesh and dust. Nack held a fleeting but fervent hope she would lose her balance and tumble into one of the waiting whirlpools, disappearing with a *fwomp* and a gurgle, just as the candle had. They had no such luck.

In fact, the pools of water helpfully moved out of the

mummy's way with each jerky step. With a wave of her paw and an impatient *Mrawr!* the rest of the whirlpools sluiced to the sides of the cave and dissolved into clouds of steam.

"Werecat mummy *witch*," mumbled Willa, adding to Barb's earlier assessment. She quickly drew her salt pouch and began sprinkling a circle around the three of them. When hers ran out halfway through, Willa plucked Barb's from her belt without a word to complete the circle.

She refocused her piercing gaze on Nack while she sprinkled, the salt falling into a perfectly symmetrical circle without her even looking.

"Now you *must* go," she said, giving him a gentle shove. "We cannot guarantee your safety here. Not with this"— she glanced backward—"werecat-witch-mummy . . ."

"Thing?" Nack offered.

"*Go*," Willa said firmly. She grabbed him by the shoulders and turned him to face the mouth of the cave.

He glanced over his shoulder to see the undead werecat closing the distance between them. Behind her, the now-empty coffin swayed on rusty hinges along one side—it really *was* a door—revealing a small opening into the darkness beyond.

Barb, meanwhile, had crouched down to hurriedly

place a defensive half-circle of candles in front of them. She whispered incantations, low and fervent, and the flames sprang to life, razor-sharp and three feet high.

Nack turned back to the cave's mouth, one foot hovering over Willa's line of salt. The gasper-cats were distracted, the werecat-witch-mummy thing had her eyes on Willa and Barb, and the remaining treacherous pools were much more visible with all of their candle-light. If Nack were quick and careful, he could almost certainly make it to the exit.

He'd make it, but he'd leave Willa and Barb to an uncertain feline fate. Leave, perhaps, without ever knowing what was in the inner chamber of the cave.

And leave without having completed his quest. With yet another chance at regaining his honor gone, snuffed out like his now-cat-goo-covered candle.

The werecat's cries grew louder, and soon, the gasper-cats joined in. Seeming now under the werecat's control, they fanned out around Barb's and Willa's candles. They inched forward, hissing their icy breath, trying to blow out the candles without getting too close. The mummy lurched forward again, now less than twenty feet away . . . now ten . . . now five . . .

Willa launched herself at the werecat.

Nack looked at the moonlight streaming into the

cave mouth, and then down again at his foot. Quickly and carefully, he leapt over the line of salt, disturbing not a grain of Willa's handiwork.

And just as quickly and carefully, he darted around the dueling knights and werecat and ran, full tilt, toward the tomb door.

———————◆———————

Though the outer chamber echoed with the gasper-cats' growls and the knights' battle cries and the whooshing of swords through the air, the inner chamber was as silent as . . . well, the grave. The battle outside seemed like a distant memory as soon as Nack stepped around the werecat mummy's coffin. He edged into the tomb proper.

Candles resting on ledges all around the room flared to life as Nack entered. He took a step back, expecting them to trigger yet more defenses, but nothing in the room stirred. He took another tentative step inside.

It was much smaller than the chamber outside and felt even tinier due to the size of its most prominent feature: a giant stone sarcophagus. The stone was rough and unadorned, but the simplicity of the structure couldn't disguise the power within. Even Nack, who considered his own magical skills to be blunt at best, could feel the power radiating from it, so strong and so cold it was like an icy vise around his chest, like being held yet again under the gasper-cat's paw.

Then he noticed the sword. It stuck straight up out of the stone—right about where the body's heart should be, if there was indeed a body inside of it. The sword was huge—at least three feet long, and that was only the part he could see. Its hilt gleamed in the flickering candlelight, decorated with swirling carvings of silver and gold, but its blade was a deep purplish black. It was a black so deep and dark it seemed to suck the light right out of the air around it, as easily as the whirlpools in the cave sucked down anything that dared get too close. The edges of the blade looked fuzzy, as if black smoke were rippling up and down them.

A shout from outside pierced the quiet of the inner tomb, jarring Nack back to the present. He took a great gasping breath. It was like he'd forgotten to breathe since he first set eyes on the sarcophagus, like he'd nearly lost himself staring into the darkness of that blade. He blinked furiously, trying to clear his head and remember why he was here in the first place.

His brain didn't seem to want to look at the sarcophagus—his eyes kept sliding away as soon as he refocused them—and so he reluctantly looked back at the sword instead. Much to his surprise, it no longer looked quite so large . . . or quite so threatening. Its hilt looked much less like a coiled silver snake and much more like the simple cross-shaped guards Nack was used to. The blade he'd mistaken for black was just plain steel, if a bit darker than usual. And all around the blade, the strange fuzziness he'd seen earlier was really a quickly brightening, teal-tinged glow. The color was almost like . . .

Like an angel blade.

A gust of wind rustled through the cave, though Nack had no idea where it could have come from. The candle flames shivered in their ancient sconces. And with the rustling, a whisper traveled on the breeze.

You could save them . . .

Nack whipped around, expecting to find the werecat witch or some other creature poised in the door, ready to strike, but there was no one there.

"Who said that?" Nack demanded, his voice cracking.

You could save them all . . . and I can help you . . .

Nack swept the shovel from his shoulder and held it aloft, spinning on the spot. Still, he saw no one, and the whispering grew louder. The words began to blend into each other—*sword . . . save . . . your friends . . . only way . . .*

The sword. It glowed brighter and brighter as the

whispering increased—and even brighter when Nack took a step toward it.

"AAAAAARGH!"

"BARB!"

Willa's cry echoed from the outer chamber, her gentle voice gone raw and rough. If the werecat witch had hurt Barb . . . or worse . . .

GRAB AHOLD OF MY HANDLE, said the whispering voice, suddenly as clear as if someone were speaking right into Nack's ear.

The sword. Nack knew it was the sword, as readily as he'd know the sound of his own voice.

GRAB HOLD, AND ALL WILL BE WELL.

The sword's voice was silky smooth, with a faint echo that reminded Nack of a crowd all speaking at once. Strangely, it had the same lilt to its voice that Nack's father had . . . that Declan had, too . . .

They wouldn't hesitate to accept an angel blade's help. They wouldn't hesitate to do anything that might save the knights outside and the gasper-cats' innocent victims.

Nack strode forward as confidently as he could manage, grasped the hilt of the sword in both hands, and tugged with all his might.

6

Of Your Own Free Will

Nack blinked. The tomb was gone.

He stood at one end of a great marble hall. At first, it seemed as large as one of the grassy pastures on the Furnival lands, but the more he stared into the distance, the more he realized he couldn't see any end to it at all. On either side of him, lining the length of the hall, were tall stone pillars that felt strangely familiar to Nack, like he'd seen them somewhere before. The dark stone was carved with such intricate designs that Nack could not make out exactly what they were. One moment, they looked like climbing vines and bursting blossoms—the next, horned beasts with mouths open wide in sharp-fanged screams . . .

Nack jumped back and the monstrous faces

disappeared, replaced by geometric patterns that seemed to swirl and change the more he stared at them. He looked at his feet, which were suddenly cold on the hard, polished floor. It was covered in giant square tiles, alternating black and white marble in a checkered pattern, stretching onward and outward for seemingly the entire length of the hall.

The sword appeared in front of him, popping into existence just as suddenly as the hall itself. The weapon floated in midair, still glowing a bright blue.

The whole hall was bathed in a dim, pearly light. Though there didn't seem to be any windows in the room, Nack knew, just as he'd known the voice in the cave belonged to the sword, that it was moonlight.

"Where are we?" asked Nack.

SOMEWHERE WE CAN TALK, said the sword. Its voice echoed inside Nack's head, flat and full all at once, and much louder than the whispers in the cave. BUT WE DO NOT HAVE MUCH TIME. YOU MUST DECIDE.

"Decide . . . decide what?" asked Nack. "What about the tomb? What about Willa and Barb?"

DECIDE WHETHER YOU WILL BE MY NEW MASTER, said the sword, as if this were the most obvious thing in the world.

"Your . . . your new master?" asked Nack, casting his

mind back to the tomb. Was the body inside the sarcophagus this sword's last master? What had happened to them? The way the sword had been thrust *through* the coffin was certainly strange . . . And Nack had always thought angels moved on after their masters passed, back to whatever plane they came from, to wait for a new knight and new sword to inhabit.

"Who are you?" asked Nack. If he recognized the sword's name, that might tell him something about its unusual history.

I AM ASPERIDES, said the sword.

The name struck a chord in Nack's mind, as if he'd heard it in some childhood fairy tale long ago, though he couldn't remember where. But of course, he'd heard about dozens of famous angel blades in the tales passed down through the Furnival generations. Even Lenira, Willa's sword, had sounded vaguely familiar to him.

And yet something about the name niggled at the back of his mind. He had never heard of an angel staying in a sword without a master before. He had never seen an angel blade quite this *color* before— a similar bright blue as the others he'd seen, but slightly . . . off, somehow, with the slightest green tinge.

And most of all, he'd never known angel blades could talk.

It didn't *surprise* him, necessarily. He knew the bond between angel and blade and knight was a sacred one. He knew much of angel blade lore was kept secret, available only to the knights who possessed such blades themselves. And he understood why: angel blade knowledge in the wrong hands—in the hands of those who practiced dark magic—would be a terrible thing.

But now, face-to-face with a possible angel blade of his own, Nack wished he'd been more prepared for what to expect.

"How can you help me?" Nack asked. "I'm not a knight . . . not a knight *yet*. And Sir Willa—back in the cave—*she* has an angel blade, too, and she's a much better fighter than I am, but that werecat . . ." Nack's thoughts jumbled together in a panic, twisting his tongue inside his mouth.

I AM VERY OLD, said Asperides, *AND HAVE POWERS THEY DO NOT.*

"I . . . I don't know . . ." Nack said. This whole thing— the tomb, the murderous werecat-witch-mummy thing, the apparent transportation to an *alternate dimension*— was all a bit much. He wanted to believe Asperides. He wanted to save Willa and Barb. And yet . . .

If only his father, or his mother, or even Declan were here. A true knight, a true Furnival, would know what to do. He could almost picture them here, standing by his side, as he took a few cautious steps toward the sword.

Come on, Nack, Declan would say, his bushy eyebrows furrowed together. *Don't be such a coward.*

Not like last time. Not like he'd been at Castle Clyffidil.

"What do I need to do?"

———————◆◆———————

The boy was unsure. Asperides could tell.

They did not have time for unsure.

Though every part of his rational mind wanted to scream, *RUN, BOY, RUN NOW, AND NEVER LOOK BACK,* he said no such thing. He couldn't. The urge to make the contract was too strong. The pull to once again be *wielded,* to cut his path of darkness and destruction, was overpowering. The souls inside of him shrieked and writhed, clamoring for one more to join their number. He would do anything to drown out those cries, to sate their hunger.

After the contract was made, he would have to get the boy out of here—and quickly. He did not know what dark powers now animated Amyral Venir, nor how quickly his former master would return to full strength when Asperides was inevitably yanked from Amyral's undead chest. Asperides did not trust this young boy to be a match for even a recently resuscitated Amyral Venir, even with Asperides at his disposal. If Amyral were to overpower them and kill the boy, Asperides would have no choice but to claim Amyral as his master yet again.

Falling once more into Amyral Venir's hands was not a risk he was willing to take.

There was a very, very small upside. If Asperides were once again to move freely in the daylight world—well, as freely as a demon sword could—he could search for more information on the prophecy of the Missing Moon. Perhaps he'd even be able to track the Seer down . . . to hear the prophecy himself . . .

But first, there was the boy. Nack Furnival. Asperides drew him in closer, the better to read Nack's soul. He sifted through the boy's memories. Nothing extraordinary there. He was a good kid. Not much of a swordsman, but short of taking on Amyral Venir, he didn't really need to be—not with Asperides in his hands. He lacked the sheer hunger for *power* that most of Asperides's masters had, but there was time to cultivate that yet. And there *was* something . . .

Ah, yes. Approval. Belonging. A bit of glory. And— far enough back in his mind that Asperides had to coax it out to say hello—just the hint of desire for revenge.

These were the things that Nack Furnival wanted most in the world.

Asperides dug further into the boy's memories. This Lord Solonos, who featured so prominently as the villain in the Furnivals' story, might prove to be a bit of an obstacle, but he could be easily dealt with. But the brother, Declan . . . it was he that Nack clearly cared about the most. Asperides conjured up the burly young man's image. And then, like clockwork . . .

"What do I need to do?"

It really was too easy sometimes.

WE MAKE A CONTRACT, said Asperides.

The boy gulped but nodded.

PLACE YOUR HAND ON MY HILT.

Nack did so, and a chill breeze rustled around them. It was admittedly overkill, but as opportunities to lure in new souls were so few and far between, Asperides couldn't help relishing in the showmanship just a bit.

ARE YOU THE HUMAN CALLED NACK FURNIVAL? Asperides asked.

"I am."

DO YOU ENTER THIS CONTRACT OF YOUR OWN FREE WILL?

The boy let out a short huff of a laugh, perhaps

considering his predicament back in the cave, but he didn't press the point.

"I do."

THE TERMS ARE THUS: BY ENTERING INTO THIS CONTRACT, WE ARE BOUND AS WEAPON AND WIELDER. YOU WILL HAVE SOLE COMMAND OF MYSELF, THE SWORD ASPERIDES, AND ALL THE POWER CONTAINED WITHIN ME, UNTIL THE TIME OF YOUR DEATH, AT WHICH POINT THE CONTRACT WILL END AND YOUR SOUL WILL BE FORFEIT.

The boy jerked backward. He would have torn his hand free from Asperides's handle but the sword's magic held him fast. He would either have to accept the contract or verbally refuse it to let go.

"My soul?" asked the boy, his eyes wide. "Forfeit to . . . to whom?"

TO ME, OF COURSE.

"B-but . . ." the boy stammered, his face pale. "I've never heard of angels taking people's souls . . . at least, no one's ever mentioned it . . ."

THERE IS MUCH YOU DO NOT KNOW, said Asperides. He must be careful. He could not *lie* to make the contract—or, in fact, tell an outright lie, in response to a direct question, to anyone who was his master. (That had made organizing Amyral's downfall a *right bear*, of course, but it had also made Asperides very, very good at saying at least some version of exactly what people wanted to hear.) Asperides could tell that this Nack Furnival, aspiring knight, tiresome do-gooder, and heir to a storied noble family that he was, would never knowingly sell his soul to a demon sword.

So Asperides had carefully made himself a little less demon-like. And if the boy could convince himself that Asperides was, in fact, an *angel* blade . . . well. So much the better. (Asperides was only slightly offended that anyone could possibly mistake him for an angel blade. Angels were *notoriously* dumb, as anyone with half a brain themselves knew.)

DO YOU UNDERSTAND THESE TERMS? Asperides pressed.

"No!" said the boy, his face twisted with indecision. "I mean, yes. But . . ."

Clearly, a little more finesse was in order.

He showed the boy images of himself holding Asperides, standing tall and proud (and, it must be said, a little taller and handsomer than he really was). The phantom Nack slayed the werecat mummy and defeated a whole host of monsters, scores of them fleeing from his blade like waves parting in the sea. He returned home and was welcomed back with open arms; his mother hugged him, his father clapped him on the shoulder, the people of the Furnival lands cheered for him—and Declan smiled widest and proudest of all. Some time later—who needed the details, really?—the walls of Lord Solonos's castle fell, presumably crumbling to the ground from the sheer weight of their inhabitants' evil deeds.

Or something. Asperides didn't think showing the gory details of battle was going to persuade this innocent marshmallow of a boy.

All the while, through all these visions of glowing successes, Asperides gleamed at Nack's side.

It could all be his.

All he needed to do was *agree to the contract.*

"I . . ." And yet, after all of that, the boy still hesitated. Asperides watched the sweat drip down his furrowed brow as indecision gripped him. After seeing all that glory, all his achievements celebrated by family and strangers alike, he was *still* reticent?

Perhaps a bit of gore was exactly what this situation called for, then.

Asperides called on a handful of souls to assist him; he was going to need a bit more magic for this.

He dissolved the hall around them, bringing both his and the boy's awareness back from the underworld and into the cave proper. A chaotic scene greeted them: the knight Willa lay unmoving on the ground, a nasty gash across her head. A gasper-cat inched closer and closer to her injured form, icy paws already reaching for her throat. Meanwhile, an exhausted Barb battled furiously with the werecat-witch-mummy. (The latter was a layer of security that Asperides had always considered in poor taste, but the witch in question had specifically requested such a role before her death. She'd hated all knights when she'd been alive, but she'd hated Amyral Venir even more.)

Barb, covered in scratches, barely kept out of the werecat witch's much longer reach. She fought with her partner's angel blade, but the sword flickered bright and then dull again, nearly ineffective without its bonded master. The knight could have left Lenira at her wife's side, so the angel blade's healing magic could work on Willa's head wound, but that would have taken time— time they did not have. (Again: *angels.* Asperides would never understand why humans loved them so much.) But without a functioning angel blade, Barb would never be able to dispatch the werecat witch for good.

Nack stood rooted to the spot, horror etched on his young features as he looked from Willa to Barb and back again. He tried to run to the unconscious knight, but his feet floated like clouds along the floor; they were not really *here*, after all.

Asperides let the souls inside him whisper to the boy, their voices overlapping until they formed something like a ghostly song.

You can save them . . . You can save everyone . . . You must do it . . .

How will you escape? . . . Would you leave them to die, Nack? . . .

You can save them . . . if only you are brave enough . . .

The boy's chest heaved. "I'll do it!" he finally shouted. "I'll make the contract!"

Now they were getting somewhere.

Asperides yanked them back to his own realm. The werecat's cries still echoed across the now-empty marble hall.

YOU UNDERSTAND THESE TERMS? Asperides repeated.

"I do, I do!" said the boy. "Now help me help them!"

DO YOU AGREE TO THESE TERMS?

"YES, I DO! I AGREE! HOW MANY TIMES DO I HAVE TO—"

THEN I AM YOURS, AND YOU ARE MINE, said Asperides.

Honestly, young people these days. No appreciation for doing things properly.

Asperides's magic exploded outward, a thousand tendrils of darkest black and brightest white, weaving around Nack Furnival's arm, up around his torso, and then his neck, and then his entire body. Sinking into his flesh. Binding him to Asperides until death took one or both of them.

Considering he was thousands of years old, Asperides had a pretty good idea whose time would come first.

Back in the cave, Asperides felt his edges scrape the inside of Amyral Venir's tomb as he soared upward, finally freed from his three-hundred-year imprisonment. For one brief, glorious moment, he floated, suspended in the air—beholden to no one and nothing—before he fell, hilt-first, into the hands of his new master.

Asperides sighed. Well, first things first.

TELL ME, YOUNG FURNIVAL, HOW HANDY ARE YOU WITH A SWORD?

"Erm . . ."

FORTUNATELY, Asperides said, *THERE IS MORE THAN ONE WAY TO SKIN A CAT.*

And fortunately for Nack Furnival, Asperides knew all of them.

7

And Now,
Survival

Asperides didn't know which was louder: the sound of the gasper-cats shrieking as they were cast back to hell in a million little pieces, or his own self-hatred-filled voice mentally berating him with every stroke of his blade.

You swore Amyral would be the last, that small voice inside of him said. How could such a small voice be so loud?

WHOOSH. He sliced himself through the air not a second too soon, sending another cat exploding in a shower of crackling ice and smoke. Nack shouted in alarm, but Asperides ignored him. He'd probably wrenched the boy's arm with that one, but Nack was too slow and untrained to win this fight of his own accord. (Asperides would get to working on *that* straightaway.) Training could come later. First, they had to survive the night.

You swore it to the others, the knights and sorcerers who died fighting Amyral Venir, so that others might live. You swore that with Amyral's death, you, too, would never trouble the world again.

How had that voice even gotten in his head in the first place? He was sure it had never troubled him before . . . or perhaps just once, all those years ago, with Amyral . . .

WHACK. He dispatched another gasper-cat and led the boy on, toward the werecat witch and freedom. It would be nice, to be free. To feel the air running across his blade, to see something in the daylight world other than the utter darkness of that tomb, to adventure in the hands of a capable (or eventually capable) wielder. And when the time came, to consume yet another soul. It had been so long . . .

It was supposed to be forever, said that annoying voice, a touch of grumpiness to its tone.

It added, *You have failed. Failed in your mission to stop Amyral Venir. Even now, he awakens, and all of your work, all of your promises, will have been for naught. And for what? This boy? One more measly human soul?*

SLASH. Asperides could hear the boy gasping, nearly sobbing with surprise and exertion, but they couldn't stop now. If the werecat witch didn't kill them, then Amyral Venir certainly would. Asperides didn't know how much time they had before Amyral succeeded in escaping from his tomb, but he knew it couldn't be long. They needed to get as far away from this cave as possible, and fast.

The werecat witch loomed over the knight Barb, who seemed to have recently fallen—the other knight, too, still lay prostrate on the floor—but the easy, angel blade–less prey didn't interest her for long. She looked up just as Nack lunged at her (of his own accord, Asperides noted with mild surprise). She scampered backward, leaping onto one of the ledges of the cave walls to gain higher ground. Asperides would have to end this quickly. He sent his own energy through Nack's arm, swinging with deadly aim for the witch's neck before she could strike out with her claws—

Asperides felt himself freeze. Just for a moment, but it was long enough for him to lose his chance. The blow glanced off the rock wall with a bone-jarring *ping* that might have shattered a lesser blade.

Nack had resisted him.

The boy took several long steps back.

"I can't . . . I can't *kill* her," he said, his breath coming in gasps. "Were-animals aren't . . . they're not demons. They're people!"

Sometimes, in moments like these, Asperides wished that he had a head to shake in despair. Of all the knights in all the lands, he just had to get paired with the sentimental child who paused mid-battle to contemplate the finer points of personhood.

The werecat witch regarded Nack through desiccated eye sockets, stalled only by her sense of Asperides's power.

NEED I MENTION, Asperides said, *THAT SHE IS ALREADY DEAD?*

"*MWRAWRRRRR*," shrieked the werecat witch, one of her fangs coming loose from her shriveled jaw. It hit the cave floor with a little *doink*.

The werecat dove for them. Asperides yanked Nack's arm again, but the boy was already moving of his own volition. He rolled across the cave floor, dangerously close to one of the whirlpools. This time, Asperides pointed himself not at the cat but toward the water.

TOUCH ME TO THE WATER, BOY.

"What?" shouted Nack, undoubtedly thinking of the fate of the earlier objects to touch those inky surfaces. Nack narrowly dodged another pounce from the werecat, whose mobility seemed to be increasing the longer she stayed animated.

DO IT NOW.

The boy thrust Asperides's tip into the water. In the split second before the pull of the whirlpool overtook them, Asperides called on the strength of his souls. Up, up from the depths of their eternal prison in the underworld, he called them into the blade, called enough of their magic to resist the water, and to command the water's magic as his own.

The whirlpool swept up from the cave floor in a mighty wave. With one flick of Asperides's point, the wave rolled toward the werecat, enveloping the smaller whirlpools in its path and adding them to its power. Asperides was careful to keep the edges of the wave away from the fallen knights—the boy would never trust him if they came to harm—but the werecat, as far as he was concerned, was fair game.

The wave chased the werecat to the rear of the cave, forcing her to retreat or be sucked into the whirling depths. She tried to bat the water away, but Asperides's power was greater than hers, and his control held. The whirlpool was nearly as big as the cave now. The werecat stumbled back up the stairs toward the inner tomb, her skeletal back arched and her crumbling mouth hissing with every step.

"*BETRAYER! SOUL-EATER! FOULEST FIEND!*" the werecat witch shrieked at Asperides. She may have been a shell of her former self, but she remembered enough to know who was responsible for her failure to execute her duty. *"You will rue the day you left this tomb!"*

Except, of course, neither Asperides nor Nack spoke werecat, so all they heard was, *"HSSST-SPT! MWOR-GURRR! MREOR-MREEAAAAIR!"* and a whole lot of growling. The werecat witch prowled back and forth in front of the inner tomb door, claws scratching at the ground in frustration.

THE DOOR, Asperides said to Nack. *THE TOMB DOOR. NOW.*

Nack charged forward, the giant whirlpool parting before him and Asperides, creating a clear path across the slimy cave floor. Asperides thrust Nack's arm forward in a warning strike and the werecat backed away, hissing and spitting. A flurry of strikes, every one getting closer than the last, until—

There. The werecat witch stumbled backward, past the doorway she had been guarding for three hundred years, and fell into the inner tomb in a tangle of skeletal limbs.

Nack was at the stone door in a flash. He pushed with all his might, but the door barely scraped against the ground. He made as if to throw Asperides to the side, to get a better grip—

NO, commanded Asperides. *WAIT.*

The power of Asperides's souls flowed through him and into the boy, filling the boy with the strength of three Nacks put together. Together, they pushed against the door. It ground against the floor with a sound like thunder . . .

And fell into place just as the werecat launched herself against it with a dull *thud.*

WE MUST GO, Asperides said. *NOW.*

Nack, now slumped against the tomb door, looked around wildly.

"But what about—"

THE TOMB DOOR SHOULD HOLD HER, Asperides said. He did not mention that it stood little chance of holding the tomb's other occupant. *AND IF THAT DOES NOT STOP HER . . .*

He urged the boy onward, back through their path through the surging whirlpool. The water swirled higher and higher on their side of them, resisting Asperides's magic—trying to do its duty, until the end, to keep anything living—or dead—from leaving that cave.

The water splashed down behind them, filling the cavern with a giant pool. Asperides kept the lapping edges at bay while Nack hauled the unconscious Willa out of the water's reach. Barb lay on a ledge above them, her injuries numerous, but not, as far as Asperides could sense, fatal.

The werecat witch's cries echoed from the inner tomb, her claws scratching ineffectually at the stone door.

YOU MAY SAY WERECATS ARE PEOPLE, said Asperides, *BUT I KNOW THEY ARE MORE CAT THAN HUMAN. AND IF THERE'S ONE THING A FELINE HATES . . .*

Nack slumped against the mouth of the cave, his grip on Asperides growing slack. Asperides would have to get them out of here soon. He figured he had minutes before the boy lost consciousness from the shock . . .

"Water," croaked Nack, and promptly collapsed.

———•———

"What did I tell you?" groused a voice somewhere above Nack's head.

"Gllrrrghn," said Nack.

A tentative but sharp poke in his side was enough to persuade him to open his eyes, though just barely. His head pounded and he ached all over, as if he'd been beaten by a whole den of angry trolls.

"Not. A mortuary," said the innkeeper, looming above

Nack with his customary sour expression (and his rake). Unless Nack was mistaken, though, the innkeeper's face relaxed at the sight of Nack's awakening.

"What . . ." started Nack, blinking against his confusion and his sense of déjà vu.

"*Someone* had a night of it, by the looks of things, hmm?" scolded the innkeeper.

A nearby horse whinnied in agreement. Nack scrambled to his feet, edged around the innkeeper's bulk, and found himself face to face with Sweet Bean.

Nack sighed with relief. The horse responded with a light kick against its stall and a wet snort into Nack's face.

"You have no idea," Nack said, rubbing the horse snot off his face—and massaging his sore head while he was at it. His memories of everything from the night before were . . . fuzzy. Quite literally, as one of the last things he remembered was the lunging werecat mummy, claws extended and mangy fur flying . . .

"I see you've gotten that sword of yours back," said the innkeeper smugly. "I thought you might have something planned, when you borrowed this old—" The older man stopped short and gingerly poked at the hay where Nack had been lying. "Well see, what's this now . . ."

Nack squeezed past the gaping innkeeper and dove

for the glint of metal under the hay. The hilt of the sword fit in his hand like it was made for him. The silvery blade gleamed in the morning light—gleamed with just the faintest hint of blue radiating from its core.

"Is that . . . well, that's an angel blade, isn't it?" asked the innkeeper, awe creeping into his voice. He tossed the rake to the side as if it were suddenly burning hot. "My apologies, sir . . ."

"Don't apologize!" said Nack hurriedly. Somehow, he'd have preferred being poked again with the rake to the way the innkeeper was looking at him now. "It's, uh, it's no big deal . . ."

"I'd heard rumors, from the guests last night, about knights traveling to the far hills," the innkeeper murmured nervously, "but I didn't think . . . If there's anything you need, sir, anything at all—"

"It's fine," said Nack, his head still throbbing, suddenly wishing for nothing more than to lie back down in the hay instead of standing here, facing the innkeeper's now reverential stare. Nack looked again at the sword in his hand. It glimmered from the pommel to the tip, every inch a knight's blade, thrumming with promise.

And, if Nack recalled correctly, far, far too quiet.

"Actually," Nack said, forcing down his own embarrassment. "Do you happen to have any rooms today?"

8

Doors Meant to Be Opened

The dark sorceress Cleoline was eighteen years old, very good at magic, and very, very bored—three things that most people would agree are a dangerous combination.

Cleoline could happily brag that she'd been expelled from Madame Patrizia's Boarding Academy for Magickal Girls of Quality at the age of thirteen, only to be promptly accepted into the Order of Archivists instead. She hadn't known much about the Archivists when she joined—mostly that they were sorcerers, and also librarians. It turned out she'd had it all backward, and they were, in fact, mostly librarians, with a little bit of sorcery thrown in. They hadn't taken kindly to her pyrotechnic experiments in their sacred forest (they cut the trees down for their fancy paper *anyway*, so she didn't see what the big deal was) or her necromantic experiments with corpses from the Order's graveyard (again, there were perfectly good bodies just *sitting there*) or, as the head librarian put it, her general inclination toward *practicing* dark magic as opposed to filing it away alphabetically in the darkest corner she could find.

(Why did it have to be alphabetical if *no one was ever going to see it?*)

And so Cleoline could *unhappily* say she'd been chucked out of the Order of Archivists at the tender age of sixteen, at which point she chose to rent a flat in an aging magician's tower basement and do her best to ignore the rest of the civilized world. She could have trudged home to her parents, but they were *sheep farmers*, which was not only extremely boring, but Cleoline had the unjust misfortune of being born with a wool allergy.

She'd thrown herself into her studies on her own, continuing her experiments as best she could. It helped that her landlord, Waldo the Wise, was more than a little blind and deaf at his age, and so was less likely to notice when one of his chickens (or grandchildren) occasionally went missing to further the pursuit of magical discovery.

The hidden portal she'd discovered (and widened, just a little) on her way out of the Order—that led straight to their top-secret collections—probably helped, too. (It was probably meant to be an emergency exit in case the archives ever came under attack, but in Cleo's opinion, why make a door if you didn't want anyone to use it?)

And yet, it had to be said, despite access to most of the world's magical knowledge, most of her experiments went nowhere. She was tired of burning off chunks of her long black hair while playing with fire, and she had to be careful about things with *fumes* down there in the basement, because she was inquisitive, not suicidal. Smuggling corpses down all those flights of stairs was exhausting, and most of the time, her revenants didn't do much more than twitch pathetically before launching themselves straight at her head, at which point she was forced to terminate the spell or risk her brains becoming zombie chow. (Waldo the Wise's tower lacked a proper dungeon in which to lock up one's victims, which Cleoline felt was a major design flaw.)

All her past failures considered, it came as a bit of a shock when the walking, talking corpse of Amyral Venir, the *coolest evilest sorcerer knight of all time*, burst through her doorway, sending splinters and grave dirt flying every which way and looking *very much alive.*

"Cleoline!" called Waldo's tremulous voice from up the stairs. "There's a young man here to see you!"

"*You,*" said Amyral, pointing one jagged, broken fingernail at her. His gaunt face was dirt-streaked, his gray eyes haunted-looking and rimmed with dark circles, his hair hanging in lank, greasy chunks.

Cleoline didn't think she'd ever seen anyone more handsome.

"You're the one who raised me," Amyral said, his voice deep and hoarse.

Three hundred years underground made one a little parched, Cleoline imagined.

Keep it casual, Cleo, she reminded herself, trying to strike as nonchalant a pose as possible on her couch without getting stabbed by one of the random chunks of door.

"Guilty," she said with a little shrug.

Amyral stared straight at her, breathing heavily.

"Then maybe it is you who can tell me . . ." he said, his gray eyes locking onto her violet ones, freezing her to the spot with their intensity. She understood why hundreds of knights had followed him all those years ago.

"Anything," Cleoline breathed.

Amyral's face twisted in pain, his eyes struggling to shed tears that Cleoline suspected he could no longer make. Not after she had ripped him from the jaws of death.

"Why do I feel so *empty*?"

A Quest or
a Mission?

Nack waited until he heard the innkeeper's daughter's footsteps echoing down the hall before he looked around the generous private suite, hurriedly chucked off his scabbard, and threw his sword across the room. It landed on the impressively large bed with a soft *whump*.

"Explain," Nack commanded.

The silence thickened, punctuated only by the sounds of a sudden rain shower outside. He might as well have been talking to . . . well, a sword.

But Nack knew better. He tiptoed over to the sword, drew it from the scabbard, and tossed it back onto the bed. He was on the other side of the room before the hilt hit the pillows.

"Explain to me how we got out of those caves," Nack insisted.

Still no answer. He felt queasy in addition to pummeled and realized he hadn't eaten since the dumplings the afternoon before. A few beads of sweat trickled down his hairline. Perhaps he really had imagined it . . . perhaps this was all a dream . . .

The name was on the tip of his tongue before he'd even thought of it.

"*Asperides*," Nack said, filling his voice with every ounce of authority he could muster. "Answer me!"

The sword glittered. A low *thrum* echoed through the air, so soft that Nack wasn't even sure he'd heard it.

I REMOVED US SAFELY FROM THE CAVE, the sword said, each word appearing in Nack's head as if it were his own thought. *I BELIEVE THAT WAS THE GOAL?*

"But . . . but *how*?" asked Nack. "The last thing I remember . . . and wait, what about Sir Willa? And Barb? We have to—"

ALL SAFE, said Asperides. *THANKS TO YOU. WILLA, OF COURSE, WILL HEAL MORE QUICKLY WITH LENIRA BY HER SIDE. AND THE VILLAGERS ARE CARING FOR BOTH THEIR INJURIES AS WE SPEAK.*

"Right," said Nack, nodding. "Good, good . . . wait. How do *you* know that?" His temporary relief at the good news vanished.

JUST BECAUSE YOU HAVE LOST CONSCIOUS-NESS DOES NOT MEAN THAT I HAVE, said the sword. *I OVERHEARD THE INNKEEPER'S GUESTS TALKING IN THE YARD.*

Nack blushed. Of course. But still . . .

"Wait a minute," said Nack, "*I was unconscious.* I . . . I must have fainted, back there in the cave. I don't remember getting back here at all." Yet even as he said it, more hazy memories surfaced in his mind, like distorted reflections shimmering on the surface of a pond. He remembered striding out of the cave, Asperides shining bright as a star in his hands, the werecat howling behind them, imprisoned by the giant whirlpool, her own magic nothing in comparison to Nack's, to that of his angel blade.

Suddenly, Nack saw himself not through his own eyes, but as if he were outside of himself, watching a young man with a gleaming sword cut through two remaining gasper-cats as if they were made of air. His chest was heaving, his hair disheveled, and his eyes glowed as bright blue as his sword . . .

Nack gasped.

I . . . ASSISTED IN OUR EVACUATION, said Asperides. *I DREW UPON MY MAGIC AND DIRECTED IT THROUGH YOU SO THAT WE MIGHT ESCAPE.*

Nack didn't know how much Asperides had seen—or could see—of his memories, and Nack wasn't sure what he thought about that. He knew that angel blades could speed up their wielder's healing, but to take control of Nack's body entirely . . . there was so much about the angel blade connection no one had told him.

IT IS NOT A POWER I RELISH EXERCISING, continued the sword. *NOR IS IT A METHOD I EMPLOY OFTEN. AND IT WILL BECOME HARDER TO DO AS OUR RELATIONSHIP . . . SOLIDIFIES.*

"Solidifies?"

THE LONGER YOU ARE MY MASTER.

Asperides said nothing more. The silence stretched between them for so long Nack thought the sword had gone back to sleep . . . or whatever it was angel blades did when they weren't conversing with their masters or slaying demons. Outside, the sounds of the rain picked up. Thunder cracked overhead, making Nack flinch, and he heard cries and scurrying outside in the yard as people fled from the sudden storm.

"Are you some sort of . . . special angel?" asked Nack finally, moving from the far wall to the corner of the bed. He was awfully tired and its pillows looked only too inviting after the long night he'd had.

When the sword didn't answer, Nack mumbled, "Sorry, if that's some sort of personal question, you know, for angels. I just . . . your power . . . I've never seen anything like it. Not with the Furnival knights. And even Willa's sword, well . . . You just seem different."

I AM VERY OLD, said Asperides. It was the same thing the sword had said to Nack in . . . wherever that place had been, just before they'd made their contract.

Before Nack had sold his soul.

Nack slammed down on the thought harder than the blow of a bridge troll's club. The contract had been made, and there was no going back on it now. Besides, if this was what it took to get an angel blade, then most of the knights in the land had done it, hadn't they? He had nothing to be ashamed of.

Nothing at all.

I can't believe I have an angel blade, Nack thought. After all those years of training, he'd only just begun tagging along on missions with Declan and the others when, well, when House Solonos decided they were more interested in consolidating their power than in protecting people against creatures from the underworld, and everything had changed. But even though he'd been called into service much younger than any knight-in-training normally would, Nack had thought it would be years—decades, perhaps—until he performed a deed brave enough, until the circumstances were just right, for him to attract an angel to his sword. Some knights never managed it in their entire lives, for one reason or another. And here he was, barely thirteen years old and wielding what appeared to be one of the most powerful and ancient angel blades in existence!

"I can't believe I have an angel blade," Nack muttered aloud, finally allowing himself to sink into the pillows next to Asperides. A moment later, he shot upright with a start. "I have an *angel blade*!"

SO WE HAVE ESTABLISHED, said Asperides.

"No, no, you don't understand," said Nack. "I—well, we—rid the cave of those gasper-cats, right? That boy from the market, Arty, he'll be all right again after this, and anyone else whose breath they stole. We defeated and imprisoned the werecat-witch-mummy . . . thing. I got *an angel blade*. And I, well, I didn't part with my clan on the best of terms, you see, but this . . . this is amazing! That's a proper quest, done and dusted. They'll have to take me back after this!"

HMMM, said the sword.

"What 'hmmm'?" asked Nack testily. "What are you 'hmmming' for?"

WAS IT, THOUGH?

"Was what, er, what?" asked Nack.

WAS IT A QUEST, AFTER ALL? mused the sword. *IT SEEMED MORE LIKE A MISSION, TO ME.*

"Wha— There's a difference?" asked Nack, flopping back down onto the pillows.

IN MY EXPERIENCE—WHICH IS BUT A MERE SEVERAL THOUSAND YEARS—A "QUEST" DENOTES A GRANDER JOURNEY THAN A SINGULAR HARDSCRABBLE ENCOUNTER WITH A MUMMY.

"There were the gasper-cats, too," Nack insisted. "And the whirlpools!"

TO BE SURE, Asperides allowed. *BUT IT IS HARDLY THE STUFF OF BALLADS, IS IT?*

"Speak for yourself," Nack said, slinking down on the mass of pillows and crossing his arms. "I must be the youngest Furnival angel-blade bearer in generations! Surely, that's enough proof that I . . . well, that I'm brave enough to . . . well, that I can do what needs doing."

OF COURSE, said the sword, its voice as silky-smooth as one of the pillowcases on the bed. It said nothing more for a few moments, leaving Nack to stew in his newly simmering self-doubt. *Did* his escapades in the cave qualify as a quest? *Had* he been brave enough— or just in the right place at the right time? It hadn't taken very long, to be sure. The request for aid hadn't come to him, say, in a dream, or from a mysterious fellow traveler he met in the woods. He hadn't journeyed for hundreds of miles in the pursuit of a single, specific goal, nor had he encountered any significant supernatural roadblocks or villains along the way. (He seriously doubted that a grumbling stomach and a few local bullies were considered epic enough obstacles.) Speaking of his grumbling stomach . . .

Nack did his best to put his doubts out of his mind while he scampered down the inn stairs to the kitchen. He tried to pay for a meal with his few remaining coins but was driven off with a chorus of "No trouble at all, sir, no trouble at all," and "Take it as thanks, for solving that trouble up in the hills!" and they sent him off to wait in the dining room.

The inn was full of wet people grumbling about the sudden storm, and the windows occasionally lit up with the lightning that snaked through the sky, making everyone jump at once.

"You think this is bad," said a scruffy, long-haired person with a tankard in their hand. "You should see the storms when they make landfall on the coast these days. Waves as high as mountains!" A few people looked at them skeptically, but a few others grumbled in assent. Rivulets of water from outside trickled in through the roof, as if to reinforce the coastal dweller's point.

Nack left the inn's other guests to their gossip and returned to his room with a pewter tray full of steaming pies, soup, and strong tea, and set himself up at the room's small table to tuck in with gusto. He felt bad about not paying for the food, but really . . . an empty stomach *should* be on the list of quest-qualifying obstacles. Once he'd made a dent in his dinner, he transferred some of the food from one bowl to another, put the empty one under the leaky corner of the ceiling, and went back to devouring his meal.

He had almost forgotten Asperides was there at all until the sword said, *THERE IS ALSO THE MATTER OF PROOF.*

Startled, Nack nearly choked on a generous mouthful of chicken pot pie.

"What do you mean?" he asked with a sigh. "You mean, like, that I completed the quest? Aren't you proof enough?" Nack waved his hand toward Asperides and went back to his pie.

HMM, said Asperides.

"Will you stop with the 'hmming'?" asked Nack. "I don't know what that means!"

Again, the sword was silent. But Nack couldn't help turning its words over in his mind.

"I could get some statements from the villagers," Nack mused. "Maybe from that stall owner, or Arty himself. That is, if they can read and write . . ." Nack took a fortifying swig of his tea. The grand meal in front of him suddenly seemed far less appetizing with doubt settling into his stomach instead. Surely, possessing an angel blade would be proof enough of his brave deeds. Surely, he didn't need such a very *epic* quest in order to prove himself.

Surely, he'd suffered enough.

Hadn't he?

He remembered Declan, blood-spattered and furious, pushing him so hard in the chest his breath was knocked out of him. He remembered trying not to make a sound, even though it *hurt*, not while they and the remaining Furnival knights cowered in the woods, hiding from the Solonos-allied reinforcements overtaking Castle Clyffidil.

"*You*," Declan had spat. "This is *your fault*. That 'innocent' boy you let sneak past you? He's a scout for Lord Solonos. It was he who escaped the castle, got word to his lord, and brought *those men*"—Declan pointed to the black-clad soldiers scurrying to the castle's walls—"back to claim their stolen land."

Declan had raised his voice, slightly, so that the other weary men and women might overhear. "Castle Clyffidil is lost," he said, and then, with a pointed look at Nack, added, "*Again*. House Furnival has failed to protect our allies. The moons shine naught but shame on us tonight."

"Shame shines upon us," echoed the knights, their voices barely above whispers. With dark looks at Nack, the knights each took a candle from their bandoliers, broke it in half, and tossed the pieces to the ground. Still barely able to process his brother's words, never mind use his fingers, Nack had struggled to break his candle. No one offered to help him.

Nack's candle had been the last to drop to the forest floor. Even his penance, he thought, came too little, too late.

Nack pushed his plate away from him, all traces of hunger gone. Asperides was probably right. If Nack wanted his family to welcome him back with open arms, his act of redemption had to be . . . well, it had to be at least as good as the evil he'd done, back at Castle Clyffidil.

"What do you think I'd need?" he asked Asperides. "What would be proof enough, to convince them?"

I THINK THE TESTIMONY OF A RECENTLY RESCUED PRINCESS SHOULD DO NICELY, said Asperides. *DON'T YOU?*

10

Eighty Percent Soulless

"Sooooo, I've got a theory," said Cleoline. "But I don't think you're going to like it."

A much more presentable (though admittedly still rather dead-looking) Amyral Venir stared at her from across Waldo the Wise's exceedingly long banquet table. Waldo, who had somehow been convinced to give up his seat at the head of the table for a complete stranger who had recently broken into his house, sat halfway between them, gumming away at his food and amusing himself by conjuring little whirlpools in his wine goblet, blissfully unaware of the half-shouted conversation going on over his head. (Yes, the table was that long.)

"What was that?" Amyral asked, putting a thin, pale

hand to his ear. His food sat untouched on the plate before him.

"I noticed, he does not have a hat!" piped up Waldo, gesturing to Amyral's shoulder-length locks.

They really should have just pushed the chairs closer together, but Cleoline loved the visual drama of that table and, by the Missing Moon, if she was finally going to get a chance to make *real* Evil Plans, as opposed to just reading about them, then the setting had better fit, hadn't it?

"Eat your grilled snake, Waldo," she chided him.

The old magician cheerfully returned his attention to his plate.

"I *said*," Cleoline repeated, a little louder this time. "I've got a theory. About why your resurrection didn't exactly . . . go to plan."

Cleoline gulped. The reality of *actually undead Amyral Venir* sitting at her (well, Waldo's) dining room table still hadn't set in. It was one thing to muck about crossbreeding fire-breathing lizards with Waldo's chickens, or to make animated skeletons with corpses from the local graveyard and have a rollicking dance party of one (plus skeletons), or even to try *really, really* hard to resurrect the world's most evil sorcerer knight because you'd come across the last surviving records of his misdeeds in the Order of Archivists and thought, *Cool,* and also maybe hung a portrait of said sorcerer above your dresser. It was another thing altogether to give that recently reanimated knight a bath in your basement and help him scrub what looked like bits of mummified fur out from under his fingernails. (*Blargh.* Also, it turned out that recently reanimated knights were surprisingly tetchy about their personal space and would respond to said ministrations by shouting, "Unhand me, cursed enchantress!" one minute and grumpily asking for help squeezing into one of Waldo the Wise's clean shirts the next.)

And now, sitting across this very long and dramatic table, Cleoline could appreciate that Amyral Venir might be *very displeased* with the news she was about to deliver, and she'd read enough about the dark knight to know the kind of fate that befell those who displeased him.

"Proceed," Amyral said, his steely eyes never leaving hers.

"When I resurrected you," continued Cleoline, "all I had was your portrait, about three pages of some drunk monk's notes from a few hundred years ago, and—supposedly—a scrap of the toe section from one of your socks."

"We're not eating rocks!" said Waldo, chuckling and shaking his head.

"One of my . . . socks," said Amyral.

"It had to be something personal of yours," explained Cleoline. "And those items are a bit thin on the ground, with you being nearly erased from history and all."

Amyral bristled, no doubt angry about all his great achievements being forgotten.

"I liked the purple stripes, by the way," said Cleoline. "*Anyway*, my point is, I didn't have very much to go on. And I certainly didn't know about the, uh . . . sword. Situation."

A clean shirt and one of Waldo's velvet capes now covered Amyral's chest, but Cleoline couldn't keep her eyes from straying to the spot where she knew the gaping hole was, as raw as the day the sword was thrust through him.

It certainly explained the trajectory of Amyral's career. Few people, even hundreds of years ago, seemed to believe there were any demon swords left in the world. Most people didn't even believe they existed at all. But the type of power Amyral had commanded—the hordes of men, and even demons, under his command . . . one mortal man alone couldn't have achieved such feats, no matter how skilled at combat and necromancy and moon magic.

But a dark knight with a demon sword? That was certainly possible.

And unfortunately, it also explained why Amyral Venir currently felt like there was a great sucking void inside his chest. (Grisly hole notwithstanding.)

"My demon sword knowledge is a little patchy," admitted Cleoline. "But what I can glean from the ancient chronicles is this: demon swords store their imprisoned souls somewhere in the farthest depths of the underworld. Like, *really* far. Like, possibly their own pocket-dimension-inside-a-pocket-dimension-inside-the-lowest-level-of-the-underworld kind of far. *Buuuut* they need those souls to use most of their magic, don't they? At least the more powerful stuff. So maybe they keep some soul stuff within easy reach. Maybe they keep a few souls, or some soul fragments, in a higher level of the underworld—and therefore closer to the border with our world—or even within the sword *itself*, so the sword and their master can draw on at least *some* power instantaneously."

Amyral's expression had been getting frownier and frownier—Cleoline didn't even realize it was possible to frown that hard—and she had a feeling he was starting to get the picture.

"My theory is, when I tried to resurrect you," continued Cleoline, "I was *actually* only able to grab a little piece of your soul. Which, I should mention, is still *really cool*, because that's basically why resurrections never work all that well, because the soul's too far gone into the underworld. But we got lucky!"

"Fortune smiles upon me," said Amyral acidly.

"What's that?" asked Waldo. "Did someone say 'pudding'?"

The old man looked around hopefully.

Cleoline sat back in her chair, slightly hurt. Perhaps she should have put less emphasis on the "luck" part.

"What I mean to say is," she corrected, "because your demon sword was so close to the land of the living, what with its physical presence in your tomb, when I performed the resurrection . . . well, that made it possible for me to grab the small bit of your soul that was in its . . . reserves, so to speak." It was a shame that the sword had been gone by the time Amyral had fully awakened—stolen by clueless graverobbers, no doubt, who had no idea of the power they held in their hands. Cleoline would have loved to study it.

"So what you're saying," said Amyral slowly, finally taking a long swig from his wineglass, "is that I am, essentially, soulless?"

"Not soulless, no!" Cleoline assured him, her voice high. "Not . . . entirely. I'd say about . . . eighty percent. Give or take."

"And the rest of my soul," Amyral nearly spat, "is still trapped there, in the underworld? Somewhere in that betrayer of a demon sword's prison?"

"I'm afraid so," said Cleoline quietly. "But don't worry. I'm the one who did this to you, so I'm the one who's going to fix it."

And I'm the one he'll be grateful to, Cleoline thought with pleasure. She could picture herself now—she would be the dark queen to his king, standing by his side as he ruled over his empire. She would leave smelly Waldo and her tiny basement apartment behind. She would have her *own* castle, with her own private laboratory—and it would absolutely have a proper dungeon.

"I shall do everything, and I mean *everything*, in my power to help you get your soul back," Cleoline insisted. "I'll summon the portal to the archives this very night. I'll scour every scrap of parchment in the Archivists' libraries. And we *will* find a way to retrieve your soul."

By the time Cleoline finished her impassioned speech, Amyral's eyes were blazing again, just like when he'd first bashed in her door, and Cleoline felt nearly out of breath with the excitement of it all.

"See that you do," said Amyral. "In the meantime, I will prepare for my new reign."

Cleoline raised her glass in a toast, and slowly, Amyral raised his in return.

See, she thought, surveying Amyral across the gloomy dining room and imagining what a picture they must make—the tortured dark knight on one end, and his stylish, brilliant savior on the other. *I* knew *this table would be perfect.*

"Now see here," said Waldo loudly, setting down his fork with pointed looks at both Amyral and Cleoline. "Is there any pudding, or not?"

11

The Princess in the Tower

O ut of all the lies the demon sword Asperides had told over the course of his existence, the "angel network" was amongst the most outrageous.

He'd told Nack the priestesses of the Missing Moon had kidnapped a princess who was visiting from a far-away land because they believed her to be possessed by the spirit of the Missing Moon. Her parents, too fearful of current political unrest in their home kingdom to leave, had put out a desperate plea for her safe return.

"But how did you—" Nack started to ask.

LENIRA, THE KNIGHT WILLA'S SWORD, TOLD ME, said Asperides, cutting in before Nack could finish. He normally wouldn't be so forward, but he also wouldn't have been able to lie if Nack asked him a direct question. *JUST BEFORE WE LEFT THE CAVE. IT WAS TO BE THEIR NEXT QUEST, AFTER THE DETOUR TO THE THORNY HILLS.*

"The sword *told* you?" Nack repeated, pausing in the middle of stuffing another of the innkeeper's pot pies into his rucksack. "I didn't know angel blades talked to each other. Though I suppose, until you, I didn't know angel blades talked at all . . ."

The boy was, of course, entirely correct. As far as Asperides and any other demon or resident of the underworld could tell, angels rarely did anything other than float around looking for weapons to inhabit, flash prettily, and occasionally make adorable little chirps that basically sounded like *Meep!* in varying tones. If this was indeed some sort of language, the combined efforts of human and demonic scholars over the past few thousand years hadn't yet managed to translate it. The idea that there was some sophisticated network of angel communications, swapping tips about various quests and missions and dangers ahead, was about as likely as Asperides sprouting four legs and galloping off into the sunset.

The far more likely conclusion (which the humans hadn't quite the courage to say outright) was that despite being extremely powerful mystical beings and the only true match for the powers of the underworld in the known universe, angels were *dumb as rocks.*

Fortunately for Asperides, they seemed to have some company in his new master.

Asperides had told Nack that while Willa and Barb recovered from their injuries, it was his and Nack's prerogative—no, their *duty*—to continue the knights' quest and rescue the princess. And if they just so happened to make a quick stop in the Furnival stronghold before returning said princess safely home, well, that would work out for everyone, wouldn't it?

There was no princess, of course, but not all leads were reliable, and who could blame a bunch of angels for an honest mistake?

There was, however, a young novitiate of the Mission of the Missing Moon who could tell Asperides everything he wanted to know about a certain prophecy—and what the namesake of her order had to do with it.

———————•◆•———————

Cleoline decided to take a few dozen no-crows with her to the Mission of the Missing Moon. Amyral Venir had helped her place the traps and summoning charm on Waldo the Wise's tower roof—not that they seemed to need the traps *or* the summoning charm. Amyral just kind of had to stand there, extend his well-muscled arms to the winds, and say "Come" in his low and menacing voice, and within minutes the rooftop had been filled with beady-eyed black birds.

The whole thing was so cool Cleoline almost forgot to zombify them.

In short order, however, the no-crows were made, and now their skeletal wings cut through the night sky, occasionally raining down chunks of feathers (or rotting flesh) onto the landscape below. Cleoline flew on the back of the largest former crow of the bunch; its bones had been extended with the help of some necromantic grafting to a few other skeletons she happened to have lying around. She'd also moon-magicked some cushions from one of Waldo's aging sofas to float on its back, because sitting on the back of a big bird corpse would have been far too bony for a comfortable ride. The no-crows wouldn't last long, comfy couch crow included, and she supposed the daisy print on the cushions was kind of a vibe-killer, but the undead birds were still a formidable weapon, should she need them.

And besides, she and Amyral were in a hurry. Cleoline had begun to suspect that the longer the evil knight went without his soul, the, well . . . eviler he was going to get.

And not in the dashing, charismatic, world-dominating way. More in the sneaking-live-crows-for-snacks-when-Cleoline-wasn't-looking sort of way.

The young necromancer's long black hair whipped behind her as she flew. It would all be fine. She had a bit more research to do, but if the rumors she'd heard while sneaking about in the Archivists' halls were true, this prophecy about the Missing Moon might be the key to retrieving the rest of Amyral's soul from the underworld. If the Missing Moon really were to return, the boundaries between the worlds would be at their thinnest in over two millennia.

The perfect time to sneak in, bust the soul of the greatest dark knight of all time out of prison, and sneak out, no?

But first, she had to hear the details of the prophecy, and that meant a brief errand to grab the little Seer who had started it all. She called her no-crows closer, and together they flew on, a dark cloud of decay against already darkening skies.

———— ◆ ————

Nack was nearly at the tower when the first feather fell from the foggy sky, gently wafting down until it landed squarely on his nose.

"Achoo!" he sneezed.

BE QUIET, said Asperides.

"Easy for you to say," Nack grumbled. Angel blades didn't ever have to sneeze.

The light of the two moons was the only thing illuminating his way as he crept along atop the crumbling wall that led to the Mission of the Missing Moon's tallest tower. He couldn't risk the light of a candle, and besides, he needed both hands to scoot along the top of the wall. It was a long drop down to the courtyard below.

Nack had expected to find guards at the entrances and exits to the temple complex, what with a captive princess in residence, but the place had been curiously empty when he arrived. Scurrying up to the walls in the dark, he had half expected some knight or priestess to jump out of a shadowy alcove and shout, "Halt, intruder!" but no such excitement occurred. Each and every window ledge, however, had a three-inch-thick border of salt and an ever-lasting candle—the best that money could buy and surely a drain on the priestesses' collective power, but perhaps they felt it was a small price to pay for continual protection from most demons.

The only resistance he encountered was when he first tried to dash into the inner courtyard. Under the temple's stone archway he faltered mid-step; it was as if he were suddenly trying to walk through glue instead of crisp night air, and his head began to pound.

GUARDS AND BOOBY TRAPS ARE NOT THE ONLY FORMS OF PROTECTION, said Asperides, the sword's voice almost a whisper. (Not that it made much difference if he whispered or not; Nack was fairly certain by this point that he only heard the sword speak inside his own head, anyways.) *BUT THESE WARDS WERE CRAFTED FOR LESSER BEINGS THAN US.*

He urged Nack onward, and after a few agonizingly slow steps, the invisible resistance against them vanished with a faint *pop*. (Nack also wasn't sure when he'd started referring to the sword as a "he"; when he asked Asperides what the sword used, the angel blade simply said, *I HAVE SOMETIMES FELT MORE "HE" AND SOMETIMES MORE "SHE," AND QUITE OFTEN NEITHER, BECAUSE I AM NEITHER. BUT "HE" WORKS AS WELL AS ANYTHING ELSE.* At Nack's slightly puzzled glance the sword had let out what could only be described as a chuckle and said, *WHAT A BORE IT MUST BE, NOT TO CONTAIN MULTITUDES.* And that was the last they talked about that.)

With the strongest wards behind them, it was easy enough to find a spot to scramble onto the low wall connecting the various temple buildings. Nack supposed the wards had somehow recognized Asperides's angelic nature and allowed them to pass, distinguishing friend from foe. But he didn't need wards to make crossing to the tower difficult; the top of the wall was quite narrow, and some of the stone was crumbling, and—

SPLAT.

And a bird was pooping on his face.

"Ugh, great," said Nack, blinking the wetness out of his eyes and shaking out his hair, all the while trying not to lose his grip on the wall beneath him. Getting pooped on by a passing gull was just his kind of luck.

Splat again.

"Now that is just disgusting," said Nack. "Can't you find somewhere else to do your—" He stopped, looking at the chunky residue now dripping down his shoulder, smelling the sickly stench of rotting meat. The wet patch glistened in the moonlight—glistened with the dark, reddish brown of stale blood.

Nack had never before wished so very, very hard to be merely pooped on.

NO-CROWS, said Asperides darkly. *YOU MUST FIND THEIR ANIMATOR. THE NECROMANCER CANNOT BE FAR—*

The sword's words were cut off as a great dark cloud suddenly swooped over them. Nack slammed down onto the top of the wall, making himself as flat as possible, as what must have been hundreds of no-crows made a bee-line for the tower. A few of them pecked at his ankles and shirt collar as they passed, close enough for their desiccated wings to tickle his back.

"The princess!" Nack hissed. "We've got to save her!"

He hauled himself up onto all fours again, but before he could really get going, he was forced to flatten himself yet again as another, even larger mass of no-crows swooped in from the right.

No, it wasn't a mass of no-crows. It was just a very *big* no-crow. A massive flying skeleton, with smaller no-crows flitting in and out of its ribs and its eyeholes. Nack got a brief glimpse of a rider on its back—a woman, he thought, wearing a flowing dark cape.

He had to stop her. Fear of the height and the narrow wall forgotten, Nack stood and began to run toward the tower. He'd barely taken a few steps before the woman on the massive no-crow swept over him again, her birds crying out in gleeful shrieks. Nack certainly had to shut *them* up before half the Mission woke up.

Asperides was in his hands before he realized he'd taken the sword from the scabbard. He swiped at the giant no-crow, missing the large bird but managing to cut through a few of the smaller ones encircling it. They sizzled briefly before bursting into nothingness, little flashes of bright blue popping in the air in their wake.

"It could be an assassin from House Solonos," Nack said, pausing to catch his breath. "They must have heard I'm on my own . . ." Banished or not, Nack was still one of the heirs to the clan leader. He cursed himself for not thinking of this before. Of course he'd be more vulnerable, out on his own, clan-less and friendless. One of the Solonos spies had gotten wind of Nack's angel blade, perhaps, and wanted to stamp out any potential of a rising star on the enemy's side . . .

"Stay back, foul assassin!" Nack cried as the necromancer took another dive at him. This time, he managed to swipe the underside of the monstrous no-crow. It shuddered in the air, no doubt losing a good portion of its power, and the necromancer on its back yelped. "Lord Solonos won't get the best of House Furnival tonight!"

"Whatever you say, little dude!" said the necromancer. Her voice sounded surprisingly young for such a committed agent of darkness. "Just leave the Seer to me, all right? And no one has to get—*argggh*!"

Nack used the assassin's distraction to his advantage and sliced through the giant, skeletal wing of the no-crow. He would never have been able to deliver such a blow with a normal sword, but the moment he struck out, Asperides seemed to *grow* in his hands, gaining just enough inches to perfectly catch the undead beast's wing joint. The sword glowed, its magic flowing freely, and cut through the tough sinew and bone as easily as a knife through butter.

Nack paused for a moment to catch his balance and then continued running for the tower. He felt a brief pang of guilt at the thought of the young assassin spiraling to the ground on the back of the disintegrating no-crow but quickly shook off the feeling. She'd surely been sent there to kill him, or perhaps the princess, after all.

There were still quite a few no-crows flying around, which meant that the necromancer was still alive, at least. Nack eyed them poking at the bars at the tower window. Perhaps the assassin hadn't been there for him after all? Perhaps she was some other player from the political drama back in the princess's homeland? But Nack didn't have time to worry about the necromancer's motivations now. At the moment, he was faced with the daunting task of scaling a tower and bringing a princess safely back down with him.

"There's not a chance you can transform into a flying carpet or something, is there?" Nack asked Asperides breathlessly.

I'M AFRAID NOT, said the sword. *BUT WE HARDLY HAVE NEED OF ONE. LOOK.*

Nack cast his gaze around them, dodging the occasional undead bird, until his eyes fell on something he expected to see in the Mission of the Missing Moon even less than a murder of no-crows.

"Is that . . . a flying sofa?"

———————◆———————

Sister Dawn Therin did not pay much heed to the commotion going on outside her tower prison. She could barely tell night from day there, what with its single small window so far above her. When she heard distant shouting, she could barely bring herself to care. Perhaps the Mission was being invaded by another order or clan of knights who sought to capture her and demand to hear the prophecy. Perhaps the priestesses were fighting amongst themselves over her (again). It made little difference to Therin. She was still locked in the tower, her fate still at the mercy of others.

No, it wasn't until the first of the no-crows started clawing at the window bars when she realized that, all right, *maybe* she should care a little bit, because she definitely had preferences when it came to her imminent demise, and being pecked to death by mysterious undead birds was not at the top of the list.

Therin shrieked when the first bird squeezed its way past the bars—quickly followed by another, and another. They swooped down over her, carrying their horrid stench of rotting flesh with them. She swatted at them with the long, wide sleeves of her novitiate's robe, sending them pinging off the stone walls, but they kept coming for her, dogged in their pursuit.

"Excuse me, Princess!" said a voice from somewhere up above her. "But this might actually be easier if you let them grab you!"

Princess? So now her potential kidnappers were teasing her as well as capturing her?

"Fat chance!" said Therin, ducking out of the way of another horrid-looking bird.

"Sorry," said the voice. "I should have explained. We're—I'm here to rescue you!"

Therin was about to retort, "Oh, right, a *necromancer* is here to save me," when the voice said: "Stand back, please!" and the tower was filled with a flashing bright blue light. Therin scooted back automatically, and it was a good thing—there was a great metallic sawing noise, and suddenly, the bars from the window came clanging down onto the tower's floor, only feet from where Therin had been standing moments before. One of them rolled and bonked into her toe.

"Ow!" she said, and looked up at the window, no-crows momentarily forgotten. (They had grabbed hold of her sleeves and floated expectantly beside her, their glowing red eyes flashing in the dark.) Down from the window flew a few more no-crows, but beyond them, Therin spotted the face of a dark-haired boy not much older than herself. He appeared to be floating on some-thing out of Therin's sight, and in his hands was a great, glowing angel blade.

Perhaps he *was* a knight here to rescue her, after all?

"Sorry!" the boy called. "Now, the no-crows aren't mine, but we might as well use them, all right? Otherwise I'm not sure how to get you out."

Therin gaped up at him. Some rescuer *he* was.

"No way!" said Therin, swatting at the no-crows and nearly gagging from the stench of them.

"You could always stay here, if you like!" said the boy, a little testily this time. He dipped out of view of the window again, appearing to struggle with whatever was keeping him aloft.

Out in the hall, Therin heard a door slam. Voices echoed outside—her former Sisters, she realized, undoubtedly alerted to the disturbance. Therin's lip trembled as she eyed the converging no-crows. It was either stay in here and face the Mission's judgment, or take her chances with the boy with the angel blade.

"Third Daughter, forgive me," Therin said, and extended her arms fully, the better to let the no-crows grab hold.

She was somehow gagging *and* crying—truly a feat, she thought—by the time the crows had completed their herky-jerky ascent through the tower and out the window. A thin pair of arms grabbed her around the middle ("Sorry!" said the boy, and Therin could practically hear him blush), and in a few seconds she found herself precariously perched on what appeared to be a daisy-printed couch cushion.

Over a hundred feet above the ground.

"I wouldn't look down, if I were you," advised the boy, seated across from her on a cushion of his own. The cushions were precariously connected by ropes and a few other suspicious-looking connective fibers she could only *hope* were ropes.

"You know what?" said the boy with a wince. "I'd just close your eyes, actually."

"What—"

FLASH. The sword came arcing toward her face before she even had time to scream. Therin ducked (and did, in fact, close her eyes) but the expected blow never came. Instead, the sword passed through the no-crows still insistently tugging on her robes and her hair. They disintegrated with little *poofs*.

"Other side, now," said the boy. The sword swooshed past her head, close enough to be a whisper in her ear, but to the boy's credit, not a hair on her head was harmed.

The very air itself was humming with magic—the remains of the no-crows and the necromancy used to power them, the moon-magicked couch cushions, the thrumming wards of the Mission, and something else, something heavy and ancient-feeling . . .

And, Therin realized, the moonbeams currently being gathered up by the very-much-awake priestesses, ready to hurl at Therin and her young rescuer's heads.

"Duck!" said Therin, pulling the boy down by his shoulder. The magicked moonbeam arced harmlessly over their heads as the couch cushions bobbed and weaved. More priestesses were spilling out of their quarters to line the temple's walls in defensive formations.

"How do you make these things go?!" yelled Therin, poking at the sides of the couch cushions. A bit of stuffing oozed out of one of them.

"Well," said the boy. "I've mostly tried asking them nicelyYYYYYYYYY—"

Only his screams were left behind as Therin tapped her knees against either side of the cushions, spurring the contraption onward, upward, and away into the moonlit sky.

12

No More Secrets

I t was a good thing the sorceress's couch cushions had
been animated with good old-fashioned moon magic,
as opposed to the necromancy that had created the no-
crows, because otherwise, Asperides, Nack, and the
rescued princess would not have gotten very far from the
temple complex. As it was, Asperides urged the group
onward until just before the sun's first rays poked their
heads over the horizon. The cushions had begun shuddering and losing height with the dimming of the moons'
light, but they had to get as far away as possible from
the Mission—and that necromancer assassin—before
daybreak.

They finally landed in a woodland clearing at sunrise,

miles and miles away from the temple and (hopefully) from any pesky no-crows following them—though the no-crows would have dropped from the sky even faster than the flying cushions with the rising daylight. As it was, their descent was a rough one, and after Nack and the princess tumbled unceremoniously to the ground, the cushions huffed out a heavy puff of dust and an exhausted sound that reminded Nack far too much of a human sigh. He gave the aged, beaten cushion an affectionate pat.

"Well done, you," he said. He wanted nothing more than to lie back in the grass and sleep for a week, but there was a princess in his care now, and he felt that wouldn't be very fitting for a chivalrous rescuer. He turned to the princess in question. "Don't worry," he said, with more confidence than he felt. "You're safe now, Princess. We'll find out where we are soon, and get you home presently."

"Princess?" the girl snorted, her pale, freckled nose wrinkling. "That's about the third time you've called me that, and I have no idea why. I'm starting to think you stormed the wrong tower, Sir . . ."

"Nack Furnival," Nack said automatically, forgetting, in the excitement of the moment, that he wasn't supposed to use that surname anymore. "But just call me Nack. I'm not a knight, really. Not yet."

"Well, not-a-knight Nack Furnival," said the girl.

"Thanks for the lift and all, but I'm not a princess. I'm just Therin. Well, Sister Dawn Therin, actually. Of the Mission of the Missing Moon."

Nack took a longer look at the girl—this Therin. He hadn't noticed her long robes and lopsided veil before. Granted, she hardly had the graceful bearing he expected of a princess, but then, flopping on the grass like an exhausted fish, he probably didn't look much like a noble knight, either.

"Princess," Nack said. "I understand you're scared, but you're amongst friends, now. There's no need to pretend. If you'd tell me which kingdom you're from, that'd be a great start—"

Therin snorted again—a very un-princess-like sound, it had to be said.

"Listen," she said, "I don't know what kind of story your lord, or whoever hired you to do this job, told you. But I. Am not. A princess. I'm . . . I'm a Seer. And there are a lot of people who want to know what I've been Seeing lately."

"So the no-crows . . ." Nack trailed off, wondering.

"Probably just another sorcerer trying to get in on the action," said Therin bitterly.

ASK HER ABOUT THE PROPHECY, Asperides's voice echoed inside Nack's mind. Judging by the fact that

Therin didn't *also* nearly jump ten feet in the air with surprise, she hadn't heard him.

"Wha—" started Nack.

"So, since I'm really not a princess, and you don't seem like the kidnapping type"—Therin nodded toward Nack's angel blade—"I'll just get going, shall I?" And with that, the girl got a bit unsteadily to her feet and began to pick her way across the clearing.

DO NOT LET HER ESCAPE, Asperides commanded Nack.

Nack felt his hand move to the sword, though he hadn't even thought of drawing it. He shook out his arm and the urge to move it passed, but a cold uneasiness gripped him.

"Wait!" Nack shouted. He took a few steps forward but made no move to chase after the girl. "Can you . . . can you give me a minute?"

The girl stopped and looked at him as if he had suddenly transformed into one of the flying couch cushions. "What?"

"I mean, um, can you just stay here, for like, five minutes, okay? I'll go get some firewood, see if I can't find us something to eat in the forest. We can both rest up, and then you can decide if you'd rather get going on your own. Okay?"

"I *will* get going on my own," insisted Therin. "I'm not about to let anyone—you, or whoever sent you to come fetch me, included—abuse my powers."

"No one's going to—" Nack started, then sighed. He held up his hands in surrender. "Five minutes. Okay?"

The girl looked from Nack's face to Asperides sheathed at his side, and back again, before plopping herself on the ground in the shade of an oak tree.

"Five minutes," she said, yanking her veil from her head and spreading it out on the ground before her. She snapped her fingers and it took Nack a moment to realize she was telling him to bring the couch cushions to her. He scurried to oblige and came back with what he determined was the least objectionable (though still pretty rough-looking) pillow. She lay down with a huff, her back to him.

"Thank you," said Nack. He lowered his voice as he walked into the forest.

"Now *you*," he said quietly, glancing at Asperides, "have got some explaining to do."

--------⋄--------

"Did you know she wasn't actually a princess?" Nack asked. He sat on a large tree stump in another clearing, much smaller than the one he had left Therin in. They were several minutes away, but the boy kept his voice down and the sword sheathed, just in case the young priestess went wandering.

YES, said Asperides simply.

Nack smacked the tree stump with his fist. A few beetles scurried out from under it.

"Why?" asked Nack. "Why would you tell me I was going to rescue a princess, when you knew I wasn't?"

BECAUSE I DID NOT KNOW IF YOU WOULD BE AMENABLE TO THE ERRAND'S TRUE PURPOSE, said Asperides. He had considered simply possessing Nack and questioning the Seer himself, but he had known even since the evening before that, rather surprisingly, the boy's will was stronger than he'd thought. Even now, Asperides felt himself compelled to reply to the boy's questions with more honesty than he'd planned for.

It seemed Nack Furnival was settling into his role as Asperides's new master with surprising ease.

"'The errand's true purpose'?" Nack said. "What, you mean . . . do *you* want to know what the Seer's been predicting? Is that why we came here?"

THERE IS A PROPHECY THAT I WISHED TO KNOW MORE ABOUT, YES, said Asperides, *BUT IT CONCERNS ALL OF US—EVERY BEING IN THIS*

WORLD AND *THE OTHERS. ANGELS. HUMANS. EVEN DEMONS.*

The boy shivered a little at the last word.

RUMOR OF IT HAS REACHED ALL KINDS, said Asperides. *BUT THE DETAILS LIE ONLY WITH THE MISSION OF THE MISSING MOON, AND THE FULL PROPHECY ONLY WITH THE SEER WHO CHANNELED IT.*

"You mean Therin?" Nack asked. His face fell into a frown. "Then we've lied to her. *I've* lied to her. I told her we wouldn't use her for her powers."

AND WE WILL NOT, promised Asperides. *ALL WE NEED IS THE EXACT WORDING OF THE PROPHECY. AFTER THAT, WE WILL NEED TO COMPLETE A QUEST GREATER, PERHAPS, THAN HAS EVER BEEN ATTEMPTED.*

The boy scoffed. "Where have I heard that before?"

TELL ME, BOY, Asperides said, choosing his words carefully, *HOW MUCH DO YOU KNOW ABOUT THE MISSING MOON?*

"Well . . . that it's, um . . . missing?"

YOU ARE A FONT OF KNOWLEDGE.

"Well, there isn't much more to it than that, is there?" asked Nack with a shrug. "There used to be three moons, and all of our moon magic was based around them, and it was much more powerful than what we have now. That's what the legends say, at any rate. And then thousands of years ago, the third moon just . . . disappeared. Left the planet's orbit. No one knows why. And we've had just the two ever since."

AND, said Asperides, *HOW MUCH DO YOU KNOW ABOUT DEMON SWORDS?*

For a moment, the boy froze, his usual nervous fidgeting coming to a sudden halt.

"What does any of this have to do with—"

HUMOR ME.

"Not much," Nack said, throwing up his hands in a dismissive gesture. "They haven't been around for over a thousand years, or something. My clan's tutor said there were no more than a handful to begin with, and they were responsible for so much destruction that our ancestors hid them away, or purposefully lost them, so that no one could find them ever again. And no one knows how to make any more of them, so . . ."

BUT WHAT IF, Asperides said, *SOMEONE DID?*

And Asperides, perhaps against his better judgment, explained his theory about what the prophecy contained: the possible return of the Missing Moon. His fellow angels, he said, were in a panic, because they alone were old enough to remember that demon swords could only be forged in the light of the Missing Moon. The angels had made it their mission, upon hearing rumors of the prophecy, to learn if the Missing Moon really *was* coming back—and to do everything in their power to warn the humans and stop anyone from creating a demon sword ever again.

SURELY, YOU HAVE NOTICED THE SIGNS, said Asperides. *INCREASED DEMON CROSSINGS FROM THE UNDERWORLD. BAD HARVESTS AND STRANGE WEATHER PATTERNS. MORE HAUNTINGS. MORE VIOLENCE.*

The boy shivered, undoubtedly thinking of their recent encounter with the gasper-cats—or perhaps the grim memories of battle Asperides had glimpsed in his mind.

IT IS OUR DUTY TO PROTECT THIS LAND'S PEOPLE IN THE UNCERTAIN DAYS TO COME, said Asperides solemnly. He hoped he wasn't laying it on *too* thick; he was hardly used to such heroic speechifying. *AND TO ENSURE THAT NO DEMON SWORD IS EVER FORGED AGAIN.*

"Now *that* sounds like a quest if there ever was one," Nack said, a bit shakily. The boy leaned back and rested on the palms of his hands.

"Well," Nack said after a few moments, practically

jumping off the tree stump, "if everything hinges on this prophecy, like you said, then we'd better go try and hear it, hadn't we?"

Asperides said nothing, but let out a little glowing pulse of energy in response. The boy surprised Asperides by drawing the sword and holding it up to his eyes. His voice was firm when he spoke.

"But, Asperides?" said Nack. "If we're going to be partners, we're going to do this right. We have to be honest with each other. And that means no more half-baked stories about princesses. All right?"

Partners. If Asperides could have snorted, he would have. *Right.*

YES, MASTER, said the sword. The boy made a face at Asperides's deference, but seemed too embarrassed at having given even an indirect order to say much more in response.

It was a far cry from working for Amyral Venir, that was for certain. And fortunately, Asperides doubted any more princess-related cover stories would be necessary in the future.

———◆———

Therin awoke with a jolt, her veil sticking to her face and the comforting smell of a campfire around her.

"Sorry," said the boy—Nack—sitting across from her. He sure seemed to say that a lot, for a kidnapper. "I thought you could use the sleep."

The sun had moved in the sky, and Therin guessed it must be nearly noon. She looked around, exhausted and on edge all at once. The cold heaviness she'd felt during the attack on the Mission lingered, despite the sunshine, and it made her uneasy. It was harder to feel the pull of the two moons during the day, but she reached for their reassuring presence, anyway. Though beneath *that* presence, she felt the unsettling pull of the moon that wasn't supposed to exist at all.

Nack made a great show of drinking from his canteen before offering it to her, but Therin was so thirsty she would have drunk swamp sludge, never mind being paranoid about poison. Besides, the boy—or whoever was behind him—needed her.

"I'm not going to tell you the prophecy," Therin said before the boy could ask. "I can't even remember the exact wording when I'm not . . . when I'm not Seeing. And besides, the Mission hasn't come to a verdict about it. It's up to the high priestesses to decide if it's even worth telling people or not."

OR IF THEY'RE GOING TO KILL YOU, said a voice, *AND BURY THE PROPHECY WITH YOU.*

✳ 143

Therin jumped to her feet. The canteen fell from her hands and water sloshed onto the edge of their fire, creating a small hiss of rising steam.

"Who said that?" she demanded. That heavy feeling was back, and the air tasted metallic on her tongue.

Nack stood up, too, looking almost as surprised as Therin. He held up his open hands in a gesture of surrender.

"Sorry"—again with the apologies!—"that's just, ummm—"

IT SEEMS TO ME, MY DEAR, THAT YOU ARE FAR SAFER WITH US THAN WITH YOUR…SISTERHOOD. A thinly veiled sneer echoed through the last word.

"Asperides!" said the boy, rattling the sword at his side. He met Therin's gaze once more. "Asperides," he said with a shrug, as if that explained everything, then added, "My angel blade."

Therin's heart was still pounding. "I didn't know angel blades could talk."

"Neither did I," Nack said, and strangely enough, she believed him. "Not until I had one. Though sometimes I *wish he wouldn't*." He shot another pointed look at the sword. It twinkled mischievously from inside the scabbard.

"I'm sorry he scared you," the boy continued. He picked up the canteen, peered into it hopefully, and then sighed. "But . . . does he have a point?"

"No," said Therin forcefully. Then, with a slight sniff, "Maybe?"

Nack had eased himself into a sitting position by the fire. He patted the ground next to him and looked up at Therin expectantly.

She sat down and took a deep breath, brushing her tangled ginger hair out of her face. "It's complicated," she settled on, staring into the flames.

"Therin," said Nack. "What if I told you we wanted to hear the prophecy, not because we wanted to take advantage of you, or of the Missing Moon's powers—"

"So you *did* know I wasn't a princess," Therin interrupted smugly.

"Not exactly," said Nack. "It's . . . complicated."

A tired chuckle escaped Therin's lips.

"But what if we wanted to *stop* people from doing that?" Nack asked. "To stop them from using the Missing Moon's power for dark magic?"

Therin stared into the fire again, and then into the boy's eyes. She could go back to the Mission—and an uncertain future—or she could stay with this boy, and his sword, and maybe, just maybe, have a chance at thwarting some of the disaster she felt partly responsible for predicting.

"We'll have to wait until both moons are up," she said finally, her voice smaller and softer than she wanted it to be. "My powers will be strongest then. And no jokes about being able to 'See' in the dark. I've heard them all."

"I think we can handle that," said the boy with a smile.

SPEAK FOR YOURSELF, said the sword. I MAKE NO SUCH PROMISES.

Even Therin let out a small, nervous giggle at that.

And so it was, in that moonlit circle of trees, that Nack Furnival and the demon sword Asperides became the first living beings outside the Mission of the Missing Moon to hear the following prophecy:

> Long has she traveled,
> For twenty turns a hundred times,
> But when the dead become undying,
> And the wary become warriors,
> When the seas leap to kiss the sky,
> And the two moons dance a-frenzied,
> When the days and shadows lengthen,

And the world readies herself with her
    unreadiness,
The third daughter will return.

Her light will shine upon all she has made
And that was made from her
And that was made with her
And that was made for her,
And all bathed in her light will feel her fire
And be one with the third daughter.

She will cry a tear for every day of her absence
And her tears will melt the walls
Between the worlds themselves,
Until all above and all below
Bear witness to her sorrow and her joy,
And the priestesses will dance
Until the sun rises to welcome her home.
The third daughter will return.

———— ◆ ————

It was much later that night, when they had traveled a few more miles under the moonlight to put more distance between themselves and the Mission (and, hopefully, the no-crows' mysterious master), that the demon sword

Asperides sensed the girl lying awake. Nack slept on, oblivious as ever, and that was just as well. Asperides could feel the Seer's eyes trained on him in the dark. Her pupils were large, despite the darkness—a side effect of her earlier channeling of the prophecy.

It kind of made Asperides wish he *had* made a Seeing-in-the-dark joke. Ah, well.

A few moments after the boy let out a particularly thunderous snore, Therin's whisper cut through the darkness.

"I know what you are," she said.

Asperides knew she wasn't talking to the boy.

THEN YOU KNOW, said Asperides, *THAT I HAVE JUST AS MUCH INTEREST IN STOPPING ANYONE FROM USING THE THIRD MOON'S LIGHT AS YOU DO.*

The girl said nothing, but Asperides could tell she was still listening.

WE MAY HAVE BEEN FORGED IN THE LIGHT OF THE MISSING MOON, explained Asperides. *BUT OUR LEGENDS TELL THAT WE CAN ALSO BE . . . UNMADE. SOMETHING YOUR ORDER HAS SURELY GUESSED.*

Asperides waited for the young Seer to answer, wondering if he'd said too much. Perhaps demon swords were a legend even amongst the Mission of the Missing Moon, now. Perhaps the girl had been bluffing, with her earlier confidence, and he had revealed himself for nothing— revealed himself, and his greatest weakness.

But all the girl said was, "Does he know?" She glanced to the sleeping Nack.

Asperides said, *DO YOU THINK HE WOULD BE ABLE TO DO WHAT NEEDS TO BE DONE, IF HE DID?*

Before the girl could answer, Asperides decided he had risked enough. She was a powerful moon magic user, and an even more powerful Seer, especially for one so young, but Asperides was more powerful still. He reached into the reserves of his magic, calling upon the energy of his souls trapped deep in the underworld until he had glamoured himself so thoroughly he thought even a real angel blade might mistake him for one of their own kind.

Then, very slowly, he made himself as forgettable as possible. The girl's formerly piercing gaze slid over him, her expression turning to a confused frown before her eyes grew suddenly heavy, and she passed into a troubled sleep. If Asperides had done his magic correctly, she would remember him only as the angel blade he presented himself to be, and she would never remember their conversation in the morning.

Asperides stayed awake—as he always did, since demon

swords didn't need sleep—and pondered the wording of Sister Dawn Therin's prophecy. It was a pity the prophecy didn't contain more specific details. They would have their work cut out for them, figuring out exactly when the Missing Moon would reappear. But reappear it would, and that, at least, was worth knowing for certain.

One line in particular stuck out to him, and he could only hope that he and Nack Furnival would be the only ones ever to hear it outside of the walls of the Mission of the Missing Moon.

Her tears will melt the walls between the worlds themselves.

Hadn't he and the denizens of the underworld realized the boundaries were thinning only weeks ago? Soon, he knew, they would not be the only ones who noticed.

And Asperides could think of no one who could make greater use of a thinning barrier to the underworld than a certain former master of his, who, by now, would certainly be wanting his soul back.

13

Turning
Tides

"Before we do anything else," the boy had insisted, "I have to defeat him. Lord Solonos."

See, this? This was the downside of attaching oneself to a new master with a petty revenge quest. They were easy pickings, in the recruitment stage, but then, one actually had to entertain their dull notions.

Asperides, Nack, and Therin had decided to travel north, toward the main library of the Order of Archivists. If there was anywhere in the world that would have more information to help them plot the Missing Moon's course (other than Therin's Mission, which, for obvious reasons, they could hardly return to), it would be in the Order's archives. The journey also gave Asperides the opportunity to train Nack. The thinning barrier between the worlds was creating no end of cracks for demons and spirits to slip out of, which was unfortunate for the humans, but rather good practice for a young knight-in-training.

There was so much for the boy to learn, and so little time for him to do it. If Nack was to have any chance of surviving when he faced Amyral Venir—or anyone else brave and crazed enough to mess with unpredictable Missing Moon magic—he needed to be able to strategically call on Asperides's power. He *absolutely* needed to learn to channel the existing moons, as the priestesses of the Missing Moon did with their deadly, concentrated moonbeams. Done properly, with Asperides in his hands, the boy could command several times as much magic. He must learn the strengths and weaknesses of the demons that roamed the land—demons that would only increase in number the closer the Missing Moon came. And, first and most importantly, he needed to learn not to trip over his own two feet.

Asperides pointed out that "going leagues out of their way to harass a personal but ultimately inconsequential enemy who also *has an entire army at his back*" was nowhere to be found on that list.

If it weren't for the presence of Therin, Asperides wasn't sure the boy could be swayed from his revenge, imminent end of the world or not. But though Nack talked with fervor about going after Lord Solonos, Asperides knew the boy saw himself as Therin's protector and was unlikely to abandon her or lead her right into the lion's den of Solonos's domain. Asperides was rather surprised Nack didn't suggest taking her back to the Furnival clan. She was no princess, it was true, but surely, presenting his lord with the gift of a major player in the games ahead would be more than enough to restore him to favor?

Nack made the point that there was quite a difference between "Look, Mom and Dad, I rescued an imprisoned princess in distress!" and "Look, Mom and Dad, I sort of kidnapped a highly wanted and controversial priestess of the Missing Moon without her superiors' knowledge or consent," however noble one's motives. But that Nack did not seriously consider returning to his family to seek their aid in any part of his quest told Asperides more about the current state of the Furnival clan than the boy said outright. It was clear that though Nack Furnival wasn't about to bargain with the priestess's life, he didn't have *quite* enough confidence that his family wouldn't, either.

And so, despite the boy's grumblings, they continued toward the archives and the promise, however slim it might be, of the knowledge those tomes might contain.

Asperides feared they wouldn't be the only ones looking.

The plan was simple. Asperides simply had to train a thirteen-year-old boy to beat a several-hundred-year-old zombie sorcerer knight who had only been previously defeated in a multi-layered, decade-spanning effort involving about two dozen co-conspirators. All without said boy realizing exactly what he was being trained for.

Like he said. Simple.

———————— ✦ ————————

If it weren't for Sister Dawn Therin—which she planned to remind them of frequently from that day forward—they would have all likely died horrible, swampy deaths on their very first day of adventuring. (Well, she assumed the angel would simply pass on to another sword and let his current form sink to the bottom of the murky waters with his master, but then again, she wasn't sure. This angel blade didn't seem to act like any others she'd seen before.)

For one thing, he was exceedingly rude.

WHAT PART OF "SLAY THE PLAGUE LIZARD" DID YOU UNDERSTAND TO MEAN, "WALK STRAIGHT INTO A PIT OF SLEEPING SAND AND SUFFOCATE US ALL"?

"I didn't . . . see it . . ." protested the boy, yawning

widely every few words, sunk nearly up to his chest in the enchanted sand.

Therin, perched on a nearby log, was surprised he could still talk. Even the small bits of sand that flew into her eyes were enough to make her eyelids feel heavy. So very, very heavy . . .

"Nack!" Therin shouted, more to wake herself up than anything else. "Stay awake! Use the sword!"

The next moment, the monstrous plague lizard they had been looking for in the first place slithered onto the other end of her log.

Therin was wide awake now. She dove—right into the sleeping sand pit, and nearly on top of Nack and Asperides.

A flying Therin seemed to be the wake-up call Nack needed, because just as the sand closed over their heads, a searing blue glow burned past Therin's closed eyes. She felt for Nack's free hand under the sand and grabbed it tightly. Everything around her was burning hot. She could feel Nack twisting and turning, could feel a powerful energy cutting through the sand around them.

When she opened her eyes, gasping and panting, it was to find both herself and Nack standing on a rapidly cooling platform of newly solidified ground. Asperides's tip was stuck into the rippled, porous-looking rock beneath them, his magic perhaps the only thing keeping their flesh from melting right off their bones. Around them, chaotically shaped tendrils of recently hardened earth jutted out from the former sand pit—jagged, glittering touchstones in the otherwise murky swamp. The plague lizard lay several yards away, dramatically impaled on one of the newly formed crystalline rocks.

Asperides—well, Nack *and* Asperides, Therin corrected herself—had *melted* the sleeping sand into solid earth.

Their next few missions followed a similar pattern. Either Nack and Asperides would hear about a nearby supernatural enemy, or Therin would have a prophetic dream about one (she really, really wished she could predict something *pleasant* one of these days), and within about five minutes the situation would somehow devolve from Nack saying hopefully, "Well, this seems simple enough, doesn't it?" to the three of them embroiled in mortal peril. Therin helped out when she could. Unfortunately, she had been early in her moon magic training when she'd left the Mission, and she couldn't yet channel and aim her moonbeams as precisely as she'd seen her older Sisters do. The magic often left her hair staticky for hours and blistered the tips of her fingers; she wished *she* had a sword to make channeling the power easier. (Not that it seemed to do Nack Furnival much good, since he had yet to channel so much as a twinkle of moonlight.)

Therin also supplemented Nack's knowledge of candle lore. Therin's Mission, like many of the moon-worshipping orders, made the blessed candles that the knights used in their work. Nack was surprisingly receptive to the lessons: in Therin's experience, lots of cocky knights neglected their waxwork, which was mostly protective magic, in favor of hacking and slashing with their swords. Considering the boy had an angel blade already, she thought he might be the same.

"A real knight should be an expert in all his tools," he would say. "Sir Barb—you never met her, but she's amazing—she didn't have an angel blade, and she's still one of the bravest knights I've ever seen."

The study of the sword, though, clearly loomed largest for Nack. Asperides drilled him morning, noon, and night. Every time they stopped in their travels, it wasn't a rest for Nack, but a chance to run through various forms. If they didn't happen to be hunting monsters or demons that evening, Therin would fall asleep at night to the sound of Nack's labored breathing, his feet shifting in the dirt, and Asperides slicing through the air—and she'd wake up to the same sounds in the morning.

Third Daughter knew, he needed the practice. For a knight, he wasn't very light on his feet, which he was liable to trip over at the least opportune moment. He also seemed to forget that he actually *had an angel blade* far too often for a person who practiced with it for hours every day, and it would only be by some angelic miracle of Asperides's that they would escape the aforementioned mortal peril, usually by the skin of their teeth.

Therin was never a fan of these angelic interventions. She hadn't spent much time around angel blades, it was true, but she couldn't recall Asperides's name coming up in even the oldest texts she'd studied, and something about his powers set her teeth on edge. Whenever Nack used Asperides's magic, goose bumps rose on Therin's skin, and the air felt heavy with his power. It was almost like a tugging sensation, not dissimilar to what she felt when she sensed the approaching Missing Moon. And sometimes, one of them would say his name— *Asperides*—and Therin's blood would inexplicably run cold, and her heart would beat faster in her chest as she remembered her old lessons at the Mission, and where she'd heard that name before—

And then Therin would blink, and Nack would be looking at her expectantly, and that dreadful feeling she'd had just moments before would be nothing more than a fuzzy memory, like a spooky old wives' tale she'd heard about from a friend-of-a-friend, but couldn't remember where.

But if the occasional funny feeling and frequent flirtations with death were all she had to be concerned about, well, Therin thought there were worse places to be—like trapped in a tower by her own fractured sister-hood, or trapped in somebody *else's* tower until they got the prophecy out of her and she outlived her usefulness. She didn't fully understand Nack Furnival, but for some reason, she did trust him.

It helped that he eventually started getting better at the whole slaying demons thing, too.

———— ◆ ————

The first time Nack called down the moons, he was much too focused on saving an entire orphanage from being swept away by a raging wraith-wave to fully appreciate his success. Therin and Asperides had taught him the theory—how to guide the moonbeams toward himself and into Asperides, where the sword could magnify them and extend the magic far beyond the tip of the sword itself. But Nack had never practiced channeling the moon at this scale until now.

Asperides had taken them on a special trip to the

eastern shore, taking a slight detour from their journey to the Order of Archivists, to give Nack a chance to take a crack at it.

"And to save lots of innocent people," Therin reminded Asperides. *"Right?"*

AS ALWAYS, MY DEAR, Asperides answered her solemnly. AS ALWAYS.

The ghostly touch of a wraith-wave was just as dangerous as a real tsunami. They had the power to sweep the very vulnerable—the young, the old, the sick—into the underworld as they retreated, turning each and every soul into a restless spirit cursed to haunt the seas and shores forever. Some thought they were the ghosts of storms past, no doubt riled up by all the very *recent* raging storms due to the Missing Moon's approach.

The phantom foam had arrived first, lapping at the shores with its deadly chill. The beach had been littered with the small corpses of fish and birds when they'd arrived, the first victims announcing the larger wraith-wave's imminent arrival.

Like so often happened when push came to shove, all the drills and forms Nack had practiced sloshed out of his head like seawater from a leaky bucket. He could only watch the approaching white wave, his eyes growing wider with each passing second—the great crashing of the ocean nearly enough to drown out the cries of the orphaned children in the tottering old building perched on the shore's cliffs, but not quite.

Perhaps it was those cries that did it. Or perhaps it was the fact that for once, Asperides made no move to sweep in at the last moment and rescue them all.

"A-Asperides," Nack sputtered, watching the wave get larger and larger. "Do something!"

The sword merely glowed at his side, uncharacteristically silent.

"Asperides, it's coming!" warned Nack. "I can't . . . I don't . . ."

He sensed movement to his right—Therin and the caretaker of the orphanage, trying to evacuate the children.

YOU DO NOT NEED ME, NACK FURNIVAL.

Relief flooded through Nack at the sound of the sword's voice—only to be replaced with panic as he took in the words themselves.

"That is *highly* debatable," said Nack.

YOU NEED ONLY MY POWER, AND MY POWER IS AT YOUR COMMAND, said the sword, his voice gentler than the usual sharp-tongued nagging Nack had been getting used to.

NOW YOU NEED ONLY COMMAND IT.

The candles arranged at Nack's feet sputtered in the force of the wraith-wave's power, sensing his weakening focus and resolve. The moons, though high in the sky, felt a million miles away, never mind connected to Nack's will.

"But . . . Asperides . . ."

The wraith-wave gained height and speed, its shadow darkening the path before it into a black abyss. Someone behind Nack let out a piercing shriek.

Even if she could call it fast enough, Therin's moon magic wouldn't be enough to stop the wraith-wave on her own. The children and their caretakers would never make it. They'd never get far enough, fast enough.

And once again, Nack would be the coward who failed to help the people who needed him.

"ASPERIDES!" shouted Nack. "HELP ME!"

He swung the sword, which was suddenly glowing as hot as a blue flame, in an arc around himself. His candles sprang to life as the sword passed over them. Nack raised Asperides over his head and locked his eyes on the few shafts of moonlight piercing the dark clouds.

He'd forgotten the exact words to the spell, but it didn't matter.

"*Come,*" Nack said. His throat burned, his voice

sounding odd to his ears, as if he were several people speaking instead of one. He thrust his sword skyward.

The moonbeams came, arcing down from the sky and straight toward Nack's outstretched arm. Their power jolted through the sword, sending shocks down Nack's arm that shook his whole body. Still, he held the sword strong.

With the power of the two moons in his hands, he faced the ghostly white wave bearing down upon them and swung Asperides with all his might.

The moonlight exploded out of the sword stroke, hitting the growing curve of the wave with a crack like thunder. The wraith-wave dissolved with a hiss and an anguished wail that sounded eerily human. The wave collapsed into a heaving, frothing mass of foam that was quickly dispersed out to sea, or else seemed to evaporate in the moonlight streaming down from the sky.

It wasn't until Nack slowly lowered his sword that he became dimly aware of the children's cheers, of Therin running toward him to envelop him in a bone-crushing hug. The one thing he did hear, clear as a bell, was Asperides's voice inside his head.

NOW, said the sword, *WE ARE GETTING SOMEWHERE.*

14

A Chilly Reception

It was a strange thing indeed to be a demon sword in the angel blade business.

The first time a grateful peasant tried to press a gift into Nack's hand, Asperides nearly jerked the boy's arm back, suspicious of any quick movements on the part of a stranger. But two things happened: the first was . . . well, nothing. Asperides found he could not exert his will over Nack's anymore, not even suddenly or by surprise. The second thing was that the peasant had merely given Nack a handful of coins his village had scraped together, and though Nack tried to refuse enough times to make his voice hoarse, the end result was that he and Therin had enough money to sleep in a real bed for the first time in over a month, which, while not directly affecting Asperides, certainly made everyone else much more pleasant to be around, and Asperides thought, *I could get used to this.*

Much to Asperides's surprise, the upward trend continued. Whether it was banishing a bothersome banshee in a castle full of clan war refugees, or exorcising a whole old people's home possessed by lower demons (which had been extra creepy, even for someone with Asperides's many years of experience), the young Furnival proved a much quicker study than Asperides had anticipated. Their reputation began to precede them, and soon they couldn't set two feet inside a village before they were inundated with requests for knightly aid. Asperides could tell that the attention made Nack nervous—not to mention guilty, like he was somehow profiting off the chaos caused by others. (Which, Asperides reflected, would have been the precise *goal* of most of his previous masters.) The young priestess, for her part, wasn't enthused at playing the part of dutiful maidservant, but her disguise, combined with their unpredictable route north, had so far been enough to thwart any of the Mission's agents (or anyone else) who might be searching for her. Overall, considering the impending apocalypse and rise of his former master, Asperides was inclined to feel things were going rather well.

Never before had Asperides gained a reputation for *good* deeds instead of bad, and he wasn't quite sure what to make of his new situation. It certainly stirred *something* inside of him, seeing friendly or thankful faces instead of heads lowered and cowering in fear (or, as was more common in his days with Amyral, detached from bodies altogether).

It was probably just queasiness at the unnaturalness of it all, he told himself. Whoever had heard of a *demon* sword on the side of the land of the living?

Not, it turns out, the denizens of the underworld. To say the reception Asperides received on his brief forays back to his homeland was rather *chilly* would be an understatement. (Actually, it was quite a literal statement, as the ice imp he sat down next to at the Wet Fang one day responded to Asperides's company by freezing the bar top solid, causing Asperides's drink to slip down the gentle slope of the uneven counter and onto the floor.)

"It's jus' not natural," Thom the barkeep warned him one evening, when Asperides had nipped in for a quick drink while Nack and Therin were sleeping. (What *else* was there to do when the fragile humans needed rest?) Thom had escorted Asperides to his old darkened corner when he arrived and made such a show of looking furtively around as he did so that Asperides offered to come in disguise the next time.

PERHAPS A MUSTACHE? he'd suggested. Thom merely glowered at him.

"A demon sword, killin' demons," the barman muttered as he wiped down Asperides's table. "You can understand why it rankles a few rumps now, can't ya?"

I HAVE SLAIN HUNDREDS OF DEMONS IN MY TIME, said Asperides. He had helped dozens of evildoers rise to power. And as the humans said, if you wanted to make an omelet . . .

"Yeah, but that were different, weren't it?" asked Thom with a sniff, setting Asperides's drink down before him. It was a rather disappointing pale orange color and didn't give off any sparks or noxious fumes at all. "Then, it was all in service of your own plan. More often than not, in service of the underworld. Sure, a couple o' unlucky ones might've gotten it in the mix-up, but that was always just business."

AS IS THIS, said Asperides, though he wasn't quite sure why he was even bothering to defend himself. *I AM A DEMON SWORD. I WAS MADE TO SERVE MY MASTER.*

"Well, if that's what ya tell yourself so you can sleep at

night, don't let me stop you," said Thom, already backing out of the alcove where he'd escorted Asperides. "But I'd watch yer back—er, blade—around some of these parts, if I were you."

With that, the barman disappeared, leaving Asperides to stew with his mediocre drink and Thom's horrendous advice. First of all, demon swords didn't even need sleep. Secondly: watch his back? What was their society coming to, when not even being a *demon sword* kept one safe in the upper levels of the underworld?

Not that anything or anyone, save a handful of greater demons in the farthest reaches of the underworld—the parts that could properly be called hell—could do much harm to Asperides. No, there was only one force in the universe that could do that.

Unfortunately, that same force was currently hurtling through space, straight for them all.

———————•◆•———————

Amyral Venir surveyed the scores of men assembled before him as a farmer might view a herd of cattle. That was all they were to him, really. They called him Amyral the Undying, a title the young sorceress who'd resurrected him had spread amongst them, the better to impress upon them Amyral's invincibility. They were desperate men, or greedy men, or both—left without food, families, or protection because of the war between the clans and the chaos caused by the approaching Missing Moon. They were leaderless and desperate and looking for someone to blame *and* someone to take charge. Many of them, he knew, simply wanted to take advantage of all that chaos for themselves. In the past, he might have shared their petty desires, their thirst for blood and money and the other spoils of war. In the future, he might do so again. But now? Now, he had only one use for them. He was simply biding his time until that moment came.

He spared a glance to his right, where Cleoline stood, shivering slightly in the wind. It was she who had found the remnants of the spell that would help him retrieve his soul, with her secret passage into the Order of Archivists—she who was spending hours and hours painstakingly reconstructing it. Together they had pored over historical chronicles and records of past prophecies, the better to guess when the Missing Moon would appear, and where they would be able to channel the most of its power. There was no need to guess at the contents of the little moon priestess's prophecy now. The evidence was clear, with the roiling tides, the earthquakes that rumbled across the land, the flaming meteor showers streaking across the sky, the days that stretched longer and longer, and most especially, the thinning veil between the worlds.

The barrier between the land of the living and the underworld was so fragile, so constantly shifting, that Amyral thought he could feel it in the air, an invisible but all too physical barrier between this world and the other—between his body and most of his soul. While the demons and spirits on the other side could slip in through the small holes that occasionally cropped up naturally between the worlds, Amyral had no such option. There was only one way for someone from the living realm to enter the underworld, and it was an experience that Amyral didn't care to repeat: death.

Unless, of course, one had the once-in-a-millennium chance to utilize the powerful magic of a mythical third moon. Cleoline had told him that when she was finished with the spell, he would be able to use this moon magic, under the light of the Missing Moon, to carve a doorway into hell itself. From there, Amyral would proceed onward and downward, slaying anything in his path until he finally reached the prison where his soul was kept. Only then, when he was finally reunited with himself, would he be able to heal this raging, gaping emptiness inside of him.

The revenge against that backstabbing *Asperides* would be a decent balm for his wounds, too.

Beside him, Cleoline cleared her throat, and Amyral realized he'd simply stopped talking in the middle of a speech to his followers. That was something that happened now, in this second half-life of his. He was easily distracted, easily disinterested in the world around him. How could he be otherwise, when he could barely feel the wind on his skin, though it made the girl next to him shiver like a leaf? When food tasted like ash in his mouth? When the sound of singing, or laughter, or birdsong, sounded muffled and discordant in his ears?

But he needed these men, he reminded himself. He needed this witch. He needed her spell to open the door, and he needed soldiers to protect him when the barrier between the worlds broke. Demons would come streaming through such a large opening in a heartbeat, and Amyral wanted them distracted by plenty of other human prey. He could not be slain before he had even entered the underworld. So for now, he returned to his (hopefully) stirring speech. The men's heads followed him as he paced back and forth before them.

Like so many cattle, he thought.

"Your crops have been destroyed, your livelihoods lost, your homes left unprotected in the face of this senseless clan war," Amyral told them. "Where are the brave knights of the realm now, when demons and monsters run unchecked throughout the land? What are the clans doing, while the world turns upside down? Fighting amongst themselves!" He spat in the dirt, and a few of the men booed and jeered along with him.

"And for what?" Amyral asked. "So that Lord Solonos can have a second castle, and a third? What good are their angels when their blades are turned on one another, or on you, caught in the fray?"

A few of the onlookers yelled in agreement.

"Join me, and know this," Amyral said, lowering his voice just slightly, so the men would have to strain forward a bit to hear. For just a moment, he felt a bit of the old, tingling thrill run through his veins, the rush of manipulating a crowd to his will. "We will laugh in the face of their angel blades. *We* will have something far more powerful. Under my command, after the Third Daughter returns to the sky, each and every man here will have a blade from the *netherworld* to call his own." A whisper rippled through the crowd—a current of doubt, to be sure, but also interest.

"When our struggle is finished, there will be no more clan warfare to cause strife and suffering," finished Amyral, and more cheers went up at his words. "There will only be one clan: ours."

The din of the men shouting and cheering and banging their weapons barely registered in Amyral's brain. The speech done, he retreated into himself again. The earlier spark of excitement left him as quickly as it had come. Cleoline gave his hand a squeeze, reminding him to smile and wave to the men as they made their way back to their tent. It felt like stretching old leather across his skull.

"On second thought," muttered the sorceress after looking at him, "maybe don't smile . . ."

Amyral ignored her. She, too, would lose her usefulness soon. There was no point in getting attached. There was no point to anything, except getting his soul back.

He had the returning Missing Moon. He had the spell—or would, very soon. He had the troops to lead the charge into the underworld. There was only one thing left that Amyral needed: the only tool powerful enough to channel the Missing Moon's light and carve that door between the worlds.

Amyral the Undying sneered, his skin stretching once more over his skeletal features. He whispered into the night, wondering if the demon sword could hear him even now, even so many years after their connection had been severed.

"Where are you, old friend?"

15

The Siege
of Solonos

As Nack's reputation grew, it became more and more difficult to keep his head down on their travels—and more and more difficult to ignore the clan war. Just as often as people would approach him to ask for help with a monster or a pesky spirit, they had started to greet Nack's arrival in their towns with pleas to protect them from other *knights*. Not only had many of the knights abandoned their historic duties in the interclan fighting, some had become active antagonists of the people they were supposed to protect—they fought in the streets, using residential buildings and innocent people as cover in their battles, or else stole food and supplies. Each time, it pained Nack to hear the stories, and each time, it was harder and harder to politely decline to intervene. He had been banished from his clan, he'd say, truly enough. His business was no longer theirs, and one boy could not solve a clan war. He was part of a larger mission now. He reserved his sword for demons and the dead—not the living.

Which sounded all very good and noble and sensible in his head, but pretty thin in the face of a town half-destroyed by Solonos's rampaging troops. And there were rumors, too, of yet another force on the rise—a violent hodgepodge of knights and other soldiers who'd either abandoned their posts in the clan wars, been displaced by the fighting, or simply wanted to wreak destruction of their own. Few spoke of the group's leader, about whom people seemed to know little, but when they did, it was always with fear in their eyes. Amyral the Undying, they called him. The name sent a shiver down Nack's spine, though he knew as little about the man as anyone else.

He asked Asperides, once, if they should go looking for this Amyral the Undying. It seemed he was as likely a candidate as any to use the Missing Moon's magic for his own gains. But Asperides deflected the question, saying Nack wasn't yet ready to take on warlords singlehandedly, angel blade or no, and besides, it was more important that they reach the archives to seek out information on the Missing Moon. There was little Nack could say to that. But if he wasn't ready now, then when?

PERHAPS WHEN YOU CAN FACE DOWN A DEMON WITHOUT CRYING, Asperides said.

"That was *one time*," Nack bristled. "Okay, maybe two."

If it was possible to somehow *glow mockingly*, Nack was pretty sure Asperides was doing it.

"Doesn't it bother you, though?" Nack burst out. "Not being able to . . . save everyone?"

Nack looked around to make sure no one had seen him talking to himself, but he was alone next to a babbling stream. Therin had walked farther downstream to bathe—an indulgence she clearly wished *he'd* practice more often, but who had time for baths when there was so much to learn?

NO, said Asperides shortly.

"But . . ." Nack frowned. "You're an angel blade. You're like . . . goodness and light personified." Even as he said the words, Nack felt a little silly. Asperides was many things, but "goodness and light" were somehow not the descriptors that immediately came to mind when Nack thought of him. Still, he wanted to make his point.

"Don't you feel . . . I don't know, guilty?" Nack asked, picking up a smooth stone from the edge of the streambed. "When we have to tell people we can't help? Isn't helping what you're . . . well, *made* to do?" He chucked the stone across the stream, meaning to skip it, but merely sending it splashing to the bottom in his haste.

"Sorry," he said with a wince. "That was a rude thing to say . . . I mean, angels are probably born, just like people, right? You're not like . . . necromancers' revenants or something. You're alive. And nobody's born destined to be one thing or another."

AREN'T THEY? the sword mused, his voice quiet against the bubbling of the stream. Nack immediately thought of his own destiny—or what he'd thought was going to be his destiny, at any rate. He remembered the certainty he'd felt, even at only twelve years old, at his initiation ceremony into the Furnival knights. He'd knelt in the sacred standing stone circle on his family's lands— the Dancing Priestesses, they called it—surrounded by his family and his clan. His father had presented him with his first sword—the sword that would have, in another life, become his angel blade. Kneeling there, encircled by the humming magic of the Dancing Priestesses, surrounded by the rest of the Furnivals, he had been so sure of his place. One day, he knew, Declan would be the head of the Furnival clan, the Lord of Falterfen, and Nack would serve under him—perhaps, as he had always hoped, as the leader of Declan's knights.

That was what he had been born to do. He had been . . . *was* sure of it. So perhaps Asperides had a point.

I AM NOT HUMAN. I DO NOT EXPERIENCE THE SAME EMOTIONS AS HUMANS DO, the sword said, and it took Nack a moment to realize he was answering Nack's earlier question. *AND I DO NOT WEEP FOR THAT WHICH I DO NOT HAVE. YOUR CONCEPT OF "GUILT," FOR EXAMPLE, SEEMS LIKE A PERFECTLY USELESS PHENOMENON.*

Goodness and light. Nack snorted. *Right.*

"Nice," Nack said out loud, shaking his head.

PERHAPS I AM MISTAKEN. THIS "GUILT" SEEMS TO SERVE YOU SO WELL, AFTER ALL.

Nack scowled. He picked his way along the larger rocks on the edge of the stream, pinwheeling his arms to balance.

He could tease Asperides all he liked, but something about the sword's answer troubled him—and it wasn't just that he'd made fun of Nack. (*That* was a phenomenon Nack was fairly used to.)

I am not human, Asperides had said. Despite the fact that he and Nack had performed fantastical feats together—exorcising demons, calling down the moons' light, sending the unquiet dead back to hell—it was only now, with the mundane sun shining above and the calm burbling of the stream underfoot, that Nack really, truly believed him.

And Nack found he didn't want to think about that very much.

I MAY NOT FEEL GUILT, the sword said, his echo-y voice suddenly sounding as alien to Nack's ears as when he'd first heard it in the tomb. Nack nearly lost his footing on the slippery rocks.

BUT I AM JUST AS COMMITTED TO THIS QUEST AS YOU ARE.

Asperides's certainty thrummed through the blade at Nack's side, a current of power ready and waiting to be used.

And that, at least, Nack could believe.

"So when will we go after them? Lord Solonos? This . . . Amyral the Undying?" It seemed safer, somehow, to return to their familiar arguments, though Nack knew what the sword's answer would be.

"I know, I know," said Nack. "After we look for more information in the archives. But we'll be there in a few days, Asperides. I mean after that. And if you say, '*SOON*,' again in that spooky voice of yours," Nack warned jokingly, "I'm going to toss you in this st—"

Nack stopped in his tracks, staring at the running water winding between the rocks under his feet.

"It's running backward," he said with a gulp. His voice had lowered to a whisper. "The water. It's flowing uphill."

Nack took a deep breath and let it out slowly. He knelt down and put his fingers in the cool, bubbling water. "It's the Missing Moon, isn't it?" Nack asked, watching his fingers waver and distort through the ripples.

SOON, said Asperides.

Nack huffed out a small, sharp laugh.

———◆———

The very next night, when Therin woke up shaking and shouting so loudly she nearly scared the pants off Nack, the decision of whom to confront first was made for them.

"I Saw the man they've all been whispering about," she said, her pupils still large, her gaze far away. Nack put a gentle but firm hand on her shoulder, and Therin grasped his fingers, her grip painfully tight. For a brief moment, the blurry image of a man, his sword held aloft, flashed before Nack's eyes. Nack dropped Therin's hand in surprise and the flash faded, though the silhouette of the man still floated across his vision for a few seconds, like a strange afterimage from staring into the sun too long.

"He was calling down the moonlight, just like you . . . but it was light from the Missing Moon," she said. She made no move to share her vision with Nack again—Nack wasn't sure she'd even done it on purpose to begin with—and merely twisted her quaking hands in her lap. "It's happening, and sometime soon. I know it is. The leaves had just turned on the trees. I couldn't See much more than that, but . . . in his hands . . . he was holding a demon sword."

She sat there shaking for a long time, despite Nack's assurances that demon swords were just a myth—and if they weren't, they'd been gone for over a thousand years, hadn't they?—and his promises that they still had plenty of time before the Missing Moon took its final place in the sky. The latter statement, of course, he had no basis for at all, but, currently, with only two moons visible on the horizon, it seemed a safe enough bet.

In the morning, though, despite Asperides's many protestations, Nack decided it was time to split up. They'd told Therin their mission was to stop anyone using the Missing Moon's magic for nefarious purposes, and now, according to Therin's vision, it seemed Amyral the Undying was planning to do just that. Nack would find a suitable party for Therin to continue north with and send her on to the Order of Archivists alone, while he and Asperides went to find Amyral Venir. It was their duty to at least investigate, wasn't it?

They stopped to gather supplies and look for information in Foom, a mid-sized town that was overflowing with refugees from the clan wars *and* a nearby earthquake that had levelled an entire village. Nack kept Asperides fully sheathed and tucked under his cloak as they walked about town—it didn't take a genius to see that Foom's attitude toward knights had soured over the past few months and waving around an angel blade didn't seem like the smartest of moves.

And it seemed Nack wasn't the only knight lying low. Seated shoulder to shoulder in a packed pub, Therin sitting opposite him, and wolfing down something that could questionably be called stew, Nack heard snatches of conversation from the booth behind them.

". . . think it's too big of a job for us on our own . . . can't go around asking for help . . ."

"Isn't there . . . some Furnival men at the garrison?"

Nack's ears pricked up at the mention of his family's name. He strained to hear the voices more clearly. They both sounded feminine and oddly familiar . . .

"They won't help," said the higher of the two voices,

her voice heavy with disappointment. "They won't spare a man for anyone, not since Declan Furnival was captured by Lord Solonos. Maybe we could—"

Nack's spoon fell from his hand and onto the edge of his bowl, spattering him (and Therin) with questionable stew. He ignored her cry of surprise and got to his feet, mindlessly pushing his way out of the crowded pub until he stood in the yard, gasping for breath in the muggy evening air.

Declan Furnival was captured by Lord Solonos. His brother had been taken. His brother had been taken, and Nack hadn't been there to fight with him.

It was only a few moments before Therin followed him out of the pub. The scolding she'd undoubtedly been about to give him died on her lips when she saw Nack's face.

Small pangs of guilt stabbed at his insides, reminding him of the real reason they'd come to this town—that at any moment, the mysterious Amyral and his men could be getting their hands on a demon sword. But Nack pushed the feelings aside. He had failed to put his brother and his family first once before. He would not do so again.

"Change of plans," said Nack roughly. "We're going on a rescue mission."

Neither Therin nor the sword at his side contradicted him.

"If I don't come back," Nack said, his throat feeling suddenly thick. "Don't come after me. Keep going to the Order of Archivists, and find out as much about the Missing Moon as you can."

Therin, crouched by his side, resolutely failed to acknowledge that he'd even spoken.

"I said," said Nack, flushing, "promise me you won't—"

"You're sure you can fit in one of those?" Therin asked, eyeing the laundry carts being wheeled across the moat skeptically.

Nack sighed.

They were hiding behind one of the outbuildings on Lord Solonos's land and had been surveying Castle Ravinus for days, examining every angle. Nack wasn't sure *why* Lord Solonos was outsourcing his laundry, when he surely had enough staff and space in the castle, but he wasn't going to look a gift horse in the mouth. As far as plans went, it was a terrible one, but considering all the plans they'd come up with so far had been terrible, and this one was almost certainly the *least* terrible . . . they could have done worse, couldn't they?

"I don't know if he can," said a voice behind him. "I think our boy's grown up some since we saw him last, hasn't he, Willa?"

Nack and Therin whipped around, Nack already reaching for Asperides, when he saw the last people he expected to meet skulking around Lord Solonos's castle: Sirs Willa and Barb. They were both smiling at him, though Willa had her hands on her hips. She clearly didn't exactly *approve* of their current situation.

Therin hiked up her skirts and turned to scarper, but Nack stopped her with a hand at her elbow.

"Wait," he said. "It's okay! They're friends."

Or at least, he hoped so. He now recognized the voices he'd heard in the pub, talking about Declan—it had been Willa and Barb sitting in the booth behind him the whole time. Relieved as he was that they'd both survived the werecat encounter in the cave, he had no way of knowing if they'd gotten themselves involved with the clan wars, or with Amyral the Undying, or both. They didn't seem the type, but one couldn't be too careful, these days.

"He doesn't seem to have outgrown his tendency to dive headfirst into dangerous missions alone," said Willa, but her soft voice and smile belied her scolding words.

"He's not alone," said Therin defensively, and Nack felt such a sudden rush of affection for her that he blushed.

Willa smiled, but her eyes were tight as she looked around.

"And neither will we be, if we hang about in the open too much longer." She looked to Nack, who nodded in agreement.

Later, when they had repaired to the thick woods a good walk away from Castle Ravinus and could be more confident in not being overheard—with a rushing waterfall on one side for good measure—introductions were made. Willa and Barb filled Nack in on their exploits since the eventful night in the cave. They'd been doing much the same thing as Nack had—protecting whomever they could, wherever they could, from the ever-increasing number of demons and spirits crossing over from the underworld.

"And we've heard all about you, too!" said Barb, a teasing twinkle in her eye. She clasped her hands together and put on a bashful expression. "The brave Nack Furnival, saving all those maidens and orphans from things that go bump in the night!"

Therin snorted and Nack blushed even redder than before.

"I'm only teasin' you, lad," said Barb. "You're doin' good work. And with an angel blade of your own now, too, to hear tell of it. Did it come to you in the cave? Now that's a story we'll have to hear the end of someday. Let's see it, then! What's its name?"

Nack paused. He didn't know why. But the thought of pulling out Asperides right then, of showing him off to other knights, made his stomach tie up in knots. He just didn't want to show off, he told himself. That was it. There were so many other, more important things to be doing.

"Oh, don't embarrass the boy even more, my dear," said Willa, saving Nack for the time being. "We'll have plenty of opportunity to see his blade in action, if this rescue plan turns out anything like I fear it will."

The reminder of Declan, still captured somewhere in Castle Ravinus, hit Nack like a punch in the gut.

"How did you know I was here, anyway?" asked Nack.

"Didn't need to be world-class spies, did we, to see you storming out of that pub?" asked Barb with a chuckle.

Nack ducked his head. "Oh, right."

"All thanks to my big fat mouth," said Barb, shaking her head. "I'm sorry, Nack. If I'd known you were sitting there . . . well, I wouldn't have broken the news to you like that."

Nack shrugged, sniffing a bit at the sudden tears springing up behind his eyes.

"We'll help you get your brother back, Nack," said

Willa, putting a hand on Nack's arm. "The world needs every knight it can get in these times."

"And we couldn't help but notice your plan was absolute crap," added Barb cheerfully.

"Would you believe us if we told you it was the *least* crap of several options?" piped up Therin.

"Sadly," said Willa, "I would. Sneaking into Castle Ravinus was never going to be an easy task, especially now. But I think my wife and I can provide your plan with something it currently lacks: a distraction."

"What do you mean?" asked Nack.

Willa put a hand to her chest in mock solemnity.

"Every good cause needs more soldiers, doesn't it?"

———◆———

Fortunately (or perhaps unfortunately), Nack *was* able to fit inside one of the laundry carts being wheeled into Castle Ravinus. But those baskets, a very bruised Nack discovered shortly after sneaking into one, contained not the freshly washed linens of several hundred knights, as he expected, but hundreds of pounds of coins and treasure. Lord Solonos had been using the laundry carts to run stolen treasure in and out of his home base.

Nack would do something with that information one day, he assured himself, provided he got out of this alive.

Once inside the castle, he found a cart that *actually* contained laundry and stole a serving boy's livery out of the musty pile. Nack then proceeded to do one of the most terrifying things he had ever done in his life: walk into the darkened back hallways of his fiercest enemy's castle looking like there was nowhere else in the world he was supposed to be.

He kept his gaze down and walked quickly through the corridors, carrying a bundle of fabric scraps he'd taken from the laundry to look like he was in the middle of an errand. He followed the rest of the castle's foot traffic until he got to an outer wall with a view of the courtyard. He paused to get his bearings. There, just by chance, he saw them: a whole contingent of armed guards surrounding a well-dressed but exhausted-looking young man. They hustled him along the hall on the opposite end of the courtyard, occasionally jeering and poking him with the butts of their spears. Nack only saw them for an instant, but an instant was all it took to recognize his older brother. Their prisoner was Declan.

———————— ◆ ————————

Nack willed himself not to run, not to draw attention to himself, as he followed the corners of the building to catch up with the Solonos guards.

SLOW DOWN, Asperides warned him. Even the sword's voice was quiet, as if he, too, were worried about being caught, though they both knew only Nack could hear him. *TAKE THE NEXT RIGHT. THEN THE NEXT LEFT. TWO STEPS DOWN, AND RIGHT AGAIN.* The sword used his awareness, which Nack understood to be something like sight, but not quite, to guide him through the castle. Asperides couldn't sense the whole place— or at least, Nack didn't *think* the sword could—but his knowledge of his surroundings did seem to extend beyond what a human could see with their two eyes.

"I expected you'd need some time to think," said a nearby voice, low and oily, and though Nack had never heard it before, he knew instantly that it belonged to Lord Solonos. "But do not keep me waiting long. You, of all people, must know I do not suffer fools."

The sound of a door swinging shut echoed down the hall. Nack slowed his footsteps, eyes darting behind him to make sure no one was coming.

"My lord," piped up another man, his voice dripping with subservience. "There are two itinerant knights here to see you. Come to pledge their services, they say. They're very, erm, *insistent* on pledging loyalty to you personally, sir."

The man's voice grew louder as he spoke, and Nack

bowed his head just in time to catch the passing shadows of Lord Solonos and his servant as they strode down the hallway. Nack made himself as small as possible, nearly crouched against the wall, his gaze trained on the floor.

"Well, let's make it a party, shall we?" grumbled Lord Solonos, but there was a chuckle underneath his grumpiness. "Funny, how they all show up when you start to win . . ."

Nack expected to feel something—a rush of terror, or hatred, or simply the strange feeling of fates colliding, as he came within inches of his family's enemy, the entire reason he'd been disgraced. A part of him expected Lord Solonos to stop in his tracks, point at Nack, and shout, "Impostor!" but no such outburst occurred. Neither man took even the slightest notice of Nack, who simply stood there, trying his best to be invisible and feeling curiously empty as he watched Lord Solonos's shiny shoes tramp past him.

BE CAREFUL, said Asperides, vibrating slightly underneath Nack's oversized clothes. *THERE ARE NO GUARDS AT THE DOOR.*

"No guards?" breathed Nack, bounding forward. Sure enough, only two small candelabras stood at either side of the ebony door Solonos had just closed behind him, and those would barely keep out a determined ghost.

ALL THE MORE REASON TO BE CAREFUL, Asperides warned.

Nack wasn't listening. With one last look to check for traffic in the hall, he threw open the door to rescue his brother.

16

Rescue
Awry

"**N**ack! What . . . what are you *doing* here?"

Nack had burst through the door, closing it quickly behind him, to find Declan standing in a dark but well-furnished bedroom. His brother was unrestrained, and though he looked tired and wan, apparently unharmed. There was even a small table in one corner of the room with a glass of wine and a meal on a tray, though it had gone untouched.

Nack launched himself into his brother's arms, all stealth and fighting forms and invasion tactics forgotten. He didn't care that he was supposed to be a knight on a mission, or that he was disgraced, or that he wasn't even a Furnival anymore. Declan was still his brother, and all that mattered was that his brother was here, and whole, and talking to him. Everything else could be dealt with later.

To Nack's surprise, Declan returned Nack's embrace, shock giving way to surprised acceptance. They stood that way for a moment in silence, simply holding each other tightly, and Nack wished, briefly, that Asperides was even more powerful than he already was, and could simply transport them instantaneously, over a hundred miles away to the front hall of Falterfen, where Nack's mother, and father, and the whole family could hold each other, and be together, and forget that House Solonos or the Missing Moon even existed.

But, as far as Nack knew, Asperides had no such powers. The moment ended when Declan backed away with a cough and a clap on Nack's shoulder.

"I'm rescuing you, of course," said Nack, standing up straighter and putting one hand on Asperides at his hip. Nack was surprised to hear the confidence in his voice, but for the first time in . . . well, probably forever, he actually believed it. He *would* get them both out of there.

But the warm reaction Nack expected from this declaration never came. Declan's eyes widened, his hand coming to his brow in a familiar gesture Nack had seen so many times when the knights were in a scrape. Declan stepped away from Nack, looking around the room wildly, as if he hoped one of the ottomans might say the words he so obviously didn't want to.

"Nack, you need to leave," said Declan finally, his expression and his voice both heavy. "Get out of here. It isn't safe."

"Well, I know that!" Nack said with a scoff. "That's why I came to get you! Now come on, I've stolen some clothes for you, too"—Nack scurried over to where he'd dropped his bundle on the floor in his haste to hug Declan—"so just put these on, and—"

"Nack," Declan said, his voice firmer now. "You should never have come here. Leave me. I'll be fine."

Nack turned to face his brother again. Out of all the reactions he had expected from Declan, this hadn't been one of them.

"Look," said Nack. "I know you're probably not happy to see me. I know I'm not a real Furnival anymore. But . . . but you're still my brother. So, you can leave your . . . your pride, or your heroics, or whatever this is, at this door, and come with me now, and worry about the rest of that later."

Declan said nothing, but his face twisted, filled with anguish.

"You can't very well fight demons if you're stuck in

here," Nack pointed out, slightly desperate now. "The people need you. The Furnivals need you. Your knights need you!"

I need you, Nack thought, but did not say.

"I *know they do*," said Declan, his voice a soft snarl. "And that's why I need to stay here."

It was like the time Declan had knocked the wind out of Nack all over again.

"What?"

"You need to go," said Declan again. "Get out of here, if you still can. I don't know when Solonos or his men will be back."

"Declan . . . what do you . . ." Nack's brain couldn't seem to form the words. When it finally did, he didn't want to say them.

"Are you . . . are you *surrendering* to Lord Solonos?"

Declan looked away.

"Declan, there has to be another way," Nack said, panic rising in his chest, hot and acrid. "You've seen how they've treated the other clans. They've *wiped them out*. It's too late for us to surrender, not after the resistance we've put up. And what about our allies? House Clerides, the Masaris, the Hintlians—"

"Do you think I don't know this?" spat Declan.

"N-no," backpedaled Nack. "But . . . I just . . ." Nack's

thoughts whirled inside his head. He imagined the gardens where he'd played as a child, overrun with Solonos's knights. The Dancing Priestesses, where he'd sworn his oaths to his clan, no longer the initiation site for Furnival knights, but Solonos ones. He imagined Castle Falterfen, with Lord Solonos sitting at the head of the hall, instead of Nack's father.

"What did Father and Mother say?" Nack demanded. Surely, if the order to surrender had come from them, there must be a reason. Some guarantee of their people's safety . . .

One look at Declan's face was all it took to cast that idea out the window.

"They don't know, do they?" asked Nack softly. "Our parents. They don't know you're surrendering."

Declan's silence was all the answer Nack needed. He watched his older brother stalk over to the side table and take a fortifying swig of the wine there, as if looking at a stranger.

Declan finally turned to face Nack. He jutted out his chin.

"We're not surrendering."

Hope fluttered in Nack's heart, almost painful in its brightness, until the true meaning of Declan's words hit him.

"You . . . you're not *joining* him?" Nack said, his voice cracking at the end of the question.

Declan crossed his arms.

"It's the only way, Nack."

"No," said Nack, his panic returning. "I can't believe Mother and Father would want this. I can't believe the other clan elders would support this. They wouldn't—" Nack stopped short as he watched Declan shift guiltily from foot to foot. "But they haven't agreed to this either, have they?"

Declan's head twitched, as if he were tempted to look away from Nack again, but was fighting against it. He planted his feet.

"Father would never understand," said Declan, his voice rough. "He and Mother are both too determined to cling to the past, to refuse to see which way the wind is blowing, Nack! House Solonos is going to win this war. I know it, and you know it. Isn't it better, then, to take our chances with the winning side?"

"The winning side who *killed* their neighboring clans," Nack reminded him, disgusted. "The winning side who raids villages for their supplies and spends more time running money than they do fighting demons—"

"Oh, it must be so easy for you, the famous 'itinerant knight' Nack Furnival, to stand there and judge me," spat

Declan, his face twisted in a grimacing sneer. "But you don't have other knights to protect. You don't have a clan. You don't even have a *family*!"

Declan's chest heaved as he stared at Nack, defiant. Nack could only stare back at the brother who'd trained him to be a knight, who'd practically raised him . . . and who thought joining a tyrant was his family's only way to survive the fight ahead.

Maybe Declan was right. Maybe it was foolish to resist. Hadn't the other clans' resistance, including the Furnivals', made this whole mess drag on even longer?

And yet Nack couldn't believe that House Solonos, after all they'd done, would simply let the Furnivals join their side without reprisals. What would happen to the tenants who lived on their land? What would happen to the knights, should they refuse to carry out Lord Solonos's destructive dirty work for him? And what was the future of the knighthood, period, now that House Solonos had sullied the institution and reduced formerly noble knights to bullies, thieves, and worse?

For how much longer could they say they fought on the side of the angels, if all they fought was one another?

Nack couldn't let himself think about Declan's last words. *You don't even have a family.* It was clear, then, that Declan's position hadn't changed one bit since the incident at Castle Clyffidil. Though Nack had spent the last few months trying to be the best knight he could, had even gotten an *angel blade*—and risked his life to rescue Declan from Solonos's clutches—in Declan's eyes, it still wasn't enough. It would *never* be enough.

"I hope all this shouting means you've faced whatever demons you need to face, and are prepared to make a wise decision," said a voice behind Nack.

Nack whipped around just as the door closed. Lord Solonos himself stood there, not three feet away. He was a large man, several inches over six feet tall, with an abundance of voluminous and thick dark hair, threaded with stately slivers of gray. He wore all black, except for a coat of dark navy, ornately embroidered with silver stars, suns, and moons. His eyes widened at the sight of Nack, but his face rearranged itself into a pleasantly smooth mask in seconds.

"I had meant *inner* demons just now, but it seems I may have misspoken," said Lord Solonos wryly. "Though if this *is* a demon harassing you, it's certainly rather scrawny, isn't it?"

Nack drew Asperides before Solonos had even finished speaking.

"Not a step closer," said Nack, his sword pointed straight at Lord Solonos's chest.

The man didn't even blink. He looked Nack up and down, taking in his disheveled stolen uniform. "Bit heavily armed for a stable boy, aren't you?" he said. He took half a step closer, ignoring Nack's warning. "Now, before I call my guards to come in here and gut you like a fish, boy, how about you tell me who you really are, and why you're bothering my newest recruit?"

"My name is Nack F—" Nack stopped, the weight of Asperides suddenly heavy in his hands. He swallowed the lump in his throat, did his best to ignore the sweat suddenly dripping down his face, and spoke again. "Nack. Just Nack. And I'm here to kill you."

———— ✦ ————

Finally, the demon sword Asperides thought, *things are about to get interesting.*

Asperides felt the familiar thrill that preceded a good comeuppance. He had to give Lord Solonos credit—the old fellow hardly batted an eye in the face of Nack's naked steel. But it was time for Lord Solonos to meet his end. This whole "revenge quest" of Nack's had been an unwelcome distraction from the boy's training since the moment he had become Asperides's new master. With the clock ticking on the return of the Missing Moon and a very angry Amyral Venir out for blood, Asperides needed a Nack unbothered by such pesky distractions as family ties and restored honor. It was time for the source of his master's anguish to die.

Asperides admitted to himself that he was just a *tad* disappointed over the Furnival brother's betrayal. He understood the young man's reasoning—would probably have made the same decision himself, and in less time than this. Many years of experience had taught him that most of the world's "noble" families were noble in title alone. They were as filled with backstabbing and cheating, with money-grubbing and murder, as any of the levels of hell. And yet, somehow, after so many days with young Nack, Asperides had expected . . . more, perhaps, from the rest of the Furnival clan.

But the traitorous brother was of no concern to him now. What mattered most was that Nack kill Lord Solonos, and kill him quickly, so they could return to their more important quest. The unquiet souls inside Asperides fed off Nack's anger and resentment, power seeping into the blade and the boy. Together, they were an unstoppable force of wrath. Solonos didn't stand a chance.

. . . Or, he wouldn't, if Nack would just chop off the man's head already.

WHAT ARE YOU WAITING FOR? Asperides asked Nack. *KILL HIM. KILL HIM NOW.*

The boy's grip slipped, ever so slightly.

"I . . ." Nack's voice shook. The sword point dipped in the air. "I'm *going* to . . ."

"Kill me?" prompted Lord Solonos, who looked as if he were barely restraining himself from rolling his eyes. "Yes, you've said."

Nack raised Asperides again, but made no move to strike. Of all the times to hesitate! Asperides wished he still had control over Nack's limbs, so he could do the deed himself. But if the boy wasn't motivated enough by hatred alone . . .

WE MUST FLEE, Asperides urged Nack. *KILL HIM QUICKLY, OR YOU AND YOUR BROTHER WILL NEVER MAKE IT OUT OF HERE ALIVE.*

"Any time now . . ." said Lord Solonos with a heavy sigh.

Nack's hands now shook so much he could barely hold Asperides steady in the air. The boy's breath came in shallow gasps. Hell's bells, was he *crying*?

Asperides really had to make sure his next master was actually committed to the dark arts. These heroic types were a truly nonsensical bunch.

Asperides sensed Solonos's movement just in time.

DODGE, NOW, he said to Nack, just as the older man dipped under Asperides's point and lunged.

For once, the boy obeyed him without question. He twisted to the right, just out of reach of the older man's grip. Lord Solonos lost his footing and barreled into Declan, and the two of them fell to the floor in an ungraceful tangle of limbs.

"Lord Solonos!" cried Declan as he tried to right himself. "I'm so sorry. This—this boy, I've never seen him before—"

"LORD SOLONOS."

The booming voice was as familiar to Asperides as his own, so loud it sounded as if the speaker were standing in the room with them, shouting in their ears. Amplified by magic, no doubt.

"I AM AMYRAL VENIR, AND I HAVE COME TO TAKE YOUR CASTLE."

Nack, Declan, and Solonos all froze as the menacing voice continued.

"SURRENDER THE DEMON SWORD . . . OR DIE."

17

Angels and Demons

C leoline stood on the hilltop outside Castle Ravinus, Amyral the Undying's legions of soldiers spread out below her on the hillside, ready for the order to charge. It amazed her how quickly they'd been able to advance once her band of revenant decoys had scattered Solonos's scouts. It turned out that her typical zombies, while utterly useless as loyal servants or window-shopping buddies, were pretty great at scaring the crap out of other people's armies. What seemed like minutes earlier, this hill had been empty, save for Cleoline and her small armory's worth of candles, bones, and other tools. Now that Amyral's troops had moved in, it was as if the soldiers had suddenly sprung from the ground, like clusters of so many pointy, ill-tempered daisies.

She and Amyral had considered the invasion carefully. On the one hand, he couldn't afford to decimate his forces with a defeat so close to the arrival of the Missing Moon. He would need those men to protect him from the more . . . *excitable* elements of the underworld, after all. On the other hand, if Cleoline's research had taught her anything, it was that he *absolutely* needed a demon sword to carve the doorway that would let those creatures out—and, more importantly, let Amyral *in*. As far as Cleo knew, a demon sword was one of the few creatures in existence that was truly of both worlds, and certainly the only one capable of channeling enough of the Missing Moon's magic to carve a hole in the fabric of the universe.

Cleoline had despaired when she realized they needed a demon sword, convinced her quest to retrieve Amyral's full soul was ended before it had even begun. Amyral's former sword could be literally *anywhere*. But Amyral, ever full of surprises (most of them, it had to be said, being dead stuff he had squirreled away in his pockets that Cleoline stumbled upon when she was doing the laundry), had been curiously calm.

"Where does the most power lie in this land, in this

time?" he asked her, then clarified: "The most power . . . alongside the most death."

Which, honestly, was such a poetic turn of phrase Cleo just had to take a second to appreciate that *this was her freaking life now* before she answered him. But she was equally surprised to find the answer came easily to her lips.

Lord Solonos was such an obvious candidate for a demon sword master, Cleoline could have kicked herself for not thinking of him before now. (Cleo had considered joining him, many moons ago, but then she got word that he fired a whole laboratory full of scientists and experimental sorcerers on some of his conquered lands just so he could use their building for storage or something, and *that* was an act Cleoline could never forgive.) But when she thought of Solonos's obvious power-hungriness, of his reputation for violence, of his recent sweeping victories across the land that had only accelerated within the last few months . . . if the demon sword Asperides had indeed fallen into the hands of a new master, as Amyral seemed convinced it had, then Lord Solonos seemed as likely a candidate as any.

Asperides had a way of making itself known, Amyral told her—of encouraging its masters, manipulating them, into using the sword's power obviously and publicly, the better to draw attention to its master . . . and make them the target of other envious, would-be demon sword wielders. Sooner or later, one of those aspiring evildoers would get the best of the current master—usually in the most underhanded and violent way possible—and the demon sword would have another soul to add to its well of power.

It sounded like a pretty good living, Cleoline had to admit.

And also like a pretty good trap.

But they didn't have a choice, did they? They needed the demon sword for the Missing Moon ritual. They needed it to get the rest of Amyral Venir's soul back.

Cleoline shivered in the cool night air as they waited for the moons to rise—and noticed she wasn't the only one shivering. The soldiers whispered and stirred restlessly around her. Cleoline could feel their fear in the air, like a contagious miasma floating over the crowd, not dissimilar from some of the clouds of funk she'd accidentally conjured in her basement once or twice.

It turned out being a zombie sorcerer knight's dark queen was a lot more complicated in reality than it had seemed in her daydreams back at Waldo's.

She hadn't considered, for example, that a queen had to have subjects.

"Are you all right then, my lady?" asked one of Amyral's knights, approaching her from the side—a graying man with a face like an old leather boot. She thought his name might've been Terrance. There were a lot of men around her these days—Amyral Venir tended to attract the biggest, burliest, most desperate or most ambitious fighters the land had to offer. Until tonight, Cleoline had mostly kept clear of them.

They weren't going to be around very long, after all. No reason to get attached.

"Fine, thank you," said Cleoline, trying to look like the battle-ready warrior witch she so desperately wanted to be, as opposed to an eighteen-year-old girl who'd never taken on more than a single knight in combat. (And that hadn't exactly gone smoothly.) Every time she looked at one of Amyral's knights, every time they spoke to her, she remembered most of them would meet a messy end as demon chew toys.

Cleoline took a steadying breath. There was no use thinking about that now. Not when they didn't even have the demon sword in hand yet.

One thing at a time, Cleo.

Even if Solonos didn't have a demon sword, he at least had a very nice castle. After spending the past few months on the road, they could definitely use one of those.

It probably had a real dungeon and everything.

Strips of moonlight played across the weapons of the soldiers around her. The sun had finally set.

Amyral looked over the lines of the assembled troops to Cleoline and gave her the signal. She bent down and lit the large, multicolored candle at her feet, mumbled a few words, and angled the candle toward him. When he spoke, his voice would carry over the entire castle and beyond.

"LORD SOLONOS," he began . . .

———◆———

RUN, Asperides said to the boy. *RUN, NOW.*

The demon sword had thought, after undertaking an ill-advised and ultimately unnecessary rescue mission into the castle of the most murderous human this side of the veil, in which their likelihood of escaping said murderous human's many, many soldiers was already slim to none, that things couldn't get much worse for him and his new, motley crew.

It turned out he was wrong.

Hearing his former master's voice after so many years sent a shudder of fear down Asperides's blade. He heard the boy gasp in surprise, but he could barely spare a thought for Nack. Asperides was back on battlefields long since past, his blade alight with green and red flame—hellfire summoned from the depths of his underworld prisons. He was trying to look away as Amyral Venir slaughtered everything in his path, but of course, he did not have eyes to close. And Amyral had forbidden him from allowing his consciousness to retreat to the underworld—he needed every ounce of Asperides's focus and power. He could not have his blade's mind wandering off when there were enemies to be slain. Enemies that just so happened to include scores of women and children . . .

It was clear to Asperides that Amyral made him bear witness to the dark knight's atrocities simply *because* Amyral knew it bothered the sword. No one was immune to Amyral's petty exercises of power—not even the sword to which most of that power was owed.

Amyral's voice echoed through the room again, once more demanding Asperides's retrieval. How on earth did he even know Asperides was there?

Asperides's awareness blurred, and it took him a moment to realize that for once, the boy had taken his advice. Nack was running through the castle's halls, dodging the defending knights and the chaotic press of servants and courtiers scrambling to safety. Asperides called up his mental map of the castle—or as much of it as he could sense—the better to guide Nack out of it.

They could not be here when the castle fell to Amyral—and fall it undoubtedly would.

YOU ARE GOING THE WRONG WAY, Asperides warned Nack.

"Not if we're getting Willa and Barb out, too," said Nack through gritted teeth.

Honestly. These heroic types really were going to be the end of him someday.

FORGET THEM, said Asperides. *WHAT ABOUT THE YOUNG PRIESTESS? YOU LEFT HER IN THE CLEARING. IF AMYRAL'S FOLLOWERS HAVE NOT FOUND HER BY NOW—*

"Stop those women!" cried a deep voice somewhere to their left. "They claimed to be pledging loyalty to our lord, but they led the enemy straight to our door!"

A breathless Willa and Barb rounded the corner in front of them, nearly crashing straight into Nack and Asperides. A couple of angry Solonos knights were hot on their heels.

"Oh, hello there!" said Barb brightly.

"Do *you* have any idea what's going on?" Willa asked. Her question was directed at Nack, but her gaze fell squarely on Asperides. She grabbed Nack by the shoulder and shepherded him and Barb down another corridor.

(Once again, in the wrong direction. What was *with*

these humans and their inability to think clearly when faced with certain death?)

"Not at all," said Nack, ducking into a deserted alcove. Asperides, so attuned to Nack's emotions by now, sensed the lie in the boy's voice. *That* might mean trouble later— if there was a later.

The three humans stopped to catch their breath; other castle dwellers ran back and forth but otherwise took no notice of them.

"Where's Declan?" Willa asked, her deep brown eyes filled with concern.

Nack merely shook his head, unable to form the words. Again, Asperides felt the surprising wrench of disappointment. He did feel sorry for the boy, he supposed, for having such a brutish nincompoop for a brother. The Nack Furnival he knew deserved better family than that.

Willa put a comforting hand on Nack's shoulder.

Barb ducked her head out of the alcove. "Looks clear, for now," she whispered. "What do you think? Laundry chutes? It'll at least get us out of the fray. We can sneak out the way you came in."

"It wasn't laundry I came here in," Nack clarified. "Solonos was bringing in gold. Lots of it."

"Hmmm." Willa nodded. "Whether it's ferrying laundry or treasure, I don't see that Amyral fellow letting anyone out of this castle anytime soon. We might be hiding in the sheets until we starve. Second-best option?"

"There they are!" A redheaded knight with a sneering thin face skidded to a halt directly in front of them. "Thought you could betray our lord, could you?" He made to draw his sword, but Barb didn't give him the chance. The stocky knight launched herself at the taller man, sending them both sprawling.

"Go!" Barb shouted at them, her round face red with the effort of holding down the larger man.

"*Barb*," said Willa, her face twisted with pain. She took a step forward to help her wife but stopped short as the sound of more running footsteps echoed down the hall.

"I'll be right behind you!" Barb insisted, giving the Solonos knight a good punch in the nose to emphasize her point. Willa hesitated only a moment before grabbing Nack's hand and dragging the boy in the opposite direction.

"But—" said Nack.

"You heard her," said Willa, her voice breaking, just a little. "Right behind us. Let's go!"

"Third best option?" Nack asked as they ran, dodging a gaggle of panicked kitchen maids.

Asperides was not about to let the humans in his charge wander off in the wrong direction again. Not bothering to restrict his voice to Nack's hearing, he spoke so that the knight Willa would hear him as well.

NOW, said Asperides, summoning piercing blue flames to dance along his blade and light their way through the gloomy castle, *WE FIGHT OUR WAY OUT.*

———◆———

"I . . . I swear! I don't know where it is!" pleaded Lord Solonos. "I don't know anything about any demon sword!" The bearded man wept like a child.

"Lies," hissed Amyral. Asperides was here. He could feel it. He and the sword were tied together—perhaps not as strongly as they had been in life, but it appeared the bond between demon sword and master lasted even into death. Perhaps it was Amyral's soul, calling to him from all the way inside the sword's hellfire-filled prison. At any rate, he knew the sword was, or had been, in this castle, as surely as he knew his own name.

Some time later, when Lord Solonos wasn't the lord of anything anymore, Amyral had to concede the man may have been telling the truth.

"Please," Solonos had murmured near his last

moments. "You have to believe me. I didn't know it existed. I wish I did. But I never had it. *I NEVER HAD IT!*"

Which, of course, begged the question: if Lord Solonos—sacker of cities, destroyer of entire clans, the most feared conqueror in all the land—did not have the demon sword Asperides . . . who did?

18

No Going Back

"I have to go back," Willa had told them, tears flowing freely down her face. "If there's a chance, I have to get her back."

And so she'd left Nack and Therin at their hideout near the creek, the angel blade Lenira's glow bobbing up and down as Willa retreated. She'd advised them to keep going, to not stop until they were miles away from Castle Ravinus. At the moment, traveling in the dark was safer than encountering the forces of Amyral the Undying.

"And you," Willa had said before she left, her eyes boring into Nack's. "When we meet again, you have some explaining to do."

And I'm not the only one, thought Nack as every event of that night, everything that had happened since he'd picked up Asperides, every dark suspicion he'd been pushing out of his thoughts since that night in the cave, all began to coalesce in his mind. He couldn't put it off any longer. He needed to know the truth.

It must have been nearly three in the morning before Nack and Therin, exhausted and footsore, had traveled as far from Castle Ravinus as they could. They even chanced a stretch on the main roads and fell in with a band of refugees fleeing the fighting—the clan wars and the approach of the Missing Moon had upended nearly everyone's hesitance to travel under the two moons—but they didn't stay for long. Solonos's, or Amyral's, or even Furnival spies could be anywhere. Nack made them peel off from the group before sunrise. It wasn't until Therin nearly fell flat on her face from exhaustion, simply too tired to go on, that Nack finally accepted they weren't going to travel any more that night. With Therin tucked safely in the hollow of a large oak tree, along with plenty of whispered assurances that he was only going to get firewood for the morning, Nack walked deeper into the forest. It was only when the tree cover blocked out most of the moonlight and Nack could have easily broken an ankle in the darkness that he unsheathed Asperides.

He made sure he was well outside of shouting distance of the sleeping Therin before he spoke.

"First question," Nack said roughly. He didn't need to address the sword to know Asperides was listening. "Who, exactly, is Amyral the Undying?"

A LOCAL WARLORD, said Asperides quickly. *A DARK KNIGHT AND A NECROMANCER, IF THE RUMORS ARE TRUE—*

"Who is he *to you*?" Nack fought to keep his voice even.

The sword's glow wavered. Nack gave him a small shake.

"Asperides!"

. . . MY FORMER MASTER.

Nack gritted his teeth against the hysterical laugh that threatened to burst from his throat.

"Your former . . ." He took a deep breath. "That first night. In the cave. That was Amyral the Undying in that tomb, wasn't it? And when . . . when I took you out of there, he somehow came back to life?"

HE WENT BY AMYRAL VENIR, THEN, said the sword with a sigh, *BUT . . . YES.*

A very un-knightly word escaped Nack's lips.

"We said *no more lies*, Asperides," said Nack. He wanted to pace, but the undergrowth on the forest floor was so thick he merely succeeded in stubbing his toe a few times. "After Therin joined us, you agreed. You said we'd work *together—*"

AND I DID NOT LIE TO YOU, the sword insisted. *NOT AFTER THAT DAY. NOT . . . DIRECTLY.*

Nack scoffed. "Oh, right! You just conveniently *failed to mention* that the murderous undead knight amassing enough forces to take down the most powerful clan in the land was your last *boss!*"

AMYRAL VENIR WAS NOT MY BOSS, Asperides said, his voice as sharp as his blade. The sword grew suddenly hot in Nack's hand. Nack shoved it into the ground, point down, with a yelp of surprise.

HE WAS MY MASTER. AND I HAD NO CHOICE BUT TO DO MY MASTER'S BIDDING.

Unease coiled in Nack's stomach, a slithering snake of anger—at Asperides, at Amyral, and at himself. And underneath that anger: guilt. That most useless of emotions, according to his sword. Nack, too, had probably commanded Asperides to do things against the sword's will. *You will have sole command of myself*—it was right there in their contract. Nack hadn't questioned it. He hadn't thought to. Not after seeing so many angel blades over the years. He had never stopped to think about how the angels felt, once they had chosen a sword.

And yet whatever their relationship was, it hadn't stopped Asperides from manipulating Nack since the moment they'd met. From telling him which missions to take, and which ones to ignore, and where to travel . . . Nack shook his head. How could he have been so *stupid*?

"You were keeping us away from Amyral," Nack said. "On purpose. You kept me from stopping him! Whenever we talked about going after him, it was always, 'No, Nack, we must continue on to the archives—'"

I HAD HOPED TO TRAIN YOU, YOU FOOL, said Asperides, stopping Nack in his tracks. *YES, I KNEW OF AMYRAL'S RESURRECTION. AND I KNOW WHAT KIND OF MAN—OR RATHER, MONSTER— HE WAS WHEN HE WAS ALIVE. EVENTUALLY, YES, I GUESSED HE PLANNED TO USE THE MISSING MOON FOR HIS OWN ENDS. AND SO I DID ALL I COULD TO KEEP YOU AWAY FROM HIM—*

"You admit it, then! We could have, *should have*, stopped him sooner . . ." Nack thought back to their first few days together, when Asperides had advised him against going back to his family, back to the Furnivals. He clenched his fists. "If you ever really cared about stopping him at all! For all I know, you . . . you could be on his side!"

YOU WOULD NOT HAVE STOOD A CHANCE AGAINST AMYRAL VENIR, the sword said flatly. *THAT*

IS WHY I TRAINED YOU. THAT IS WHY I INSISTED YOU FLEE, AND THEN WHY I COACHED YOU—YOU, WITH YOUR PETTY DESIRES FOR REVENGE AND FOR GLORY. YOU, WITH YOUR MEDIOCRE TALENT. I PUT UP WITH IT ALL, PUT EVERY OUNCE OF MY POWER AND EXPERTISE INTO TRAINING YOU, SO THAT YOU MIGHT HAVE EVEN THE SLIGHTEST CHANCE OF SURVIVAL, THE SMALLEST HOPE OF STOPPING AMYRAL FROM . . . FROM . . .

"From what?" prodded Nack.

The sword abandoned its traditional blue glow. Suddenly, green and red flames began to lick the length of the blade. The ground around the point smoked, the acrid smell of the thick black plumes nearly making Nack choke.

BUT IT SEEMS MY EFFORTS WERE WASTED, the sword's voice spat inside Nack's head. *FOR HOW COULD I EXPECT YOU TO KILL AMYRAL VENIR, WHEN YOU COULD NOT EVEN KILL YOUR WORST ENEMY? WHEN YOU DID NOT EVEN HAVE THE STOMACH TO PUNISH THE MAN WHO RUINED YOUR FUTURE? THE MAN WHO WOULD KILL YOUR ENTIRE CLAN WITHOUT BLINKING?*

"STOP IT!" shouted Nack, clapping his hands over his ears. He knew it was useless, that Asperides's voice was inside his head, but he couldn't help it. It was true. He hadn't had the guts—hadn't had the *courage* to do what a real Furnival heir would have done. To do what Declan would have done—or else, what Nack *thought* Declan would have done . . .

Suddenly, he was back in Castle Ravinus, the tip of his blade at Solonos's chest, the man's bushy eyebrows quirked in borderline *amusement* at Nack's posturing. Solonos had known, as Asperides did, that Nack was never going to kill him. They'd all known. Everyone in that room knew that Nack Furnival was a coward, could never do what needed to be done . . .

WE MUST RUN, AND NOW, said Asperides, *OUR ONLY HOPE IS TO BE AS FAR AWAY FROM AMYRAL VENIR AS THE EARTH ALLOWS. YOU MUST LEAVE THE PRIESTESS, LEAVE THOSE KNIGHTS, AND RUN. BECAUSE THERE IS NO HOPE FOR YOU, NO HOPE FOR ANY OF US, IF YOU CANNOT KILL THOSE WHO WOULD KILL YOU FIRST—*

"Stop it!" Nack cried. "Stop messing with my head!" The vision of the castle dissolved, and Nack was back in the forest, his chest heaving. He sat down on a nearby rock with a huff. He couldn't think of that room, or anything that had happened in it. Not yet. He couldn't let Asperides distract him. Because as he'd just discovered, apparently, Asperides couldn't refuse a direct command or question forever.

"From what?" repeated Nack, his voice barely a whisper.

PARDON? asked the sword. Nack could hear the sneer in his voice. But Nack would not be intimidated this time.

"You said you were training me to fight Amyral Venir," explained Nack. "You said you wanted me to stop him from doing something. And I asked you, to stop him from doing *what*?"

The flames running along the sword dimmed until they were barely visible. They could have been twinkling fireflies, the last remnants of night before a swiftly approaching dawn. But Nack knew better.

AMYRAL VENIR PLANS TO USE A DEMON SWORD, LONG AGO FORGED IN THE LIGHT OF THE MISSING MOON AND SOON—WITH THAT SAME MOON'S RETURN—MADE AS POWERFUL AS ANY TOOL KNOWN TO MAN, DEMON, OR ANGEL, TO CARVE A DOORWAY INTO THE UNDERWORLD.

Nack stared at the blinking hints of flames, allowing them to transfix him, the better to keep calm. He knew that now, in this moment, if he really wanted answers . . . he was going to get them.

"And why does Amyral Venir want to carve a doorway into the underworld?" he asked, straining to keep his voice even.

Nack felt Asperides hesitate again. He narrowed his eyes at the sword.

TO ENTER THE DEPTHS OF WHAT YOU HUMANS CALL HELL AND TO . . . RETRIEVE THE GREATER PART OF HIS SOUL.

Nack shuddered as remembered Asperides's words from earlier. *I did not lie to you.* He also remembered that night in the cave, a night that felt like so many years ago, though it had only been months.

The night he'd sold his soul for a chance at an angel blade's power.

Just as suddenly as before, he was back inside that strange black-and-white-tiled room. The great stone pillars looming on either side of him looked even taller now. They seemed to lean toward him, like tree limbs reaching for the sun. The words of the contract he'd made echoed in his mind.

THE TERMS ARE THUS: BY ENTERING INTO THIS CONTRACT, WE ARE BOUND AS WEAPON AND WIELDER. YOU WILL HAVE SOLE COMMAND OF MYSELF, THE SWORD ASPERIDES, AND ALL THE POWER CONTAINED WITHIN ME, UNTIL THE TIME

OF YOUR DEATH, AT WHICH POINT THE CONTRACT
WILL END AND YOUR SOUL WILL BE FORFEIT.

Nack had never heard of such a thing before.

He should have run screaming from that room.

"My soul?"

Nack watched his past self ask the question as if watching a character in a play.

"Forfeit to . . . to whom?"

The sword answered, *TO ME, OF COURSE.*

Nack's vision of his past self dissolved, but he and the sword remained. The moonlight in the hall was dimmer now. And there was no mistaking the sickly greenish tinge that tarnished Asperides's blue glow.

"Why is Amyral Venir's soul trapped in hell?" Nack asked softly.

BECAUSE THAT IS THE PRICE OF ENTERING A CONTRACT WITH . . . A BEING SUCH AS MYSELF.

A being such as himself. Nack snorted. Hot tears formed in the corners of his eyes. He let them fall. He knew the answer to his next question. He'd known it all along, hadn't he? But the promise of power, of a tool that would help him rejoin the Furnivals, help him regain his honor, help him . . . yes, he admitted it now, even attain a bit of fame and glory along the way . . . that had been enough to make him ignore his instincts, ignore the warning signs and the sword's unusual appearance and behavior and *powers*. By the angels, his powers. No wonder Nack had never seen an angel blade like Asperides in his life.

It was because there was no such thing.

"And what sort of being are you?" Nack asked, staring straight at the glowing sword.

I THINK YOU KNOW, said Asperides. *I THINK YOU HAVE ALWAYS KNOWN, IN YOUR HEART OF HEARTS, NACK FURNIVAL.*

Nack lost his temper. The scream erupted out of him, scratching his throat, clawing across the mysterious chamber's walls like one of the angry gasper-cats back in the cave.

"TELL ME. WHAT. YOU ARE."

The sword's glow dimmed until Nack stood in near-total darkness.

I AM A DEMON SWORD, said Asperides.

The cool winds of the wood blew around them. Nack smelled decaying earth. The sky was pink with the early light of dawn. He thought he could hear Therin calling his name.

Nack could almost picture the sword sweeping forward in a mocking bow as he added, *MASTER.*

19

Homeward Bound

*T*HIS WILL NOT WORK, Asperides assured the boy. *NO MORTAL METHODS CAN BREAK THE MYSTICAL TIES THAT—*

Sploosh. Asperides hit the raging river water with an undignified splat.

So that was how it was going to be, then.

Asperides let the current of the River Spide sweep him along. This wasn't the first time one of his masters had tried to be rid of him without fulfilling their end of the contract, and it wouldn't be the last. It wouldn't be long before the fickle hands of fate placed him back into his master's arms. If only the boy hadn't been so impulsive, so ridiculously *ashamed* of his bond with Asperides, they might have come to an understanding. They might have even stood a chance against Amyral Venir. Sure, Asperides had tricked the boy into selling his soul. That had to sting a bit. But they'd made a good team, hadn't they? They'd both gone from being lost to history and obscurity to being one of the most famous demon-slaying teams in the land! Asperides saw no reason why the arrangement couldn't continue, once Nack had time to cool down a bit. But now, Nack had left himself and the girl priestess vulnerable in the most dangerous of dangerous times—not to mention losing precious time in their preparations for the arrival of the Missing Moon.

And the Missing Moon *was* coming. Asperides could feel it. Never mind the earthquakes and the rising tides and the torrents of spirits and demons streaming in and out of the underworld. Asperides could sense the Missing Moon's approach, deep down in the place where other beings might've kept their souls. Asperides had no soul, of course, but he was starting to understand what one might feel like—like everything that made him *himself,* concentrated and hard as a diamond, and yet as invisible as the wind. This was what the pull of the Missing Moon felt like—and it was getting stronger. Stronger and closer.

Asperides could almost sympathize with the longing

Amyral Venir must feel, to be reunited with the part of himself that was lost.

But only *almost*.

For now, he was faced with a situation he hadn't encountered in quite some time: boredom. After all those years trapped in Amyral's tomb, it had been sort of pleasant, really, to be out and about again, slaying and scheming. He could only hope Nack and Therin wouldn't get themselves into too much trouble in the meantime . . . But what was the sense in worrying? He could not move about freely here, not without a master, the way he could in the underworld. All he could do now was wait.

As he let the water carry him, Asperides's consciousness sank into depths deeper than the river water. He sank down, and down some more, into his favorite darkened corner of his favorite pub in the underworld. It had been far too long since he'd visited the Wet Fang, after all.

———◆———

"I *cannot* believe you."

Therin looked at Nack in disbelief. She was cold, and damp, and exhausted, and her dreams had been filled with disturbing glimpses of the approaching Missing Moon, and now Nack Furnival was telling her he was giving up on their *entire quest* to go shove his head in the sand and pretend nothing was happening.

Therin clutched her threadbare cloak around her shoulders and shivered as she glared at him.

"We now have proof—honest-to-goodness, straight-from-the-underworld proof that Amyral Venir is *definitely, totally planning* to use the Missing Moon's light to open up *an actual doorway* to the underworld, which is going to let hundreds, if not thousands, of demons and spirits into our world, and you're giving up and *going home*?"

"I'm not . . . I just . . ." Nack's brow furrowed. "Did you miss the part where I mentioned Asperides was a *demon sword*?!"

"WHO YOU THREW INTO THE RIVER," said Therin, smacking her forehead with her hand. She wanted to smack Nack. "What kind of numskull does that? What if we get attacked by a demon, or run into Amyral's soldiers, or Amyral gets his creepy undead hands on Asperides, hmm? What about that! Honestly, how he chose *you* as a master . . ."

"It was a right-place-right-time kind of thing," said Nack. "But also: demon sword! Asperides! Is one!"

Therin put her hands on her hips. "And you knew nothing about that, did you?" she asked.

Nack could only sputter in response.

Truth be told, Therin *had* been surprised when Nack told her that Asperides was a demon sword . . . for about ten seconds. But then, lots of things suddenly made a lot more sense. Like how sometimes, when Asperides was around, or when Nack was drawing on his power, Therin would feel this heavy, pressing sensation that would make her feel nauseous, or give her a headache, and her mouth would taste of metal. And how Nack and Asperides seemed to talk to each other unlike any other angel blade and knight Therin had seen before. And, of course, there was Asperides's power. For such a powerful angel blade, Therin had been surprised she'd never seen his name in the Mission of the Missing Moon's history books.

Of course, that was because he wasn't an angel blade at all, and someone, long ago, had done a *very* fine job of erasing him from history altogether.

But the Mission of the Missing Moon had passed down *some* lore through the ages, even if all the demon swords' names had been lost to history. Therin had spotted Asperides for what he was, that first night they had met. But her defenses had been nothing against his power. Now, with his influence gone, she remembered. He'd made her forget—that time, and a few other times, as well. And she had to admit that for the sake of their work, for the sake of the people they were and would be saving, she'd put her uneasy feelings about the sword aside, too . . .

She didn't condone what Asperides had done. She didn't condone what he was—even if some of the other stories the Mission passed down about the swords and the Missing Moon were true. But just as she'd teamed up with Nack because he seemed determined to keep people from abusing the moon's power, she still believed Asperides was committed to the same thing. And Asperides had known that a world with a permanent doorway to the underworld was one that could never be allowed to come to pass—had known it, apparently, better than the supposedly noble knight standing in front of her.

"You knew something was up with Asperides from the start," Therin said. She lowered her head. "We both did. And we both decided it was worth ignoring, at least for now, for the greater good! To stop people like Amyral Venir!"

Nack merely shuffled his feet in the dirt and mumbled something too soft for Therin to hear.

"What?" she said.

"I said—" Nack cleared his throat. "I didn't . . . I didn't team up with Asperides so I could stop Amyral Venir."

"Well, we didn't know it would be him, specifically, but—"

"No," said Nack, grimacing. "I didn't do it so I could stop people from abusing the Missing Moon's return. I didn't even know about the Missing Moon when I met him. I didn't do it so I could be a better knight and help more people, and slay more demons, and . . . and stop all the evil I encountered in its tracks, or whatever you've started to believe about me. I did it to go home. I sold my soul so I could impress my family enough to convince them I wasn't the coward they thought I was. I just . . . I just wanted to go home."

Nack sniffed, his eyes full of unshed tears. But Therin could feel no sympathy for him—not after she'd given up *her* home, and her sisters, and her education, and her entire *life* to travel with this boy and his sword, because she'd believed he was different than all the others who wanted to use her for their own gain.

"Well, safe travels then," said Therin, standing as tall as her short frame would allow.

"But you can come, too!" Nack assured her. "I wasn't going to just leave you in the forest—"

"You might as well have," said Therin, already wondering if she could catch up with the group of refugees they'd walked with earlier, and if some of them might be headed north, too. She gathered up the muddied hem of her cloak and made off in what she thought was the right direction.

"Therin, wait!" Nack called after her. "Where are you going?"

"To try and stop a zombie knight from ripping open a permanent hole in the universe," groused Therin as she struggled to find the forest path. "You have a nice time at home with Mom and Dad while the world is ending."

"Therin."

"And don't worry, Nack," she said as she left him behind. "You don't have anything to prove to your family."

"What—"

"Because it looks to me like you're just as much of a coward now as you say you were before."

He stopped following her after that, leaving her with only the soft crunch of her footfalls on the forest floor for company.

As Nack made his way across the war-torn and natural disaster–ravaged landscape, he conceded that he might have been a tad hasty in throwing his only source of protection into the River Spide. It didn't help that people occasionally recognized him from his travels with

Asperides and Therin; after they hailed him with thanks for performing some minor good deed or another, he never failed to notice their slightly askance looks at his obvious lack of a weapon. He also noticed other rogue knights and bands of men noticing *him*, and after a few days of a very jumpy existence, he finally caved and fashioned a bunch of twigs into what he hoped was a visible, sword-shaped lump in his pack. It wasn't perfect, but it did make him feel slightly less like he was walking the roads naked.

It took him nearly five weeks of walking and hitching rides on passing carts to reach the Furnival lands. He performed a few minor exorcisms to earn some coin and some food until he ran out of candles, but after that, with no sword and an empty bandolier, he was just as helpless as any other refugee on the road. Each day stretched longer than the last, the light of the two moons—and the approaching third, presumably—mixing eerily with the sun in ways that no one living had ever seen before. Meteor showers streaked through the skies at night. Watching the molten paths they cut across the sky made Nack feel out of place even as he drew nearer to his homeland, like he was walking on an alien planet. The Missing Moon's approach was nigh.

He'd expected a challenge the second he set foot onto Furnival lands—expected armed bands of knights he barely recognized, and who certainly wouldn't recognize him, to shoot him on sight, the times being what they were. Instead, he found the woods eerily quiet, the outer fields abandoned. Crops that should have been harvested in the late summer and early autumn lay dead and rotting in the fields, utterly useless to the hundreds of people they could have fed. There were even cold patches and shimmering bits of mist hovering here and there in the fields; Nack sensed and saw them more easily now than he once did, and he knew enough to give them a wide berth. His stomach sank as he walked. Rogue spirits would never have been allowed to manifest so clearly on the Furnival lands he once knew. Where were the people? Where were the knights?

It was only after walking for a solid half hour that he finally ran across another living soul—one of their old gamekeepers, a man named Grennan who had always seemed as ancient as some of the Furnival wood's oldest trees. Far from shouting, "Trespasser!" and shoving Nack off the property with the added motivation of something pointy—or his deadly slingshot—Grennan merely nodded in Nack's direction and croaked, "'Spect they'll be glad to see ya, after all. Come along, now."

Grennan wasn't exactly forthcoming with information, but the whereabouts of the land's inhabitants became clearer the closer they got to Castle Falterfen—chiefly because nearly everyone was *inside* Castle Falterfen. Closer to the castle, great swaths of the earth had been turned up or cloven in two, swallowing several outbuildings and barns that had the misfortune to lie in their path—casualties of one of the recent earthquakes, no doubt. But Castle Falterfen itself still stood proudly, offering shelter as best it could to the throngs of people within its walls.

Nack had thought he would feel different the next time he set foot inside his childhood home. He thought he would feel braver, more confident, more worthy of the name he sought to restore. But mostly? He felt nervous.

Nervous and ashamed.

"Nack!" a voice called, tremulous and uncertain.

His mother.

"Nack, is it truly you?"

———•◆•———

"We've heard quite a few tales of your bravery, my son."

"My son." His father's words settled over him like a warm, comforting blanket. As he sat at his family table for the first time in what felt like forever, Nack couldn't believe it was really happening. He couldn't believe he was really back here, sitting at his father's side, his mother smiling across from him, servants scurrying back and forth bringing mountains of hot, comforting food that was more than Nack had even seen in one place in months. He couldn't quite believe that he was full, and comfortable, and not about to sleep on the wet ground or in someone's barn for the night. There was a bed waiting for him—*his* bed—and he was back home with his family, where he belonged.

He couldn't help but notice, of course, that even this food was less plentiful and varied than the usual fare of his childhood, but he didn't expect much else in such difficult times. They took dinner in one of his father's sitting rooms as opposed to the castle's great hall, the better to keep their first meal together a family affair—or so Nack's mother had said. A small voice inside of him (which sounded far too much like Asperides for Nack's liking) said that they'd also kept Nack out of the public eye on purpose, perhaps because they hadn't *really* decided what to do with him yet. Nack wished he could chuck that small voice into the river, too, but his father's mention of these "tales of his bravery" didn't do much to quell his anxiety.

"It's nothing, Father," said Nack, ducking his head. "I was just . . . doing my duty. For the people. And for a chance at living up to your name again someday."

"And we are so, so glad that day is here," his mother said, her eyes glistening. She reached over the table and took Nack's hand. "I always thought your father was too hasty—"

"We have a reputation to uphold," his father interrupted her sternly, his tone suggesting this was not the first time he'd made this point. Nack ignored the steely glances that passed between them. Now *this* was starting to resemble the family dinners he remembered.

"And now that Nack has proven himself," his mother pressed, "now that he has an angel blade—"

"I don't," Nack said quickly. Seeing his parents' faces freeze, he added, "Or at least, I don't have a sword anymore." He was careful not to specify exactly which kind of sword had been in his possession and hated himself all the more for it. It seemed Asperides had rubbed off on him in more ways than one.

"I lost it," Nack said, poking at the bits of food on his plate, "after the battle at Castle Ravinus."

"Castle *Ravinus*?" his father said, his shocked voice booming through the room.

"You may not know this, but the, uh, the new warlord, Amyral Venir—he took the castle. I don't even know if Solonos is still alive—"

"He isn't," his mother said shortly, sharing another

heavy look with his father. Nack had rarely seen either of them look so surprised. "If the gossip can be trusted."

"Why were *you* at Castle Ravinus when it fell?" demanded Father. "What business could you possibly have there?"

Bristling a bit at his father's tone, Nack raised his own voice. "I was trying to rescue Declan!"

Both of his parents looked down at their plates at the mention of their eldest son's name. The lack of his presence had been the uninvited guest hovering at the edge of their dinner tonight, and now, Nack had just asked that painful memory to pull up a chair and join them.

"Oh, Nack . . ." his mother said, her expression kind and caring once more. "You shouldn't have. Not even our knights could have gotten past Solonos to rescue your brother. We . . . when he was captured . . . well, we accepted his fate a long time ago." She sniffed, her lips thinning into a brittle line.

Now was the moment he'd been avoiding since the first step he'd taken onto his father and mother's lands, Nack thought. (Well, there were actually several moments he wasn't particularly looking forward to— such as the eventual conversation about selling his soul to an ancient demonic creature—but this was definitely one of them.) Memories from that terrible day in Castle

Ravinus rushed back to him, sharp and painful. If Nack felt this betrayed by Declan's actions, how would his *parents* feel?

He would never know unless he told them. And they deserved to know the truth.

"Declan wasn't captured," Nack said, the words leaping out of his mouth before he could think of a more delicate way of saying them.

"What's that?" His mother's brow furrowed.

"Declan wasn't captured," Nack said again, a little more firmly this time. "I . . . I did manage to get into Castle Ravinus. I saw him there. But he wasn't really . . . he wasn't there as a prisoner."

It was Nack's father's turn to bristle.

"Now, what exactly are you saying, boy?"

Nack sighed. How quickly they had gone from "my son" to "boy."

"I'm saying Declan wasn't captured by Lord Solonos. He went there of his own free will," Nack said. "And he went there to join Solonos's side."

BOOM. His father's fist slammed down on the table, sending their goblets jittering and sloshing liquid all over. The servants, it seemed, had conveniently made themselves scarce just in time.

"Impossible!" cried Lord Furnival. He waggled a

finger at Nack, a deep flush rising along his craggy neck and jowls. "If this story is some twisted way of . . . of getting your brother back, for the perfectly justified way he reported *your* treasonous behavior—"

"I'm sorry," Nack said. "But it's true."

"Our Declan would never . . ." His mother's voice wavered.

Nack insisted, "I spoke to him myself."

His father stood up, knocking his chair back. "I'm warning you, boy—"

"And I'm warning *you!*" Nack said hotly, momentarily stunning his father into silence. "Why do you think I would tell you this? Just to upset you? You have a right to know. He went behind your back with this. If he'd told Solonos anything, given him any information about our side—"

"ENOUGH," Lord Furnival said, slashing his arm like a sword through the air. Nack was wise enough to edge back out of its reach. "I will not hear another word of slander said against my son!"

"He was going to betray you, betray us—"

"THERE IS NO US," his father reminded Nack, his chest heaving. "You were banished from this clan, you ungrateful child. And it seems for good reason."

Panic clawed its way up Nack's throat, sudden

and fiery. He thought his parents would be angry, yes. Surprised, yes. But he never thought—

"Guards!" called his father, flinging off his mother, who was grabbing at his sleeve, pleading with her husband to calm down. "Take this boy out of my sight!"

Miraculously, this time, the servants and guards seemed to be just outside the door, ready to spring into action. Funny how that happened.

Nack hung his head as his father's last words echoed behind him, even louder than the large wooden door that slammed as he was dragged from the room.

"He is no son of mine."

20

Master and Commander

There were few ills, the demon sword Asperides thought as he hovered in a booth inside the Wet Fang, that could not be cured by a warm beverage and a comfortable spot by a crackling fire—even if one could not actually drink said beverage, and even if the merry flames occasionally cackled in addition to crackled, as hellfire was wont to do. Here, in his habitual haunt, surrounded by the usual bustle of hags and demons and other creatures of the underworld, it was much easier to forget all that unpleasantness with Nack Furnival and Amyral Venir. It seemed possible to forget, if only for a moment, the calamitous approach of the Missing Moon.

ANOTHER, THOM, called Asperides to the barkeep

when his drink began to grow cold. The pub was quieter than Asperides had expected it might be. Then again, with so many small pathways, even temporary and shifting as they were, opening to the daylight world lately, Asperides was surprised there were any denizens of the underworld *left* in the upper reaches.

The burly barman made his way over to Asperides slowly—perhaps still sore, Asperides thought, about their last conversation. Asperides understood he was an even less popular figure in the underworld now than he was *before* he'd made himself a reputation for slaying and exorcising its inhabitants—and that was saying something, as there was plenty of fear and resentment toward demon swords to begin with. But before, the whispers and hurried glances away from his blade had been tinged with awe, with fearful respect. Now, even Asperides noticed the malicious grumblings that followed his movements. He didn't need the half-demon barkeep to tell him not very many patrons of said bar were happy to see him.

"Surprised to see you here," said Thom when he finally reached Asperides. He dutifully swapped out Asperides's cooling drink for another—this one inky black, quietly sizzling, and requiring two coasters not to burn a hole straight through the table. (It really was an art form.)

Thom added, "Seemed like you were spending most of your time topside these days."

A DEMON SWORD GOES WHERE THEY WISH, said Asperides curtly. *He* hadn't forgotten their last conversation, either.

Thom surprised him by letting out a soft chuckle. The barkeep mumbled something under his breath as he turned to lumber away.

WHAT DID YOU SAY? demanded Asperides. A tendril of smoke lashed out from his blade and wrapped itself around the half-demon's wrist.

Thom froze where he stood. What little chatter there had been in the bar suddenly quieted. "All I said was," Thom said gruffly, "that's funny, 'cause that's not what you said last time."

PARDON? He gave the tendril of smoke some slack.

Just a little.

Thom shook off the smoke and turned to face Asperides. "Today, it's all, 'a demon sword goes where they wish,'" said Thom, his expression darkening. "But that wasn't the story last time, was it? When we wanted to know why so many of *us* were on the receiving end of that blade of yours?"

YOU HAVE NOTHING TO FEAR FROM ME,

Asperides said lazily, *IF YOU STAY IN YOUR PLACE. IN THIS WORLD.*

Thom ignored him. "Back then, it was, 'Oh, I'm just a demon sword, I've got to do what my master says,' wasn't it?" he asked.

I WILL FORGET THIS INSOLENCE, growled Asperides. *ONCE. IN RESPECT OF THE MANY YEARS OF OUR—*

"Our what?" Thom scoffed. "Our friendship? You mean the six hundred years you barely said two words to me and I gave you drinks for free?"

A few titters rose from the pub's other patrons.

In the past, Asperides might have summoned a few souls from the depths of his prison, the better to put on an impressive show of force and remind these lesser beings of their place.

Now, though, after so many times calling on his power to *stop* evil instead of enact it . . . it felt cheap, somehow, to use the souls inside him to make a point by cutting off a few fingers and toes here, or burning someone's eyeballs out there.

Especially when what they were saying was, unfortunately, the truth.

"You're losing your touch, demon sword," said Thom, shaking his head.

WHY? drawled Asperides. *BECAUSE I REFUSE TO BE BAITED BY MEDIOCRE INSULTS?*

"No," said Thom, stepping forward to take back Asperides's drink. Now *that* made Asperides want to summon all the hellfire in the universe.

"Because you haven't even noticed," said the barman, raising the glass in a little mock toast, "that I've been stallin'."

Asperides withdrew all his smoke tendrils, subdued the silvery-blue gleam of his fake angel blade glamour, took every ounce of focus out of the wider world and into himself. He knew the other bar patrons now saw little more than a black void, sucking all the light that remained out of the room. They would go mad if they stared at it for too long.

Good, Asperides thought. *Let them.*

Asperides had been an idiot. No wonder there were so few patrons in the Wet Fang. The ones that remained got out of their seats and turned to face Asperides, their faces set with grim purpose.

And up above, up in the daylight world, Asperides sensed a change in the undulating current of the water. It wasn't the current carrying him along the riverbed anymore, but several pairs of scaly, gnarled hands. He'd let himself get distracted by trading petty insults in the underworld, only to have his physical form hijacked in the land of the living.

"You might want to stay topside from now on, Asperides," said Thom. "Can't say what kind of welcome you'll have down here after today."

YOU WILL PAY FOR THIS INSOLENCE, Asperides said, though his words sounded thin, even to him. He knew where the water demons in the daylight world were taking him, and he knew the hands of fate would help them deliver him to their intended recipient. *YOU WILL WISH YOU HAD NEVER CROSSED A DEMON SWORD.*

"You know," Thom mused, his fists tensed at his sides, "you call yourself that. But I'm not convinced you're one of us at all."

And with that, Asperides's attention was wrenched back to the daylight world as those traitorous slimy hands battered him against the hull of a ship. The water demons raised him so high above the water their scaly faces broke the surface—now *that* was sure to stir up mermaid rumors in this part of the world for the next decade or two.

Clunk, clunk went Asperides's blade against the wood.

Tee-hee went the water demons.

OH, SHUT IT, said Asperides, just as another cry came from above.

"My lord! Look! There's something in the water . . ."

And then, all too quickly, the voice he had dreaded hearing for over three hundred years.

"Hello again, old friend."

Poised at the bow of his river boat, Amyral Venir considered whether or not Nack Furnival had to die. Cleoline, standing a little shakily beside him after her latest bout of seasickness, didn't think the young knight's chances looked too good.

Not finding the demon sword at Castle Ravinus had been a setback, to be sure. Cleoline shivered—whether from her seasickness and the chilly breeze on the water or from the memory of Amyral Venir's anger on that occasion, she couldn't say. When it had become clear that Solonos didn't have the demon sword—had never had it, it seemed, which made Cleoline rather admire the man's pure talent for conquest—Amyral's wrath had been a sight to behold. It was only Cleoline's words, slow and soothing, that had managed to pull him back from the blind, frothing rage he quickly lost himself to.

Cleoline had always thought those dire warnings in the necromantic grimoires about zombies eating brains had been hyperbole designed to scare off anyone except the truly committed.

Now, though? She wasn't so sure.

She had gotten kind of used to Amyral's blank stares and sullen silences. Only the mention of anything connected to retrieving his soul roused any semblance of a reaction from him these days. That purpose was his driving force, his singular focus—to the unhappy exclusion of all else, such as the provisioning, arming, and general condition of their followers, all of which tended to fall to Cleoline. (The soldiers might have started calling themselves the Undying, but they, unlike their leader, were still human, and humans needed to eat.) And then, when they'd failed to capture the demon sword, and she nearly thought Amyral would burn his throat raw with screaming, before remembering all the tissue in there was super dead and she wasn't exactly sure what dark magic even made him capable of speech these days, anyway . . . well.

They would just need to retrieve the rest of Amyral's soul from the underworld, and then all would be well, wouldn't it? Amyral could go back to being a proper evil overlord—no more of this traipsing all around the countryside business—and Cleoline could go back to lounging glamorously at his side and conducting her experiments in their very own spacious dungeon, as opposed to running logistics for an entire small army and puking her guts out over the side of a rickety commandeered boat on the River Spide.

It had been sheer luck, really, that they'd been traveling on the river at all. They should have probably stayed behind at Castle Ravinus if they wanted to actually hold the thing, but it had been Cleoline who'd urged them to travel. She'd sneaked enough crumbling scrolls out of the Order of Archivists' library by now to be able to piece together a possible location for the Missing Moon ritual—a stone circle on, quite incidentally, what were now Furnival lands. The Dancing Priestesses, as it was called, had both enough history of ancient magic *and* a good position as one of the first powerful places to be hit by the moon's light. They would need both for the best chance at opening up Amyral's doorway into the underworld.

"The boy is a problem," Amyral grunted into the wind. Cleoline didn't know if he expected her to answer or not.

Cleo wasn't sure how much of the original bond between Asperides and Amyral remained, but clearly, Amyral still held some sway over his former sword.

Perhaps the fact that even a fraction of his soul remained outside Asperides's prison was enough to give him some of the powers and privileges of the sword's master. How else could he have forced the boy's name out of Asperides?

The sword itself was locked belowdecks now. ("So the crafty demon cannot spy on us," Amyral said.) Cleoline preferred it that way. Amyral hadn't yet made the connection that the young knight with the immensely powerful "angel" blade she'd run into when trying to capture the moon priestess was this same Nack Furnival—and Cleoline wasn't in the mood to tell him. If Amyral knew the demon sword had been just within reach, and that Cleoline had missed it . . . Amyral had been angry enough that she'd failed to capture the Seer. (The scorch marks in Waldo the Wise's dungeon walls were proof enough of that.) If he realized that Cleoline had *also* let the demon sword escape out from under her nose . . . well, the less frequently Asperides was around to alert Amyral to this fact, the better.

Plus, the sword gave her the creeps. Its presence made the air around it feel heavy and brought a metallic taste to Cleoline's mouth that she only associated with the oldest, darkest magic. Not to mention the major *person* vibes it gave off, as opposed to *thing*. Amyral had spent nearly two hours belowdecks with the sword, engaging in a battle of wills, to get Asperides to divulge the identity of his current master. Cleoline's glimpse of the sword afterward gave her the impression of a beaten man rather than an all-powerful demonic weapon, and she was happy not to have to look at it anymore.

She almost felt *bad* for it. Him. Hadn't that been how the sword referred to himself?

But it wasn't her business to care, she reminded herself. She wanted this. She had resurrected Amyral Venir from the dead. She *wanted* to be his dark queen.

At least, she thought she did.

But that was before they'd started amassing real followers—real followers who depended on Amyral and Cleoline for their day-to-day survival. Real followers who weren't shy about taking what they needed—and wanted—from anyone who got in their way. That was before the battle at Castle Ravinus, before she felt the life forces of the knights beside her leave their bodies as they were slain, only to be raised again to do her bidding until they became too unwieldy to control. That was before the lady's maid who dressed Cleoline on their first night in the castle did so shaking and sobbing the whole time, so afraid Amyral's knights—or even Cleoline herself—were going to kill her at any moment. Cleoline remembered the woman's hands fumbling with the fastenings of

Cleoline's dress, her fingers fluttering against Cleoline's skin like panicked butterflies trapped in a jar.

None of it seemed to faze Amyral, though.

None of it seemed to faze him at all.

And now, he was prepared to obliterate yet another obstacle that stood in his way. Cleoline supposed she should be used to it by now. But all she felt was sick, and she didn't think the rocking boat was all to blame.

"I don't necessarily see why the boy has to die," Cleoline said to Amyral, hoping to strike just the right note of casual disinterest. She may not have been able to stop the deaths of Amyral's men, but they, at least, had signed up for a war. Nack Furnival, on the other hand . . . well, soul-binding contracts with two-thousand-year-old demonic entities aside, he was just a kid, wasn't he?

"And why not?" grunted Amyral, his steely gaze focused out over the water—or on nothing entirely. It was hard to tell with him.

"There's nothing in the lore I've read that says you have to be *master* of the demon sword in order to wield it for the portal ritual," Cleoline pointed out. "You just have to have one in your possession."

"Hmm," said Amyral.

"Plus," added Cleoline, not sure whether to be encouraged by that illuminating response or not, "I'm not so sure you're *not* Asperides's master at this point. The contract you made specified 'until your death.' It never specified what the arrangement would be if you had more than one of those—*not*," Cleoline added hastily, "that you're going to have another death anytime soon. Or, er, ever. Probably. My dark king."

Still clinging to the railing, Cleoline ducked in a kind of awkward half-curtsy.

Smooth, Cleo. Really smooth.

"It's true, I do still appear to hold some sway over my old friend . . ." mused Amyral with a small, grim smile. It quickly settled into a hard line again. "But I have to be sure. There's still no word, no sign of the boy?"

"Not that our people or my birds have seen," said Cleoline, lying only a little. The truth was, in the nightmarishly long to-do list of things that accompanied taking a castle by force and then setting out with a party of over a hundred men to conduct a complex ancient ritual, she'd *sort of, kind of* forgotten to make a new batch of no-crows and send them out searching for Nack until there was just about an hour or two of total darkness left the night before. Not one no-crow had made it back before being burnt to a crisp by the morning sun.

"Forget Nack Furnival for now, my lord," urged Cleoline. "You have more pressing matters to attend to.

You'll need all your strength for the ritual. And besides . . . we'll need to enter the Furnival lands to access the stone circle anyway. With any luck—"

"We'll just have to hope Nack Furnival's at home, then, won't we?" asked Amyral. His mouth split in a wolfish grin, and Cleoline couldn't tell if those pointy teeth were directed at her, or Nack Furnival, or both.

That night, when they made a temporary stop in a small port town to reprovision (which really meant *raid*), and Cleoline finally got her land legs back after an hour lurching around like one of her earliest necromantic experiments, the young sorceress finally had time to think. She thought about how daydreaming about being an attractive zombie sorcerer knight's right-hand woman was a lot more glamorous than actually *being* one, especially when said zombie sorcerer knight was one hundred percent gunning for the title of Actual Worst Dude in the World. True, she'd read all about his past atrocities in the Archivists' saucier volumes, but much like the panicky zombie warnings, she'd thought they were exaggerations—history written by the conquerors, who'd wanted to paint Amyral Venir as the villain because they had won and he had lost. Amyral Venir had been a knight with a vision, a man meant to rule, and his contemporaries just hadn't seen that. These were the stories Cleoline had told herself, back before she'd resurrected him.

Also, she had just really liked the idea of being a dark sorceress queen, as opposed to a nobody witch with a socially unacceptable interest in fire and dead stuff who lived in some old guy's basement.

But now, after all of that thinking, Cleoline came to an unpleasant and surprising conclusion.

Some dead things, she decided, were meant to stay dead.

She left in the middle of the night, hoping the darkness of her cloak was enough to let her blend into the shadows. If she was going to save Nack Furnival and stop Amyral Venir from ripping open a door into hell, she had a lot of work to do.

21

Witches Stick Together

I am not here, Therin told herself forcefully. She tried her best to ignore the vision of the great stone circle vibrating at the edges of her mind. Her visions didn't used to come upon her in her waking hours, but lately, it seemed like the Missing Moon had turned that rule upside down, too.

"I am not here," she said again, out loud this time. She could only hope no one was around to hear her.

I'm in the archives, she told herself. *I'm not a Seer, I'm a librarian. I'm not a Seer, I'm a librarian. I'm not a Seer—*

The vision fizzled. The great pillars of stone on the grassy hill disappeared. She stood alone at the end of one of the cold, dank tunnels that ran in a head-turning maze all over (and under) the Order of Archivists' libraries. At least, she'd thought she was alone. But there, barely visible in the gloom, sat an ancient Archivist at a desk piled so high with books the tiny librarian was barely visible behind it. A tarnished and tilted brass sign hanging above the desk began, "REFEREN—" before it, too, was obscured by a teetering tower of books.

The bleary-eyed person behind the desk held a magnifying glass in one hand and a candle in the other, the better to examine the ponderous tome on the table before them. They held the candle so close to their face a few chunks of wax had glopped off and stuck to their wiry hair. They appeared not to notice.

Therin's breath froze in her chest, but the elderly librarian didn't even look up from their book when they croaked, "Oh, what was that, dear? Did you say something?"

Therin briefly held up one of the books from her own gigantic stack piled on top of a rickety cart. The senior librarians left all the shelving to the newbies, not seeming to care if a few trainees got so lost they perished in the bowels of the archives.

The librarian squinted at it. "Unicorn-related antiquities? Two corridors to the left. Which you'd know, my dear, if you only read the signs. Young people these days . . ."

Therin scurried past the barely visible etchings in the wall (which did, in fact, mention antiquities, just not in any living language) without a backward glance. Once she'd put enough distance between herself and the ancient librarian, she stopped to catch her breath.

That had been a close one. Therin had been trying to stay under the radar and ignore her Sight as much as possible since arriving at the Order of Archivists about a month ago. She'd kept mum about her origins, and fortunately, the Archivists hadn't asked too many questions. They'd nearly turned her away ("Do you know how many young people want to be librarians these days?!") until she quickly demonstrated her literacy in a handful of languages, a smattering of moon magic, a genuine interest in history, and an ability to solemnly walk hallowed halls without making too much noise. (They'd done a lot of that at the Mission, so Therin had a practiced gliding footfall.)

Now that she was finally here, Therin was trying her best to forget the past—and forget the more unpleasant details about the future, which her subconscious seemed singularly uninterested in doing. She was trying to build a new life for herself. But she also hadn't given up on

the small hope of stopping Amyral Venir from opening his doorway to the underworld. She hoped—as she,
Nack, and Asperides had originally planned—to access
materials related to the Missing Moon prophecy, and
any spells that Amyral might use during the moon's rising. The Archivists' collection couldn't possibly rival the
Mission's library, but since she couldn't exactly go back
there, the archives were the second-best option.

So whenever her duties allowed, or when she felt she
could comfortably pretend she'd gotten hopelessly lost in
the stacks (which occasionally happened anyway), Therin
snuck off to the restricted section to search for anything
that might help her in the fight against Amyral Venir.
The Archivists had clearly stepped up security recently.
There was even a sphinx guarding one of the doorways,
though Therin hadn't failed to answer one of its riddles
yet—and she suspected it secretly liked her, anyway. She
had gotten past the section's magical protections on her
second try and taught herself how to put them back up
again on her way out by the fourth.

Not that there was too much to find in the restricted
section, especially in the books about Missing Moon
magic. The selection was pitifully small—and, unless
Therin was imagining things, *getting smaller.* She finished her unicorn antiquities shelving, parked her cart in

an out-of-the-way corner, and took a few spare minutes to sneak away for her own research—only to find fewer books on the shelves than the last time she'd been there. Therin lit the small lantern all the librarians carried on their belts and squinted into the gloom. Sure enough, book-shaped rivulets had been carved into the dust where someone had slid several volumes off the shelves. Someone had been here, and recently.

Another Archivist, perhaps? There was nothing in their rules against higher-level Archivists and select patrons accessing the section, and yet whoever had been there hadn't reported the clear evidence of *Therin's* sneaking and snooping, which another librarian, especially a senior one, almost certainly would have. It had to be someone who also didn't want to be seen . . . though that didn't necessarily rule out another Archivist. For all their claims about scholarly neutrality, they did still have an entire section guarded by a sphinx and no small collection of nasty wards. And clearly, someone had broken with the ranks at some point in their history, because there were barely any books that mentioned demon swords, Asperides, or even Amyral Venir's first life. (She did eventually find one mention of Asperides, along with two other names she presumed to be his . . . siblings? Cousins? She wasn't sure on the proper terminology. But there was no other trace of them anywhere, and since no other sword had surfaced, despite the current chaos-filled state of the world, Therin could only assume the other swords had been lost to history, the underworld, or both.)

At any rate, with every new trip Therin made down into the bowels of the archives, she had to remind herself it was entirely possible her endeavors didn't go unobserved. Whether she liked it or not, she wasn't alone.

A fact which became immediately obvious the day another girl came tumbling out of thin air and nearly fell into Therin's lap.

Therin leapt back, tripping over her long robes—what *was* it with these ancient societies and their love of voluminous fabric?—and sending her tiny lantern flying. It hit the wall with a sad crunch and flickered out, plunging both her and the intruder into darkness.

A flurry of colorful words Therin didn't think had been uttered in a library in a very long time spun out at her from the gloom. A few moments later, Therin shielded her eyes as the alcove flooded with a dim but steady light.

"If you value your life, little librarian, you never saw me here," said the girl who appeared out of nowhere.

"There are *lamps* in here?" Therin asked indignantly.

Sure enough, lining the walls, little spots of light bobbed behind frosted globes dulled with a few hundred years of dust. They were mounted high enough that she'd never have noticed them in a million years. It wasn't much light, but it was still better than squinting into the dark like a mole rat. "Why didn't anyone tell me?" Therin complained.

"You must be new," said the strange girl, pursing her lips and staring Therin up and down. Therin took the opportunity to stare back; the girl was tall and willowy, with long, tangled dark hair and a silky black cloak that looked like it had once been nice but was now in need of a washing. She might've been in her late teens or early twenties; it was hard to tell in this light, and Therin, having never lived around many women who were much younger than sixty, couldn't say for sure. There was something familiar about her, about the way her magic felt as its leftover energy crackled through the air, but Therin couldn't put her finger on it.

"The older librarians get a kick out of hazing the newbies, I think," mused the girl. "Must think everyone should go as blind as they have. On the other hand, it's totally possible they just forgot the lanterns were there at all . . ."

"Can I *help you*?" asked Therin, gesturing to the sizzling hole in the universe behind the intruder.

"No, thanks," said the girl cheerfully, hiking up her cloak to stride past where Therin sat, still sprawled on the floor. "I've been breaking into this place for years."

Therin skittered back, away from the girl's stomping boots.

"It's you!" Therin said. "You've been taking all the books!"

"Now *that* is an exaggeration," said the girl as she stepped around Therin. "I see plenty of books left around here, don't you?"

"All the books about the Missing Moon," clarified Therin, scrambling to her feet. She wasn't sure how she'd be a match for this older, taller, and all-around *cooler* sorceress, but she wasn't about to stand by while someone so clearly interested in the Missing Moon just swanned in and robbed the world's oldest library.

At Therin's mention of the moon, the girl paused in her perusal of the shelves. She narrowed her eyes.

"What part about the whole 'if you value your life, you never saw me here' speech did you not understand, little librarian?"

"I'm not a—" *librarian*, Therin had been about to say.

Except she was now, wasn't she? Or at least, that's what she'd been trying to convince herself.

"I can't just let you . . . march in here through your . . . whatever that was—"

"Portal, and it's not mine, it was *basically* already here—"

"And steal a bunch of knowledge to abuse the magic of the Missing Moon!"

The other girl sighed before turning her back on Therin again. "That *was* the original plan," she admitted. "But it's not anymore. So, don't worry about it."

"'Don't worry about it?'" echoed Therin, mouth agape. "Who are you, how did you get in here, and tell me one good reason why I shouldn't send out a distress flare right this instant!" She fished in her cloak for her spelled signal candle and waved it threateningly in front of the girl's nose.

The girl proceeded to snatch it from Therin's grip and snap it in half.

"Hey!"

"Of *course* luck would have it, the first time I run into someone down here is *now*," grumbled the sorceress. She chucked aside the broken candle. "Listen, little librarian, why don't you run along and busy yourself with what-ever onerous, endless shelving they've given you to do, or go dust or de-mold something, and we can pretend we never saw each other? Not that there's much left of use to me here . . ."

"I am *not* a librarian!" Therin burst out, thrusting her arm between the sorceress and the books on the shelves.

The girl's look lazily dragged from the shelf to Therin's face—and for the first time, Therin thought she detected a hint of interest.

"Oh?" said the girl. "What are you, then?"

Therin gulped. If this sorceress was an agent of darkness and decided to make Therin her prisoner—or worse—she'd find out eventually. Might as well get the revelation over with now.

"I'm a Seer," said Therin, lifting up her chin.

And at that, the girl looked *very* interested.

"You don't say . . ." she said with a grin.

22

A Real Knight

Nack Furnival was busy trying to find the least uncomfortable position to sleep in while on a bed literally made of rocks when a sudden groaning and thunderous crumbling of stone alerted him to the fact that someone was trying to pull the bars off his window.

"I would really appreciate it," said a voice above him, huffing with exertion, "if you could be a little bit more cooperative than I was, the last time we met like this."

Nack blinked at the moonlight now streaming onto him, dodged a few loose stones raining down on his head, and nearly screamed at the sight that filled his window.

Therin was perched precariously on the window

ledge, surrounded (and possibly held up?) by two of the largest, ugliest trolls Nack had ever seen.

"Therin!" Nack shouted. "Watch out!"

"Oh, them?" Therin asked, bracing herself against the building while the trolls continued to rip at (and chew) the remaining bars on the window. Sparks flew where their rock-hard skin chafed against the metal. "Well, Cleo's got a lot of contacts, and it turns out, not all the magical creatures out there are that excited about Amyral Venir, either—"

"NRRRGH," said one of the trolls.

"And so these guys offered to give us a lift! Which would normally be terrifying, but in this case, was also super helpful. Watch your head!"

Nack barely had time to duck under his hard slab of a bed before a deluge of stonework rained down from above.

"Are you trying to rescue me or kill me?" Nack exclaimed. By the time he got to his feet, Therin was standing in front of him, having been deposited surprisingly gently there by one of the troll's tree-trunk-like arms. She looked dirty and out of breath but curiously happy to see him.

"The first one," she said. "But mostly because you're the only one who can stop him."

Nack's heart sank. "Listen," said Nack. "I appreciate the rescue, but I'm no match for Amyral Venir. Especially not without . . . without Asperides."

"Amyral has Asperides," Therin said, her face grim again.

Nack sat back on his stone bench, his knees suddenly jelly—only to stand up again when a sharp bit of masonry poked him in the rear.

"Well, then I really have no idea why you're here," Nack said. "Because if that's true, then we're all done for."

"Cleoline doesn't think so," Therin said, perking up a bit. "She thinks you might be the sword's true master—"

"Who . . . who is Cleoline?" Nack stuttered, willing his brain to keep up with the events of the evening. "Does this have something to do with why you're suddenly hanging out with trolls?"

"Says the kid who sold his soul to a demon sword," Therin pointed out. "No need to be so judgy."

"I hate to break up a good banter," interrupted another voice from above. "But I suggest we take this conversation elsewhere? There are some burly-looking knights headed in our direction, and surprisingly, they don't look too happy to see us . . ."

Nack looked up to see the necromancer who'd attacked him while he had been trying to rescue Therin, bobbing just outside the window. She sat astride the thick, hairy neck of a third troll. The troll gave Nack a snaggletoothed grin. (Or possibly a grimace. It was kind of hard to tell with trolls.)

"Wha . . . she . . . you?" was all Nack could manage.

"Later," said Therin firmly, grabbing his hand.

"I can't go," Nack insisted. "I just got home—"

"And I can see that's going great for you!"

The troll had once again lowered his arm through the window. Therin shoved Nack into his chair-sized palm.

"Climb up onto his shoulders," Therin urged. "And do it quickly, before he decides to crush *you* instead of window bars. They're big fans of crushing. Go!"

"They came this way!" a shout echoed from the hallway. Footsteps pounded on the stairs below the tower.

Nack looked down at the pile of rubble littering the tower floor, at the doorway that would soon burst open, filled with Furnival knights ready to . . .

To what? Save him, or use their swords against him instead?

"Do you want to stop Amyral Venir *or not*?" Therin insisted.

Nack sighed. It was true, he'd made a contract with a demon sword, and his reasons for making that contract hadn't been noble. And it was true that his soul was destined for eternal damnation. Nothing he did would save him from the fact that many, many lifetimes of suffering were waiting for him after he died. Joining Therin now, and trying to stop Amyral, would almost certainly end in his own early death—a hastening of his inevitable punishment.

But maybe that, Nack realized, was what being a knight really meant. Doing the right thing—trying to save people—when there was nothing at all to be gained. When there was no promise of glory, or bounty, or a shiny angel blade. Even when you had no good reason to—had, in fact, several good reasons *not* to—help at all.

He held out his hands to help Therin up the troll's arm first.

"I'm right behind you," he assured her.

"Ugh, *knights*!" Therin snorted, shaking her head as she accepted a boost up through the window.

But Nack could see her grin all the same.

———————◆————————

Nack held one of Therin's hands, the necromancer Cleoline the other. As the young Seer shared her full vision with them, the silvery standing stones known as the Dancing Priestesses materialized before Nack's eyes. It was nighttime in the vision, though he could hardly tell; the light of the two moons shone brightly in the sky, and after a few moments, their light was joined by the first tentative beams of the Missing Moon—the infamous Third Daughter—trailing across the sky, caressing the standing stones with the affection of a long-lost friend.

The sight would have been almost beautiful, if not for one interloper marring the landscape. Amyral Venir stood in the center of the Dancing Priestesses, Asperides raised in his hands. He chanted low, blistering words that made black and silver smoke pour out of his mouth, eyes, and ears. His lips cracked, growing drier with every syllable, until the flesh began to sizzle and burn.

Amyral raised Asperides higher, and then, with a sound like the crack of lightning and the scraping of dried bones combined, he began to cut a hole into the universe.

Nack looked away, and even Cleoline, all five feet eight inches of dark, sorcerous intimidation, made a little choking noise. Therin gave each of their hands a squeeze, reminding them to loosen their grips—Nack had nearly forgotten about her beside him, and realized guiltily he'd probably squeezed hard enough to break her tiny fingers—and he and Cleoline let go. The vision dissipated, leaving them once more in the abandoned gamekeeper's hut they'd taken temporary refuge in.

(Well, it hadn't exactly been abandoned when they'd stumbled into it. Grennan, the old gamekeeper, had been there, but at the sight of Nack and company, he merely hefted a few candles and a fearsome-looking hacksaw into his pack and shuffled away, grumbling, "I didn't see nothin', now, did I? But good luck with whatever I'm not seeing, sonny." So, it was *technically* abandoned now.)

Nack had recognized the Dancing Priestesses immediately—he'd have known those stones anywhere. He had played amongst them as a child, had sworn his oath as a member of the Furnival clan in their shadows. And he realized now what the pillars in the marble room in Asperides's . . . inner consciousness, or whatever that place was where he'd made the contract, reminded him of. They *were* the Dancing Priestesses—there were just many more of them, in Asperides's realm, and they were the stones as they had originally been carved, thousands of years ago; sculpted pillars engraved with deep grooves in dead, magical languages.

"Those stones are on Furnival land," Nack said grimly. "He's coming here."

"If he isn't here already," said Cleoline, twisting a long lock of her dark hair in her fingers. "Even before Therin could see this vision this clearly, I triangulated the rough location of the best place for the ritual weeks ago. I told Amyral right away."

"Remind me," said Nack to Therin, "why is she here again?"

Therin elbowed him in the ribs.

"Cleo's on our side now," Therin insisted.

"Well, I'm certainly not keen on letting half a hell dimension's worth of demons loose onto the unsuspecting populace," clarified Cleoline.

"Oh, great," scoffed Nack. "Glad that's clear."

Scuffling sounds from outside led to Cleoline reaching for a bag of bones on her belt (who just went around carrying a *bag of bones*?). Therin ducked behind the kitchen counter, and Nack reached for the sword at his side—before realizing there would *be* no sword there at all. Was it a band of Furnival knights, come to take him back to answer for his crimes? Or perhaps it was a group of the Undying, already taking over the outer Furnival territory? Maybe a stray spirit or demon?

"Still haven't seen anythin'!" Grennan's gravelly voice echoed from outside. "I'll keep goin' on not seeing anythin' while you go straight through that door, there—no, don't use the front door, nobody uses the front door— that one, there. Not seein' anythin', no sir! But isn't that a mighty fine angel blade on a mighty fi—"

"I thought you weren't seeing anything, sir," a familiar voice chided the man, though there was laughter behind it.

"Willa?" Nack called. "Is that you?"

A moment later, the knight herself stepped through the side door (as instructed), Lenira radiating power from its sheath at her side.

"Willa!" Therin ran forward to hug the knight, who returned the gesture warmly.

"How did you . . . Wait, where's Barb?" Nack asked.

It had been the wrong question.

Willa shook her head.

"I couldn't get back into Castle Ravinus," she said. "There were too many of the Undying around—and they, unfortunately, run a much tighter ship than Solonos did."

Cleoline scoffed from where she stood leaning against the counter.

"Not anymore," she said. "I did most of the running. But, um, sorry, I guess?"

Willa stepped back, her stance suddenly tense. Her hand floated to the angel blade at her side. She looked from Cleoline to Nack and back again.

"She's on our side now," Nack said hurriedly, holding up his hands. Willa's shoulders dropped, ever so slightly, and the angel blade stayed where it was.

"We'll explain later," Nack said, with a pointed look at Cleoline. It was times like these he sort of wished he could speak into people's minds like Asperides did.

"But in the meantime," said Nack, "how . . . *why* are you here?"

"I said I couldn't get into the castle," said Willa. "But that doesn't mean I stopped following Amyral's tracks. When I saw him and most of his soldiers leaving Castle Ravinus, I thought he might be prepping for a big showdown somewhere. It didn't take me long to figure out they'd brought a few prisoners—the ones who could fight, anyway—to throw at whatever enemy he was taking on next." Willa's lips twisted with distaste. "I just haven't been able to get close enough to their camps to try and get to her—or any of the captured knights."

Willa wrung her hands. Nack had never seen her look this worried—not even when surrounded by a pack of angry gasper-cats.

"I didn't realize they were coming here to fight the Furnivals," Willa continued. "I'm so, so sorry, Nack. I'll . . . if I can't help Barb, then I'll do what I can to help you."

Nack gulped, a lump suddenly forming in his throat. Willa had come all this way to rescue Barb, and now, she was willing not only to put her mission to the side, but also to quite possibly fight *against* the army her wife was being forced to fight for? All so she could help Nack and do her part to defeat Amyral Venir?

Nack had no words. His whole life, he'd thought men like Declan, like his father, were what *real* knights were supposed to be. But he realized that the kind of knight he should have been looking up to was standing right in front of him.

He'd do his best to make her proud. But first, he had even more bad news to deliver.

"Amyral Venir isn't here to fight my family," Nack said. "At least, that's not mainly why he's here."

"But what does he want?" Willa asked.

Nack sighed and scratched at his temple. "Oh, just, you know, to slice a hole in the universe and get his soul out of the underworld. Using the demon sword Asperides."

Wordlessly, Willa began rummaging in Grennan's cabinets until she came across a rusty teakettle.

"Can you start a fire with those witchy fingers of yours?" she asked Cleoline sharply. "Because for this, I think we're going to need some tea."

Nack paled a little under her stern gaze. "I'll just . . . start that explanation I promised you now, shall I?"

23

Really Not a Crow

The Furnivals had been expecting an invasion, that much was clear.

Amyral Venir surveyed the retreating knights before him with distaste. He wasn't even sure they were really knights—more likely they were simply lowly guards, to be stationed at this outpost on the fringes of the Furnival estates. Empty pastures and rolling hills surrounded the Dancing Priestesses as far as the eye could see. Most of the common folk had fled to the castle back when they thought Solonos was coming. Those that hadn't took one look at Amyral's troops ranging over the hilltops and scurried after their neighbors, surely wishing they'd had the sense to leave sooner.

Amyral encouraged his men to leave them (mostly) alone. Ruling the common people held little interest for him, and he had plenty of soldiers to stand between him and the demons that would come pouring out of hell in a matter of hours.

Besides, the more Furnivals that ran for the hills, the fewer there would be who might put up a stand and get in Amyral's way. After Cleoline's defection, he'd been surprised to find the land surrounding the Dancing Priestesses unguarded. (He could only assume she had abandoned him, and not been caught up in some abduction by his enemies, as the witch was much too clever to get herself captured.) He had thought the very first thing Cleoline would do would be to link up with the Furnival boy and alert his family to Amyral's plans—not that it would have mattered much, if his information about the strength of the Furnival forces after this multi-year clan war was correct. But to find the area nearly uninhabited and almost entirely unguarded? Either the Furnivals had some sort of sneak attack planned, or Cleoline's plans to save the day had gone about as well as her first hundred attempts at resurrection.

Amyral spared no more thoughts on the witch's betrayal. He owed her this second life, it was true, but she had also caused him this suffering. It was because of *her* lack of foresight that while his body lived, his soul still languished in eternal torment. It was because of her that this ritual was even necessary at all. Had she resurrected him properly, he would have plucked Asperides from his chest and carried on with the plans he had put into motion so many years ago.

Not that he could particularly remember, or care about, the details of those plans now. Another side effect of this cursed half-life of his, he suspected. But after he retrieved his soul, he could make new plans. And with the demon sword Asperides at his command, whatever he desired would be his.

Perhaps it was fate that had brought him back at such an auspicious hour. If he had been called back at any other time, would he have missed the return of the Missing Moon? Or would he have had to wait, with only remnants of ancient prophecies and blind faith, like those old priestesses in their temple, until the moon's return? Amyral shuddered at the thought. He could not imagine waiting years, or even centuries.

He smiled. It was like pulling the strings of a rickety marionette, with so little soul to feel his pleasure, but he managed it. He wouldn't have to wait long at all.

It was time.

The first beams of the light of the Missing Moon began to kiss the treetops on the hills ahead, bathing them in the pearly glow that had not graced this planet in over two thousand years.

"You must stand back," he called to his followers, waiting just outside the stone circle, "until the ritual is over. No matter what happens to me, you must not enter this circle until it is time. Then, and only then, will I have amassed enough power to forge demon swords for each of you."

LIAR, LIAR, PANTS ON FIRE, said a singsong voice in Amyral's head.

"I thought I told you to be *quiet*," Amyral hissed, squeezing the grip of the blade at his side. He looked hurriedly around at the assembled men, but it appeared none of them had heard the demon sword's words.

THAT WAS A WHILE AGO, said Asperides. Amyral could practically hear the shrug in the sword's voice. *YOUR COMMANDS DON'T HOLD THE WEIGHT THEY USED TO, OLD MAN.*

Shut up, hissed Amyral—this time, silently, but with as much force as his mind could muster. The sword's energy dimmed, and Amyral pictured Asperides retreating inside itself like a scolded child running to their room.

If only there had been another demon sword to do the deed, Amyral thought. But it was fitting, in the end, that the very sword he used to free himself from hell was the one that held him prisoner.

It took Amyral a moment to realize someone had been speaking to him for the past several moments. These followers of his were necessary, he knew, but so very *needy*.

"I said, how do we know?" asked one of his men, clearly on his second or third attempt at getting Amyral's attention.

"I'm sorry, my brother," said Amyral, though he didn't do much to disguise the growl in his voice. "What troubles you?"

The man stumbled a bit where he stood, as if, impatient as he was, he hadn't really expected Amyral to answer.

"H-how do we know, my lord? When the spell is complete, and the time has come?"

Amyral smiled again. The man took another step back.

Perhaps Cleoline had been right about the smiling.

"Trust me, my friend," said Amyral, unsheathing the demon sword at his side as he prepared to carve the first of his spell's runes into the ether. "You'll know."

————— • ◆ • —————

"I think this is really stretching the definition of 'no-crow,'" Nack said as he valiantly tried not to vomit all over his companions.

"Well," said Therin, clearly trying not to breathe through her nose, "it really *isn't* a crow. So, depending on how technical we're getting . . ." She trailed off as a meaty chunk of . . . whatever one called the undead creature-contraption hybrid they flew on . . . sloughed off and into the darkened abyss below.

"Excuse me," interrupted Cleoline from somewhere behind Nack. "But I seem to recall that so far, I'm the only one who has contributed anything of value to this suicide mission."

Nack and Therin ceased their complaining, and Nack tried not to look too hard at the mass of feathers, flesh, and pieces of Grennan the gamekeeper's furniture ("Still not seeing anythin'! Looters took that lot, sure enough!") that currently held Nack and his companions up in the sky. While Willa looked for a way to slip in with Amyral's troops moving on the ground, Nack, Therin, and Cleoline had realized they would need a speedier and stealthier approach if they wanted any hope of getting close to the Dancing Priestesses while Amyral was conducting the Missing Moon ritual. And so for the first time in his life, Nack Furnival found himself helping to *create* the undead instead of destroy them. (He had to admit his insistence that they summon birds that were already dead had been both time-intensive and the chief cause of the entire flying monstrosity being *extra super gross*, but look, he may have sold his soul to a demon of the underworld, but he was not a *bird murderer.*)

They hung back, over a mile away from the stone circle, the better to see Amyral's forces without (hopefully) being seen themselves—which was no easy task, considering how brightly the two moons hung in the sky that night.

And unless Nack was mistaken . . .

"Is it just me, or is it getting . . . brighter?"

No sooner had the words left his mouth than a great rumbling rent the air. A crack and a whispering, shimmering sound followed soon after, which Nack realized was all the leaves in the trees shaking in their branches at once. He looked down with horror to see the ground below *moving*, rolling and roiling like the waves of the sea. Great cracks appeared in the earth, sucking down unfortunate trees, a few rickety fences, and even a (hopefully) abandoned shepherd's hut. While the earth roared and crumbled below, a zigzag of lightning and a crack of thunder zapped through the air far too close for comfort. Therin shrieked at the sudden sound, grabbing onto whatever she could on their makeshift flying creation.

Nack had grown accustomed to the traumatic signs of the Missing Moon's approach over the past few months, but he had never had the opportunity (or misfortune, depending on how you looked at it) to see the destruction from above.

"It's another earthquake!" yelled Cleoline over the clapping thunder. "The moon must be getting closer. We have to—argh!"

Nack never learned what they had to do, because at that moment, a gleaming shaft of moonlight pierced the clouds, another clap of thunder cracked right above their heads, and the really-not-a-crow thing beneath them gave such a dramatic lurch as to nearly send him, Cleoline, and Therin toppling over the side.

"It's here!" Therin said breathlessly, her eyes fixed above them. Nack grabbed her tightly around the middle, as she looked a little too likely to forget they had more immediately pressing problems at hand.

"It's *messing* with my magiiiiiiiiiic!" Cleoline's

complaint dissolved into a panicked shriek as the giant no-crow lurched several feet downward again. They began to spin, first in a wide circle, and then a narrower one, as the many, many dead things currently holding them aloft apparently decided that a new moon was in town, the old rules didn't apply to them, and they'd much rather stay dead, thank you very much. (Or at least, do their own thing. This seemed to be the philosophy of what could charitably be called the tail end of the beast, which basically *dissolved* back into its former, smaller bird bits and flew off of its own volition entirely.)

Nack barely had time to register that there was a brand-new moon hanging in the sky.

Cleoline struggled to regain control of the no-crow, desperately trying to reanimate its various component parts and steer the whole thing out of the Missing Moon's light—which wasn't an easy task, considering the light was creeping forward, foot by foot, directly in the path they wanted to go.

Straight for the Dancing Priestesses and the waiting Amyral Venir.

"We're going to miss it," Nack said, almost to himself, the drop in his stomach unrelated to their loss of altitude. "We're going to miss the ritual!"

"And a whole lot of other things, if I can't keep this

thing in the air," said Cleo through gritted teeth. Her eyes glowed an unearthly red as she went back to her spellcasting. In front of him, Therin was curiously quiet, though she squirmed out of Nack's arms to get a better look at the Missing Moon. *Her* eyes went curiously dark and filmy-looking in its glow, and Nack briefly considered the possibility that it was time to get new friends.

If my eyeballs turn black or something, I am out *of here*, he thought. (But also, how would he even know the color of his own eyeballs?) His thoughts spiraling faster than their haphazard descent, Nack had just enough presence of mind to throw himself and Therin into a nearby hedge before the no-crow hit the ground.

"Shut your eyes!" he warned as he and Therin plowed into the hedge separating two fields. It was *just* soft enough to keep them from breaking anything important and just scratchy enough to make Nack feel like he'd taken off his entire outer layer of skin on impact.

A few seconds later, he heard an unfortunate squelching *crunch* that let him know Cleo had landed not too far away.

Nack and Therin huddled in the crushed hedge, breathing hard, too shocked and knocked about to speak.

After a few moments, he managed to croak, "Cleo. Cleoline! Are you all right?"

There were a few more squelching sounds before the necromancer's voice piped up.

"*Now* he asks," she said with a huff. "Fortunately, none of the pointy bits stabbed me on the way down, no."

A few moments later, a slippery hand yanked Nack out from the hedge's brambly embrace. He yelped—there went the second layer of skin.

Cleoline stood there, covered head to toe in . . . well, presumably lots of crushed no-crow. She looked basically all right, though she was even paler than usual, and Nack noticed she favored her left foot. She looked like she couldn't decide whether to hug Nack or slap him. They compromised by not saying anything and helping Therin (much more gently) out of the bushes.

Cleoline took another look at Nack and snorted.

"You really are the knight-in-shining-armor type, aren't you?" she groused, shaking out the sodden hemline of her cloak. "Who else could crash a giant no-crow and not end up covered in bird goo?"

Any retort Nack might've had was cut off by a gasp from Therin. She pointed with a shaking hand to the nearby hilltop where the seven Dancing Priestesses stood, looking like tall maidens in white gowns in the glow of the three moons. And there, in the moonlight nearly as bright as day, stood Amyral Venir, the demon sword Asperides held aloft in his hands. Nack, Therin, and Cleoline could do nothing but watch in horror as the sword cut through the air—slowly, like Amyral was dragging the blade through glue. But it wasn't glue the dark knight was cutting—it was the very fabric of the universe. A blinding light, tinged with green, even brighter than the light of the Missing Moon, poured out from the blazing jagged line floating in the ether. It was so bright that Nack, nearly half a mile away, couldn't look at it directly.

They were too late.

Nack looked at the terrified faces of Cleoline and Therin beside him. He thought of Willa, even now trying to find a way behind enemy lines. He thought of all the innocent people hiding in the castle, and even of Amyral's band of followers—they would be the first victims when the doorway to the underworld opened. He even thought of Asperides, being used against his will to start the end of the world.

They were too late, Nack told himself.

He took off running anyway.

24

A Daughter,
a Doorway

Amyral Venir could feel his soul calling to him. He could feel it, but he couldn't see it. Not yet. He had many levels of hell to traverse before he could do that, he knew. He did hope those levels of hell weren't quite as *bright* as the doorway into it seemed to be.

He turned his face away from the blinding light streaming out of the cut he'd made into the universe, but he did not let up his pressure on the sword, did not loosen his grip in the slightest. Asperides had gone silent since the ritual began. Perhaps all its power was channeled into the spell, or perhaps it had decided to sulk forever. It was impossible to tell with the demon sword.

It didn't matter to Amyral. The less he had to listen to Asperides's chatter, the better. The sword would speak again to navigate them safely through the underworld. Then, Amyral would *make* it talk.

Amyral's arms shuddered against the force of . . . the universe, he supposed. Powerful ancient spells notwithstanding, it didn't seem too keen to be carved into. Even with the words of the witch's spell pouring from his lips, each cursed syllable burning his mouth, blistering his lips until they would have bled if he still had any blood to bleed, cutting his doorway was slow and difficult work. Amyral's muscles quivered with exhaustion, but he thrived on the sensation—it was a sensation, after all, and he could feel it. It had been so long since he could feel. That must mean his soul was close.

But so far, he had only managed to carve the very top of his doorway. He began to cut the corner, roaring with exertion as he pulled even harder on the demon sword. Red sparks shot out from the blade, stinging his skin and sizzling in his hair, but his efforts paid off—the sword sliced another two feet down, much faster than it had through the top.

Hell knew he was coming now. And at any moment, the demons on the other side would realize that doors worked two ways. Amyral would either have to slip in quickly or wait until the first wave of demons subsided and were too busy slaughtering his followers to notice a single man running in the wrong direction. Amyral had positioned his soldiers directly in front of the future doorway, clustered together on one side of the hill—a neat package gift-wrapped just for the denizens of hell.

"AMYRAL VENIR!" a voice called from close by.

Much too close.

Amyral opened his eyes just enough against the glaring light to glimpse Nack Furnival dashing into the Dancing Priestesses' circle—straight over the runes Amyral had so painstakingly carved into the ground to make his spell possible.

Noises of alarm rose from Amyral's men.

"Sir!"

"My lord!"

"How did he—"

"We couldn't see—the light is so bright—"

"Someone stop the boy!"

"NO," Amyral roared.

The men took a collective step back. The awkward clinking of their armor and weapons filled the silence.

"Not one more person steps into this circle!" Amyral warned them, straining to keep the rage out of his voice.

He still needed these men. But honestly, even though they'd undoubtedly been dazzled by the ritual, they had had *one job.* "Leave the boy to me."

"Amyral Venir, by order of . . . House Furnival, and all of the knights in the service of the living, I order you to stop!" said the boy.

It was a laughable declaration made even more ridiculous by the fact that the boy was still doubled over, gasping for breath from running.

Amyral chuckled. See? That was genuine amusement, wasn't it? More feeling was coming back to him every moment he got closer to his soul.

"And how do you propose to stop me, Nack of House Furnival?" asked Amyral, giving another tug on Asperides for emphasis. The sword moved only a few inches this time, probably reacting to the pause in the spell. Best to get this over with quickly. The boy could be the first to feed the demons.

"I don't have to stop you," said Nack, finally standing up straight, though still breathing heavily. "I just have to stop him."

The boy's gaze fell to Asperides for a moment before he, too, was forced to shield his eyes at the doorway's brightness.

For the first time since he realized he had been

betrayed, all those hundreds of years ago, Amyral Venir felt a flicker of fear.

"Asperides," said the boy, extending a shaking hand, "to me."

Amyral froze, gripping the sword so tightly he thought his undead bones would snap, waiting for the sword to be ripped from his hands, to obey the command of its new, rightful master. The ritual would be ruined, the doorway would not be big enough, the sword would turn against him, and . . .

And nothing happened.

Other than a brief vibration, so slight it barely jarred his already aching arms, the sword showed no sign of even having heard the boy's command. And it certainly showed no inclination to leap into Nack Furnival's pitifully small and shaking palm.

Amyral chuckled and spared a glance in the boy's direction. Nack stood with his mouth open, staring first at the sword and then down at his hand, as if not quite sure what to do about either of them.

"So the witch was right," Amyral said. "I am the sword's true master. Your contract was null and void the minute she raised me from the grave. Give her my thanks, will you? Assuming you survive."

Amyral turned back to his grim work. He pressed

harder against the sword. The edges of his clothes were so hot from their proximity to the sizzling void that they had started to smoke.

"Nack, don't!" someone called.

Amyral barely noticed the boy barreling toward him until it was too late, but he managed to brace himself in time. He kept hold of the sword with one hand while easily batting Nack away with the other. The strength of the undead lent his blow the extra force he needed, and the boy was flung backward against one of the Dancing Priestesses. He crumpled to the ground and stayed there, groaning faintly.

"You!" Amyral called to him. "Who are you, to think you could possibly command this much power? I have heard stories about you, Nack Furnival. The brave knight, the knight of the people—the knight who ran away, who betrayed his own family to their enemies. I *know* your heart, Nack Furnival, and contract or no, you are the last person in the world fit to wield this sword."

Memories of the boy making the contract surfaced in his mind—a different room, but also same one, where Amyral himself had stood, all those years ago. He saw the boy's trivial fears, his petty desires for *family* and *acceptance* and *glory*. They were not Amyral's memories, but he wasn't surprised he had access to them. He was more than the master of the demon sword Asperides—he was part of the sword now, too. Though it was a mere glimpse, Amyral saw all he needed to see. If Amyral's blows could not keep the boy down, then his words would do the job.

"Only a real knight, a true knight, could ever hope to be master of this sword," said Amyral. "And you, my boy, are no knight."

Amyral turned back to his spell. He'd been distracted by this interloper long enough, and unless he was mistaken, the height of the moon had already reached its peak. He would need to finish the doorway, and soon.

Though his very eyeballs seemed to boil with the effort, Amyral succeeded in making yet another deep cut in the doorway. One long side was now nearly complete, in addition to the top. He plucked the sword from the ether with difficulty and noticed he was sweating, which he didn't think was possible, before he realized he was actually sweating *blood*, which he didn't think was possible either.

It was also apparent that he was no longer alone at the boundary of the worlds. The ends of long, pointy fingers, tipped with even longer and pointier nails, appeared along the narrow gap between this world and the next. If Amyral listened closely, he could hear faint whispering, scrambling, scraping sounds.

Amyral took a shuddering breath and raised the sword again, this time on the other side. His arms felt like two hunks of lead, and he could barely see for the brightness and smoke pouring out from the underworld, but he had one last, long cut to make before his doorway was a real gateway—large enough for him to enter, and not just for demons and spirits to exit. He would have to be quick.

"You know, the thing I learned about working with Asperides," Nack's slightly quavering voice came from behind him, "is that if you really want him to do something, you've gotta be *really specific* with your instructions."

Amyral spun around. The boy stood ten paces away, bruised and battered, but standing all the same.

"DEMON SWORD ASPERIDES," the boy called, thrusting his arm straight into the air, "I, NACK FURNIVAL, YOUR TRUE MASTER, COMMAND YOU TO COME TO ME. *NOW.*"

NOW THAT'S MORE LIKE IT came Asperides's mocking voice, quick and clear as a bell.

The demon sword Asperides soared out of Amyral Venir's hand and straight into the waiting arms of Nack Furnival—just as the denizens of the underworld apparently noticed that this tear in the barrier to the land of the living was the largest any of them had seen in thousands of years—and that even if it was a trap, it was just too good a chance to pass up.

Amyral Venir only got one glimpse of those clawed hands ripping and tearing at his precious doorway, forcing his jagged cut open wider and wider, before the first wave of demons exploded out of the underworld.

They did not spare much thought for the silly, defenseless, (mostly) human man standing right in their way.

———— ◆ ————

The first few demons through the tear in the universe merely contented themselves with trampling straight over Amyral Venir. The fourth, apparently, decided that being in a hurry was no reason not to stop for a snack and swallowed the dark sorcerer whole.

"Um, Asperides," said Nack. "Nice to see you, sorry about the yelling—"

I'M VERY TOUCHED, said the sword. *ALSO: LATER.*

Nack hefted the sword and, nearly without thinking, swiped several heads off a lunging, many-headed hydra that had just squirmed through the partial gateway. Asperides's blade very obligingly turned blazingly hot with every cut, cauterizing each headless lump before it had the chance to grow back into two more toothy, venomous monsters. Nack turned from the flailing hydra and immediately ran through a patch of frosty air hanging to his left—malevolent spirits, looking for a host to possess. Holding the sword before him, he was protected from the bone-chilling cold (and, more importantly, possession). Little sizzles, pops, and faint shrieks punctuated the air the blade touched as the spirits were sent back to the underworld. He wasn't quite fast enough, though, and couldn't stop one of the spirits from diving into a hapless Undying soldier who got too close; a moment later and the man's eyes had turned black. He ran from the fray, a hungry look in his eyes. Nack took a step forward to follow—

LEAVE HIM, said Asperides. *YOU WILL NEED CANDLES AND TIME TO EXORCISE HIM NOW. AND THERE ARE MORE COMING.*

Asperides was right. More and more demons squeezed out of the partial doorway Amyral Venir had carved into the underworld. Nack backed against one of the Dancing Priestesses to take stock of the situation around him. He yelped when his back touched the stone. A tingling shock, like built-up static, had zapped him, making his hair stand on end. The stones were still surging with magical power—from Amyral's spell, from the Missing Moon's arrival, or both. It was impossible to tell.

Nack put a few inches between the stone and himself.

He reached for the pouch at his waist and hastily sprinkled an arc of salt on the ground in front of him. It wouldn't keep out any mid-level or greater demons, but it would buy him time and keep any rogue spirits away.

Nack took stock of the hilltop. The Undying had immediately scattered, fleeing into the nearby hills. But the open pastures left them little place to hide. A handful of the knights appeared to have angel blades. Their blue glow flashed against the darkness of the hills, bright even in the light of the moons. Some of the soldiers appeared to be trying to organize a more purposeful retreat but struggled to both hold the demons off their comrades and corral the fleeing fighters at the same time.

A *thump* next to him made Nack jump. It wasn't the fleshy hellbeast Nack expected, but rather a sweaty and white-faced Cleoline. She sank to the ground, clutching the ankle Nack suspected she'd hurt during the no-crow crash. If the magical shock from leaning against the standing stone bothered her, she either didn't show it or she was in too bad of a shape to notice.

"For a mediocre knight," she half-shouted to make herself heard over the screams of men and demons, "you sure can run fast."

"You're hurt," Nack said, immediately stepping in front of Cleoline and extending his salt line. He gave a nosy gasper-cat that had started sniffing at the necromancer a hard bop on the nose with Asperides. It shattered into a billion dissolving pieces. "Why didn't you stay behind and hide? What's Therin doing?" Nack's stomach twisted at the thought of the tiny moon priestess out all alone in the hills.

Before Cleoline could answer, a beam of moonlight so concentrated it looked like a sword itself slashed the ground in front of Nack, leaving a patch of singed grass (and the severed, wriggling tentacles of whatever had been about to make a grab for him and Cleoline) behind.

"Saving our butts!" said Cleoline, sloppily gesturing to the center of the circle. Sure enough, there stood Therin, closer to the doorway than Nack had dared get, directing moonbeams with her bare hands, sending demons exploding into tiny bits left and right.

"She really got a handle on this new moon magic thing," said Cleoline, a little ruefully. "Devoting your life to it probably helps," she conceded.

SHE IS NOT THE ONLY ONE WHO CAN CALL DOWN THE MOON, Asperides reminded Nack, which Nack appreciated as a gentler way of saying, "Get your butt moving!"

Nack looked from Cleoline to Therin to the fleeing soldiers and back again, indecision gripping his gut.

"Go," said Cleoline firmly. "Not all of us need sparkly moonbeams to fight." The necromancer closed her eyes and thrust her fingers into the earth at her side. Dark veins sprouted on her arms, twisting down her wrists and fingers like vines. Beneath them, the earth shifted in an unpleasant way that Nack was fairly certain was not an earthquake, but the sudden shifting of many, many bones buried near the standing stones over the millennia.

"Which is code for, 'there is a lot of dead stuff here and I will be fine!'" she grunted, her eyes opening, red as glowing rubies. Nack caught a glimpse of a skeletal hand thrusting its way up from the earth before he forced himself to turn away and make his way toward Therin.

How do we reach for it? Nack thought, and though they'd never spoken this way before, he knew Asperides could hear him. He chanced a quick look up at the Missing Moon—the Third Daughter of the prophecy, returned at last.

ALLOW ME TO MAKE THE INTRODUCTIONS, said Asperides. Nack detected a certain hesitancy in the sword's words, despite his confident quip. But whatever Asperides did must have worked, because a moment later, Nack felt a power unlike anything he'd ever felt jolt through his arm and down his entire body. He staggered under the weight of it and was nearly chomped in half for his carelessness. He rolled and brought Asperides up, ready to face his attacker. A silvery beam several feet long extended from the tip of the sword. The enormous, horned snake demon with a face like a court jester never stood a chance. The moonbeam burned its eyes and flesh, making it rear back, and Nack and the sword's blade did the rest.

"Aw, leave some of the cool ones for us, why don't you?"

Nack looked through the steaming pile of demon remains to see a battered-looking but otherwise healthy Barb and Willa striding toward him.

"Barb!" said Nack, relief flooding through him. "You're okay!"

"And even better now," said Barb, "now that I've got something to fight for other than that zombie warlord!" She grinned, ducked under a passing cloud of spirits that her wife quickly dispatched with her angel blade, and came up still smiling.

Nack supposed that, to be a knight, you had to be a certain kind of crazy.

He, Barb, and Willa eventually made their way to the center of the stone circle, careful not to get zapped by Therin's moonbeams. Willa and Nack hurriedly poured a circle of salt around them. They used up most of their

remaining supply, and even so, the line was pitifully thin—
Nack didn't think it would survive a stiff wind, never mind
a full-fledged assault from the underworld. Barb, he was
chagrined but not surprised to see, didn't have any salt of
her own; apparently Amyral Venir hadn't even deigned to
supply his soldiers with the most basic protections.

Nack moved to put a hand on Therin's shoulder, but
the girl interrupted him, her voice echoing with the power
she was channeling. The candles she had arranged at her
feet flared and shot sparks into the air as she spoke.

"Don't," she warned him. "I'm not sure how long I can
keep this up, and I'm also not sure I won't barbecue you
if you touch me."

"Fair enough," Nack said, settling for standing with
his back to her. Willa and Barb took up positions on
either side of them. Behind him came vague sounds of
gnashing, cracking, and chomping that Nack fervently
hoped were Cleoline's zombies doing their duty to protect their creator.

Nack took a deep breath, trying to channel even
more of the Missing Moon's power. It was a strange feeling, like shaking hands with a friend he hadn't seen in
a while—and then promptly yanking on that hand and
praying it held on to yours as you catapulted off a cliff.

It worked. Nack and Asperides unleashed wave after

wave of concentrated moonlight against the onslaught of demons. Nack ducked and weaved and silently thanked Asperides when the sword seemed to move his arm of its own accord, often saving him (or Therin, or one of the knights) from a grisly end. It was different from the times Asperides had seemed to control him, when they first met. This time, it felt more like a reflex. With the power of the Missing Moon flowing through them, they were finally fighting as one.

But they were also losing. Nack didn't know how much time had passed before he realized he could hardly lift his arms. His legs began to shake beneath him. He looked to his right and saw that Therin's moonbeams were not as long nor as solid-looking as before. To his left, Willa covered Barb as the curly-haired knight took a moment to rest, her hands on her knees, her head hung low.

And still, the demons kept coming. Amyral Venir had failed to create a doorway into the underworld, but he had heartily succeeded at creating a portal *out* of it. And more of the demons were sneaking past Nack and his companions entirely, escaping into the countryside beyond.

"There are too many of them," Nack gasped. Asperides suddenly seemed much heavier in his arms as the realization set in.

"Too many?" scoffed Barb, nearly losing her footing

in the process. "I don't know about you, but I'm just getting started."

Over her head, Nack caught Willa's worried look.

A moment later, things got much darker—literally. It took them all a moment to realize Therin's moonbeams had stopped flashing. A pile of spent wicks and blobs of wax littered the ground in front of her.

"Nack . . ."

Therin's voice came softly from Nack's side. He just managed to shift his grip on Asperides enough to catch her before she fainted.

Willa sprang into action, leaping in front of Nack and Therin to confront the bat-winged demon who'd chosen that brief moment of weakness to swoop down from above.

DO YOU TRUST ME? Asperides's voice echoed louder than usual in Nack's head, and Nack could tell the sword was speaking to the group at large.

At first, Nack could only think of the silvery voice that had lured him into the tomb all those months ago. He had trusted that voice, had trusted its promises of redemption and victory and glory. And what had it gotten him?

A gory death in vain in the apocalypse, probably. Plus an eternity in hell afterward.

But also, if he admitted it to himself? He'd gotten a good teacher—and, for reasons he didn't fully understand—a powerful ally. Against all the odds, against his very nature, Asperides really was just as determined as any of them to stop Amyral Venir.

"What do we do?" Nack asked.

EVERYONE, TOUCH THE BLADE, Asperides instructed. *NOW.*

Willa looked back at Nack, her eyes desperate. She grabbed her wife's hand, and Nack grabbed Willa's. They quickly knelt on the ground, circling around the sword, an utterly defenseless little puddle of people. Nack hoisted the unconscious Therin closer, being sure to keep contact with her as he reached forward.

The instant they all touched the sword, a blinding green light exploded around them.

A moment later, only a circular scorch mark in the center of the Dancing Priestesses left any clue that they had been there at all.

25

All Souls

They landed in Asperides's hall again. It wasn't the hall of Nack's original contract. That strange realm had been full of shiny marble tiles and impeccably carved pillars, sharp corners and diffuse moonlight. In this hall, the pillars were entirely replaced by the standing stones, each Dancing Priestess as weathered as it looked on the hilltop outside . . . wherever they were. The floor was still tiled, but slightly curved, as if the hill had followed them into Asperides's private world. Weeds, grass, and vines burst from cracks in the tiles and grew around and over the standing stones—nature reclaiming the efforts of men. Or swords, Nack supposed.

A stunned Willa and Barb got slowly to their feet. Nack gently rested Therin against one of the pillars.

Moss helpfully sprouted up around its base and formed a little pillow under her head.

"Where *are* we?" whispered Willa reverently, as if she were in a temple or other sacred place.

Nack noticed the angel blade in her hand was curiously dim—practically unidentifiable as an angel blade—and fervently hoped they'd be out of there before the knight noticed.

A nearby groan made Nack, Willa, and Barb all jump until the moonlight—much brighter in this version of the hall—illuminated another figure slumped against one of the stones.

"Whoa," said Cleoline. "I like the decor. Very shabby chic."

She wasn't even touching the sword, Nack thought, impressed with Asperides's skill. But the sword confirmed Nack's worries before he even had a chance to voice them.

WE DO NOT HAVE MUCH TIME, said Asperides to them all. *IT HAS COST ME MUCH POWER TO DO EVEN THIS.*

"Thank you, Asperides," said Willa. She looked to the sword at Nack's side, and then around the room, as if unsure where she should direct her words. "Honestly."

"We need a plan to close that hole," Barb said bluntly, all traces of her earlier sense of humor gone. "Otherwise they'll just keep coming on through forever."

"Is that something you can do, Asperides?" asked Willa. "Would it be within your power?" If Willa had any misgivings about dealing with a demon sword, the urgency of the situation was apparently enough for her to put them to the side for the moment.

YES, OF COURSE, said the sword. *I HAVE BEEN ALLOWING US ALL TO FIGHT FOR OUR LIVES MERELY TO AMUSE MYSELF.*

"What Asperides *means* to say," Nack interrupted as Barb's mouth opened and closed in shock, "is that, um, no. He can't."

Can you? Nack asked privately, looking at the entire . . . pocket universe, or whatever it was, around them.

SEE MY PREVIOUS STATEMENT, answered the sword churlishly, tendrils of black smoke sprouting from his blade in his indignance.

"What about the spell?" suggested Willa. "Cleoline, you put it together. Surely there's a way to reverse it."

The necromancer shook her head, her stringy hair falling over her face like a curtain.

"Not once it's started," she said with a grimace. "The

ritual was never meant to be interrupted like this. And there wasn't exactly an 'undo' option in the ancient scrolls I was piecing together. I don't think anyone making the doorway wanted to chance someone would close it behind them."

Her words hung heavy in the air. Willa and Barb seemed stunned into silence. Nack hadn't really expected much to begin with, given how the whole night was going.

"Sorry," Cleo added with a wince—whether from the pain in her leg or for dooming them all, Nack wasn't sure, but he supposed it hardly mattered anymore.

MAKE A PLAN TO FLEE, THEN, said Asperides. *I CANNOT HOLD YOU HERE MUCH LONGER. MY POWER—*

"Is exactly what we need."

Nack spun around to see Therin sitting up against the pillar, looking pale and wan, but very much awake.

"Therin!" Nack ran to her side and helped her sit up a little more. "Are you okay—"

Therin waved him off impatiently.

"Asperides," she said, her voice cracking. She cleared her throat. Even speaking seemed to tire her. "You know the legends are true. The reason Amyral needed you for this ritual was because you were forged in the light of the Missing Moon. You were made from pieces of both the worlds, but only the Third Daughter could bind you together."

"And?" Nack asked, a tad exasperated. They knew all of this already.

"The Missing Moon's power made you," said Therin softly. "It can unmake you, too."

Nack didn't think it was possible, but the air seemed to grow even heavier. He shivered against a sudden chill that rippled through him.

"Asperides . . ." he said. "What does she mean?"

———————◆———————

The demon sword Asperides had really been enjoying his early retirement before a certain scrappy, young knight came along and ruined everything. He realized, with some sadness, that he might never have another steamy drink in his favorite darkened corner of the Wet Fang again, and then was embarrassed he was sad about that, firstly because it was silly, and secondly because the barman had betrayed him and delivered him into the hands of his greatest enemy, and one's last thoughts should surely be devoted to a worthier subject.

Shouldn't they?

Asperides had never really considered the fact that he might *have* last thoughts.

It was all happening very fast.

Fortunately, they didn't have time for Nack Furnival's Big Dumb Hero act, because they were all about to be eaten by a bunch of angry demons if they didn't do something. That saved a lot of time that would have otherwise been spent moaning and groaning over Asperides's probable fate—a situation Asperides had also never really considered, as none of his masters had been much concerned with his fate unless it was connected to their own. But Nack Furnival, surprisingly, seemed uniquely troubled by the fact that Asperides might use so much power he would functionally cease to exist.

"There's got to be another way," the boy had said.

There wasn't. And the seconds were ticking by. And the aforementioned hungry demons were waiting.

"It's your choice," Nack finally said, his voice thick but surprisingly calm. "Is this what you want to do?"

It took Asperides several moments to realize the boy was addressing *him*.

It then took him several more moments to realize he could never remember anyone asking him that question.

WHEN WE RETURN TO THE EARTHLY REALM, Asperides said to Nack, *YOU MUST NOT HESITATE. DO YOU UNDERSTAND ME?*

The boy merely nodded. Asperides could practically

see the lump in Nack's throat and felt curiously choked up himself at the sight—not that he had a throat, of course, but perhaps the souls he was currently summoning from the deepest levels of the underworld, creating an unprecedented bottleneck of power, were partially to blame for the sensation. Yes, that was surely it.

The Third Daughter's light bathed Asperides's blade as they surfaced into the circle of Dancing Priestesses once again. Willa and Barb sprang into action, defending Nack and Asperides and the young priestess, as Nack and Asperides prepared to seal Amyral Venir's tear in the universe for good.

Well, Asperides supposed it was more like patching the tear than actually closing it. The necromancer was right—there was no "undo" option on creating a permanent doorway to the underworld—but that didn't mean they couldn't stop up the gaps.

Which was exactly what they planned to do, using each and every last soul inside of Asperides.

He called upon them all. He called upon every murderous warlord, every ambitious dark knight, every evil necromancer he had ever called master. He called up the brave and the cowardly, the smart and the gullible—the souls who had known what a contract with a demon sword meant, and the souls who hadn't. Some of them resisted, more out of surprise than anything else, as they had not been called upon for years and years. But Asperides called them all up eventually. No matter the cruelties they had asked him to execute, the enemies they bade him slay, the evil spells and demons they had summoned through him . . . at the end of the day, their souls belonged to him.

He had no idea what would happen to Nack's contract if their plan succeeded. Would Asperides, who had no soul of his own, merely blink out of existence the moment all his power was used up? Would his contract with Nack then be null and void? Or someday (hopefully many years from now), would Asperides simply reappear in the universe, Nack's bright soul burning inside of him, and be forced to start collecting souls anew, forever trapped in his cursed mission?

Trapped. He had never really thought of the compulsion that way before. It was just how things were. But now . . . the thought of adding even one more soul to his "collection" sickened him.

He could only hope to put the souls he'd already claimed to good use. It wasn't the eternal rest they would have wished for, of that he was certain, but it was . . . fitting, in a way. The power he'd used to unleash so much evil on the world would now be used, quite literally, to stop it.

Nack's hands shook as he gripped Asperides, striding closer and closer to the bright, weeping tear. There was a brief pause in the crush of demons pushing through, and the ones who had just surfaced steered well clear of Nack, sensing the power surging from the boy's sword. Nack planted his feet and placed the tip of Asperides's blade as near to the tear in the universe as either of them dared.

Then, one by one, Asperides let each of his souls go.

He imagined the closest comparison, for a human, would be . . . well, rather fittingly, a sword wound. He felt the souls oozing out of him as one might feel the loss of blood from . . . perhaps a minor wound, to start with. Each soul traveling out of his deepest depths, down the length of his blade, and out into the world was something he watched with detached interest, rather than felt—at least at first. Then, he began to notice he felt rather . . . empty. Weak. A sensation like a door closing inside him let him know that the last of the souls had left the underworld entirely.

The souls latched onto the tear in the ether, each a tiny, bright pearl of light. The opening narrowed where they touched it, edges shrinking like a healing wound closed with careful stitches. The boy slowly guided the blade over and across the opening, inch by inch, so each pearl was connected to the last, like beads on a string.

The empty feeling was overwhelming now. Asperides's sense of awareness dimmed as the souls rushed out of him. He had previously been able to sense the whole clearing, the whole stone circle, and everyone in it, not to mention see as far as the humans could. But now his senses dimmed; one second, he saw a flash of Nack's face, and then another shining soul, added to the string hanging in the air. The next, he heard a voice—maybe the young priestess?—calling a name. Could it have been his? He wasn't sure. The next few seconds would be blackness, or merely mist, or silence, or a strange, familiar thrumming sensation he could not place.

The very last soul to leave was, predictably, Amyral Venir's. It put up a bit of a fight on the way out, moving far slower down Asperides's blade than the others. Asperides used what little energy he had left to give it an extra shove.

And good riddance, he thought.

A moment later, Asperides realized two very important things: the first being that despite his best efforts, despite using up every single imprisoned soul within him, there was still a small but noticeable gap left in the tear between the worlds.

The second realization was that *he was still having realizations.*

The emptiness inside of him smarted. He felt small, and alone, as if he'd been standing in the center of a bustling crowd on a cold day and hadn't noticed the chill in the air until the heat, the motion of all those other bodies had gone. The strongest sensation other than that was . . . a strange tug, outward and upward and all around himself at once. He supposed it could be the underworld, clamoring to devour the remnants of a being who had lorded too much power within it for far too long. But if he was still here at all . . . if he was still capable of thought and feeling, either he had failed to send every last one of his captured souls to hell, or . . .

Or perhaps, for the last several thousand years, he had been wrong, and demon sword or not, there *was* a part of him, however small, that was entirely himself.

Perhaps the demon sword Asperides had a soul after all.

"Asperides!" A voice called his name again. Nack, desperate and urgent.

I HEARD YOU THE FIRST TIME, BOY, said Asperides. His voice sounded tinny and high, unaccompanied by its usual echo. *IF AMYRAL VENIR'S PORTAL DID NOT RAISE THE DEAD, YOUR SHOUTING CERTAINLY COULD HAVE.*

"Asperides, you're alive!" Nack said, and even with his new, diminished vision, Asperides could see the relieved smile spread across the boy's face—though it was quickly overshadowed with apprehension as Nack noticed the remnant of Amyral's portal still floating in the air. "But . . . the doorway . . ."

IT APPEARS ONE MORE SOUL IS NEEDED TO FINISH THIS TASK, Asperides said. This time, he felt no fear at the prospect. *SO I SUPPOSE I'D BETTER BE QUICK ABOUT IT, SHOULDN'T I?*

Already a few tendrils of swirling white mist had started leaking out of the remaining gap—sneaky spirits determined to make their way back to the land of the living.

That mysterious pulling sensation was even stronger now, making it harder and harder for Asperides to ground his awareness to the task at hand.

A moment later, he realized what that pull was: the Missing Moon, returned to full strength at last. The Third Daughter who had made him was calling him home.

But first, he had a job to do.

Nack opened his mouth to protest, but Asperides stopped him.

I HAVE LIVED A LONG LIFE, NACK FURNIVAL, Asperides said.

And for the first time, it did feel like a life—not just an existence.

IT IS ABOUT TIME I LIVED IT WELL.

The last things Asperides saw were hope, and determination, and—unless he was mistaken—just a little bit of love, shining out of Nack Furnival's eyes, bright and brilliant as the moon.

26

Armies and Angels

When the first Furnival reinforcements appeared over the hilltop, Nack thought he must be dreaming. He must have fallen asleep in the middle of the battle, finally overcome by the bone-crushing exhaustion and being skinned alive by a shrub and the searing, sharp pain in his side that he was pretty sure was from being launched into the standing stones by Amyral Venir—though by this point, it was honestly hard to tell.

But when the old gamekeeper Grennan appeared at the front of the charge, riding a llama instead of a horse and yelling, "I didn't see nothin', but I brought some help, just in case!" Nack decided that, as strange a sight as that was, it was still pretty low on the list of strange things that had happened to him that day, and simply let the relief rush through him.

If some part of his brain recognized it was rather odd to be fighting alongside some of the knights who'd thrown him in a dungeon mere hours ago, he didn't give it too much attention. He merely fell in alongside them, as he had so many times in practice, and did his best to steer the especially nasty critters in the direction of someone with an angel blade.

His own sword—he couldn't think of it as "Asperides," not anymore—was just that: a normal sword. An empty shell of what it had been. It took Nack longer than it should have to realize that he couldn't just slice through demons like butter anymore. More than once, it was only the quick reflexes of Willa, or Barb, or one of the Furnival knights—even, one time, a man he recognized as belonging to Amyral Venir's forces—that saved him from a sticky end.

Dawn snuck up on them all. One moment, they were surrounded by hungry demons and vengeful spirits, every second filled with the clash of swords and the cries of humans and beasts alike. The next, their swords began hitting empty air, as the demons fled for cover and the spirits fizzled in the air, and a faint blush crept over the horizon. The light of two of the moons disappeared. Only the third remained in the sky, long after the sun had begun to rise. Nack wondered if it would ever really set.

It was during a pause in the early morning fighting, when someone was shoving water from a canteen down Nack's throat to make sure he had had enough to drink (he had not), that the first shimmering blue lights appeared on the battlefield.

As far as Nack could tell, they simply popped into existence. One moment there was nothing, and the next, the air was filled with a faint chirping and buzzing and Nack was surrounded by several blue, glowing orbs. They bobbed around the Dancing Priestesses, occasionally bonking harmlessly into the knights, or the stones, or each other.

It wasn't until one of the orbs bumped into one of Cleoline's defender zombies and turned it into a pile of ash that Nack realized what they were.

Angels.

One of the floating blobs of light made straight for his head. Nack ducked, but it still clipped his ear, and suddenly, it was as if he'd gained several hours of energy. His head felt clearer, and he was steadier on his feet.

"What the . . ."

Another one nudged at his elbow, like some sort of ethereal dog asking for a pat.

"I think that one likes you," joked one of the Furnival knights near him—Yosta, Nack thought she was called.

Nack held his arm very still as the angel nudged it again. The glowing orb made its way down to his hand and hovered there expectantly.

"What?" Nack said. He wasn't sure if it could understand him—though he was fairly confident now that it wouldn't talk back.

The angel merely bobbed up and down, bathing his hand in a pleasant, fuzzy warmth whenever it boinked against him.

"You have to invite it in." A steadying hand landed on his shoulder. Willa looked down at him, her face tired but still warm as ever.

"Oh," Nack said. Now *he* felt like the stupid blob.

The angel wasn't just here to make friends. It had chosen him.

It had chosen his sword.

"People say they're attracted to great deeds," Willa

said softly, nodding toward the angel. "Feats of bravery, and things like that." She held up Lenira, still pulsing with faint blue light, though the sword was covered in demon ichor.

"Personally," she said, leaning in to squeeze Nack's shoulder, "I suspect it's all the bloodshed and the noise and the chaos that really gets their attention." She shrugged. "But don't tell any *real* knights I said that." She shot Nack a conspiratorial look.

"I . . . I can't," Nack said, still staring at the angel— and at the sword that mere moments ago had been Asperides. It felt like . . . a betrayal, somehow. Nack knew that was ridiculous, but he couldn't shake the feeling. "I'm not . . ."

He wasn't even sure how to finish that sentence. Not brave enough? Not smart enough? Not good enough with a sword?

Not worthy?

A few months ago—even a few hours ago—Nack might have said those things. Now?

The floating blue blob in front of him certainly didn't seem to have any objections to his character—and the firm hand on his shoulder told him he had a good teacher to learn from.

"You are," said Willa, before Nack could finish the thought. "You *are.*"

Nack gave the angel a gentle nudge with his wrist.

"Sword's that way, friend," he said. He took a deep breath.

"Come on in."

———◆———

Nack and his friends spent a full day sleeping in Nack's old quarters in Castle Falterfen before any of the household staff dared to crack the door open. After Cleoline's ankle had been set by the Furnivals' doctor, Nack's ribs and leg seen to, and the rest of them generally patched up, Nack had barred the door, installed Cleoline in the adjoining guestroom and Therin in his bed, and took up his own place on the floor, directly in front of the door. If Therin, or anyone else, thought of arguing with this arrangement, they didn't get far, mostly because they were too tired to argue about anything.

He lay there with his angel blade at his side, letting its warmth spread through him. The closer it was to his bruised side or his scraped skin, the quicker he healed. By the end of that first full day of rest, he felt much less like he'd been hit by a tornado, which was a good thing, as Nack imagined he'd need all his strength for the days—and most importantly, the nights—ahead. It was certainly a perk of angel blades that had been vastly understated.

As little shafts of sunlight filtered through the gaps in the room's thick curtains, Nack lay on his back, turning the blade this way and that in the light. The sword's ever-present blue glow turned whiter in the sun. Though he couldn't say precisely how, he knew its name was Iremidus, just as surely as he knew his own name was Nack. He would have to look up the name in the Furnival family records, or perhaps in the Order of Archivists, to see whom it had been partnered with in the past.

If he lay very, very still, he thought he could hear a faint noise emanating from the blade. It didn't sound like words, so much as an intermittent sort of *meep meep*. Nack got the distinct impression of contentment, with just a touch of boredom, as if the sword were saying, "This is nice and all, but come on, lazy bones, you've been lying about long enough. Let's get up and defeat some evil!"

But maybe he was projecting. Just a little.

His own pulse thrumming in time to the energy of the blade in his hand, Nack took a quick look around to make sure everyone else was still asleep. Slowly, he brought Iremidus so close it was almost touching his lips.

"Hello?" he whispered.

Meep meep, said the sword.

He supposed that would have to do.

Later, when he was feeling more ambulatory, he tried to use Iremidus's powers to heal Cleoline's ankle, with pretty disappointing results. Nothing happened except the sword glowing a brighter, more threatening blue in the necromancer's presence—sensing, no doubt, her ties to the darker magical arts.

Willa explained later that all angel blades worked that way, unfortunately. As far as anyone knew, their healing powers only helped the owners of the swords they bonded with. ("And that's as close as you're ever getting to this fine specimen with an angel blade in your paws, anyway," said Cleoline, and that was the end of that experiment.)

It wasn't until the sun was nearly setting the next day, and Nack and his friends were sitting on every available surface in his room, munching on some chicken and rolls he'd pilfered from the castle kitchen, that his family apparently decided waiting any longer would just make an already awkward conversation even more awkward. There was a soft knock on his door, and then someone very official outside it said, "The Lord and Lady Furnival!" as if they were introducing Nack's parents at a ball, and not their own son's bedroom doorway.

The door opened, and Nack was on his feet, but he kept his angel blade in his scabbard, and so, he was glad to see, did Willa.

There would be no more angel blades drawn around other humans, Nack decided. Not if he had anything to say about it. (The small part of him that he assumed would be forever Asperides-shaped, even though the sword's presence was long gone from his mind, said, *Best start carrying a second weapon, then.* He did his best to ignore it.)

And then his parents just kind of stood there, hovering in the doorway, with a bunch of servants around them, until Nack said, "Um, come in," and they did, and his mother made a face at the undeniable funk of a room filled with five battle-weary people who'd had slightly bigger concerns than bathing for the last couple of days. At least she had the good sense not to say anything about it.

What she *did* say nearly knocked Nack flat onto the floor again.

"Your father and I have come to the decision," she said, "that you will be the senior heir to House Furnival. We will be riding west soon, to negotiate with the other clans, and we wish you to remain here, as head of the family, in our stead."

To which Nack promptly replied, surprising everyone in the room (himself included): "Um, no."

(He later conceded he could have been slightly more diplomatic in his refusal, even if in the end, the sentiment was the same.)

There was a lot of flustered hemming and hawing at that. Cleoline and Barb, still munching on their chicken legs, swiveled their heads from Nack to the rest of the Furnivals and back again.

"But, sweetheart, we thought you'd be pleased . . ."

"The leadership you displayed during the attack . . ."

It all sounded like *meep meep* to Nack, especially when it became evident that nowhere in his parents' pleas lay anything resembling an apology. No "We're sorry we banished you from the family on a flimsy pretext for failing to kill another child, son." No "Turns out you were right about your brother and he really was going to sell us out to the enemy on our doorstep." No "Sorry we ever doubted you!"

It wasn't that Nack desperately needed to hear these things. Not anymore. But he still thought it was important someone say them. He wasn't sure he *wanted* to be part of a clan whose leaders couldn't admit they'd been wrong even when the world had been ending.

They also eventually got around to a point which

Nack suspected from the minute they first asked him to stay, which was that by "negotiate with the other clans," they meant "try and step into some of the power vacuum left by Lord Solonos's and Amyral Venir's deaths."

"Your place is here, Nack," his father had insisted. "With Declan holding Castle Ravinus—"

Barb made a chunky gargling noise as she nearly choked on her chicken. Lord Furnival shot her a dirty look.

"Declan *what*?" asked Nack.

"Your brother and his men turned the castle," explained Nack's father. Nack detected a barely concealed challenge in his voice—*Prove him a traitor now, why don't you?*—but Nack was too tired to rise to the bait. "He holds it now, in the Furnival name, and I expect he will for quite some time, if we are to bring stability to the realm once more."

And there it was. Nack couldn't *prove* his older brother was a traitor who would sell out his entire clan to a murderous tyrant, and no one was ever going to admit anything of the sort—but that wouldn't stop his father from giving Declan a shiny castle of his own to play with that just so happened to be comfortably over a hundred miles away, and hope it would be enough for everyone involved to forget the whole thing had ever happened.

"You made it very clear to me—not once, but twice," Nack reminded them, lowering his voice, "that I was not a Furnival anymore."

"That was before you *proved yourself*, son," said his mother, placing a hand on his arm. "But we were . . . now we know, don't we, that you're truly a knight, a real Furnival, deep down."

A "real" Furnival. What did that mean? The idea was even wobblier to Nack than that of a "real" knight, especially now. And the thought of being penned up in Castle Falterfen, trying to get lots of people who had tossed him in a dungeon mere days ago to follow his decisions . . . His parents and Declan seemed keen to take advantage of the current political situation. And Nack supposed someone had to sort those things out. But him? He couldn't imagine himself sitting home at Castle Falterfen with all those new demons still loose in the world.

Iremidus said, *Meep meep.*

I agree, Nack thought back.

"I'm sorry, Mother," Nack said, "but I'm not sure I am."

Knights of the Road

The last time Nack Furnival had left Castle Falterfen, it had been with nothing but the clothes on his back, a bandolier of candles, and a heart so heavy he thought it would sink down, down, and through his body, into the earth and whatever mysteries lay beneath, because surely, he could not survive with it feeling like this. The sun had been shining, then, as if to mock him, as if to purposefully shine its light on his guilt and his shame.

Now, it was drizzling, but not pouring, which felt quite fitting, actually. His heart was still heavy, but now, at least, it was because he had a purpose.

And this time, he had more people at his back than he knew what to do with.

Though the doorway to the underworld had been patched closed, there were still more demons and evil spirits out in the world than there ever had been before. Nack understood that he had played his own part, however small, in making that happen. (Lesson learned: he would never, ever throw a sword in a river again. Mostly, because they were very expensive.) He knew that Amyral

Venir would probably have found another way to get to Asperides, or even have found another demon sword, if any of them still existed. But it didn't change what had happened. And so until every last demon who had come through that doorway was back where it belonged, Nack had a job to do.

He was pleased, though not entirely surprised, when Willa and Barb invited him to travel with them. Nack still had a lot of learning to do with Iremidus, and he'd been trying to gather up the courage to ask to study under Willa ever since the battle at the Dancing Priestesses. It didn't make much sense for him to go off on his own and probably get eaten by the first greater demon he came across. And thanks to that very battle, Barb had an angel blade now, too. Nack thought they'd make a good team.

He was a bit more surprised when three of the Furnival clan decided to join him—including the full-fledged knight he'd fought next to at the stones, Yosta, and her apprentice, Rill. The third was a distant cousin who uncomfortably reminded Nack of the pimply blond who'd stolen his first sword.

"Why would you want to come with *me*?" Nack asked. They all stood in the drizzle, already late to start out, because Yosta and the rest had showed up just as they were about to leave, and Nack had to take the time to try and convince them that they really shouldn't.

Pimply Cousin nodded roughly toward the castle.

"You seem nicer than this lot," he said.

Nack supposed he couldn't argue with that.

Their first quest wasn't really a quest—they had little intelligence, so far, about where most of the demons had run off to—but Nack had little doubt it would be quite the adventure simply to travel across the countryside after all the tumult of the recent months. He was going to escort Therin—and, much to his surprise, Cleoline—back to the Mission of the Missing Moon.

"Are you sure you want to go back there?" he'd asked Therin. "Didn't they kind of try to, uh . . ."

"Sell me to the highest bidder?" Therin supplied helpfully. She sighed. "Yeah. But I was still raised there. The Mission is still *my* mission." She scrunched her nose up at her own corniness, making them both laugh. "The Missing Moon's returned now, but there's still so much we don't know. About the moon. About her magic. I don't think it's an end for the Mission. I think . . . I think it's time for a new beginning."

She said it with such conviction, Nack could have sworn her voice had the ring of prophecy.

"I, on the other hand, am merely a reformed sinner,"

said Cleoline, putting her hands together and bowing her head in mock solemnity. Therin elbowed her in the ribs.

Nack had to admit there were worse ideas than hiding Cleoline away in a convent, at least for a while. There were lots of people—both followers *and* enemies of Amyral Venir—who would have a bone to pick with his former right-hand woman. (Though, if there were ever *actual* bones involved, Nack wouldn't be the one to bet against Cleoline.)

"Seriously though," said the necromancer under her breath as Therin turned again to packing, "that new moon magic is *wicked*. I have got to learn me some of that."

"Plus," Cleo added. "Someone's gotta keep an eye on this one while she rebuilds a church from the ground up." She looked affectionately at Therin. "Don't worry, kid. Anyone tries to mess with her, I'll harvest them for parts myself."

It must be said that Nack would not be entirely sad to see the back of Cleoline. At the very least, his life would probably contain a lot less rotting organic matter.

They were mere miles from the gates of Castle Falterfen when a commotion at the edge of one of the fields stopped them in their tracks.

"Nack Furnival! Wait!"

The party halted as four people stumbled out from

behind the overgrown stalks of wheat—two burly, bearded men; a tall, reedy person; and a woman with a long ponytail, her skirts pinned up to her knees, and— Nack did a double take—a pair of twin angel blade daggers glowing at her hips.

They all looked the worse for wear, as if they'd been camping out in the fields.

Or, as Nack immediately realized, hiding out.

"I recognize those two," said Barb, her normally cheerful expression turning sour, gesturing to the big men. "They're Amyral Venir's soldiers."

The men made grumbling noises and the woman widened her stance.

"So what?" scoffed the woman. She glared daggers at Cleoline, who was standing at Nack's side. "So is *she*."

Nack took a step in front of Cleo, but the tall person held up their hands in a peaceable gesture.

"We *were* Amyral Venir's soldiers," they corrected Barb. "But not anymore. We were . . . led astray by his promises. We knew he was going to harness the power of the Missing Moon. He even promised demon swords for us all."

Beside Nack, Therin stiffened.

"Judge all you like, little miss," said the woman in an amused, drawling voice. "But tell me this: world being what it is, wouldn't *you* jump at a chance at a few square meals and a chance to defend yourself properly out there? A chance to change your fate to what you make it?"

Nack, for one, could say nothing to that.

"We *didn't* know he was going to open that portal to the underworld," said the tall person.

"And sacrifice us all," scoffed the woman, fingers trailing to one of her blades, as if she hoped a *re*-resurrected Amyral Venir might pop out of the bushes, just so she could have her shot at him.

"We'd . . . we'd like to try and make right what we did," said one of the bearded men, his voice surprisingly quiet and shaky. The man next to him shuffled a little closer and gave his hand a comforting squeeze.

Cleoline shot Nack an amused look that plainly said, *I can actually see your big, dumb heart melting.*

Nack looked to Willa and Barb. Though this mission was personal, he wasn't its leader, and honestly, he was quite content with that arrangement. Willa paced back and forth along the path, surveying the newcomers carefully.

"There will be no looting in this group," Willa said finally, her eyes fixing on every one of the party—even Nack—until he was sure they all felt like pupils being raked over the coals by a particularly strict teacher. "There will be no solo missions. There will be no asking for payment from civilians. If hospitality is offered, then we gladly take it. If not . . ."

By the time she'd finished her list of rules, Nack thought he'd be able to hear a pin drop. (Yes, even though they were in a wheat field. It was *that* quiet.)

"These are the rules an itinerant knight lives by," she said, straightening up to her full, impressive height, one hand on Lenira at her side. "And you will, too, if you wish to stay in good standing as a knight of the road. Do you understand?"

DO YOU AGREE TO THESE TERMS? Nack remembered another voice asking, what felt like so long ago.

A knight of the road. Nack had never heard the itinerant knights referred to like that.

He liked the sound of it.

"Yes," Nack piped up. The angel blade at his side hummed in agreement.

"Yes, I do."

Acknowledgments

After the publication of my last novel, *The Dark Lord Clementine*, it was very much *not* a sure thing that I would publish another novel any time soon. It's been a bumpy few years, from my own personal health issues to a global pandemic. But the wait has made me all the more excited to finally share Nack, Asperides, and their adventures with the world. This novel came to me fast and fun and exactly when I needed it, and if there is even one reader who opens these pages at precisely the moment *they* need it, I'll consider the whole thing a rollicking success.

Many thanks to the following folks for making this book possible:

The fine people at Champion PT and Performance, for taking my pain seriously and teaching my arms how to be arms again. I literally could not have written this book without your help, care, and patience. (Extra thanks to Theresa for connecting me with Champion and coaching me through my fitness journey during those tough times.)

Harvard John, Alex Trivilino, and Elizabeth C. Bunce, for their kind and expert beta reading.

My agent, Victoria Marini, for always being game.

My spouse, David, for listening (*so much* listening), and for marking fight choreography in the living room with me, because that is a totally normal thing that couples do.

My Transpatial Tavern crew. Keep it weird, y'all. You make an old crone feel young again. Special thanks to Chris Panatier, without whom Willa would not be Willa.

James Firnhaber and Carla Weise, for working their illustrative and design magic. Nack's creepy eyeball will live rent-free in my brain forever, and I love it.

Krestyna Lypen and the whole team at Algonquin Young Readers, for making this book a book, and for not laughing in my face when I came to them with the idea, "So, there's this two-thousand-year-old talking sword..." I am very lucky indeed to tell stories with you all.